THE CONCRETE GROVE

Also by Gary McMahon

Hungry Hearts
Pretty Little Dead Things

THE CONCRETE GROVE

GARY McMAHON

SOLARIS

First published 2011 by Solaris
an imprint of Rebellion Publishing Ltd,
Riverside House, Osney Mead,
Oxford, OX2 0ES, UK

www.solarisbooks.com

ISBN: 978 1 907519 95 6

A CIP catalogue record for this book is available from the
British Library.

Designed & typeset by Rebellion Publishing

Printed in the US

This one's dedicated to Mark West,
who always sees the wood for the trees.

Acknowledgments

Thanks always to Emily and Charlie for showing me another world; to Mark West for his beta-reading skills and enthusiasm; Sharon Ring for taking chances; John Haslam and Mick Parkinson for moral support and match-day drunkenness; Emily again for allowing me to use our romantic weekend away to do some valuable research; Jon Oliver for commissioning a mad idea for three books from a one-page synopsis; and the whole talented team at Solaris for helping me pursue this vision and get a story that's been in my head for decades onto the page.

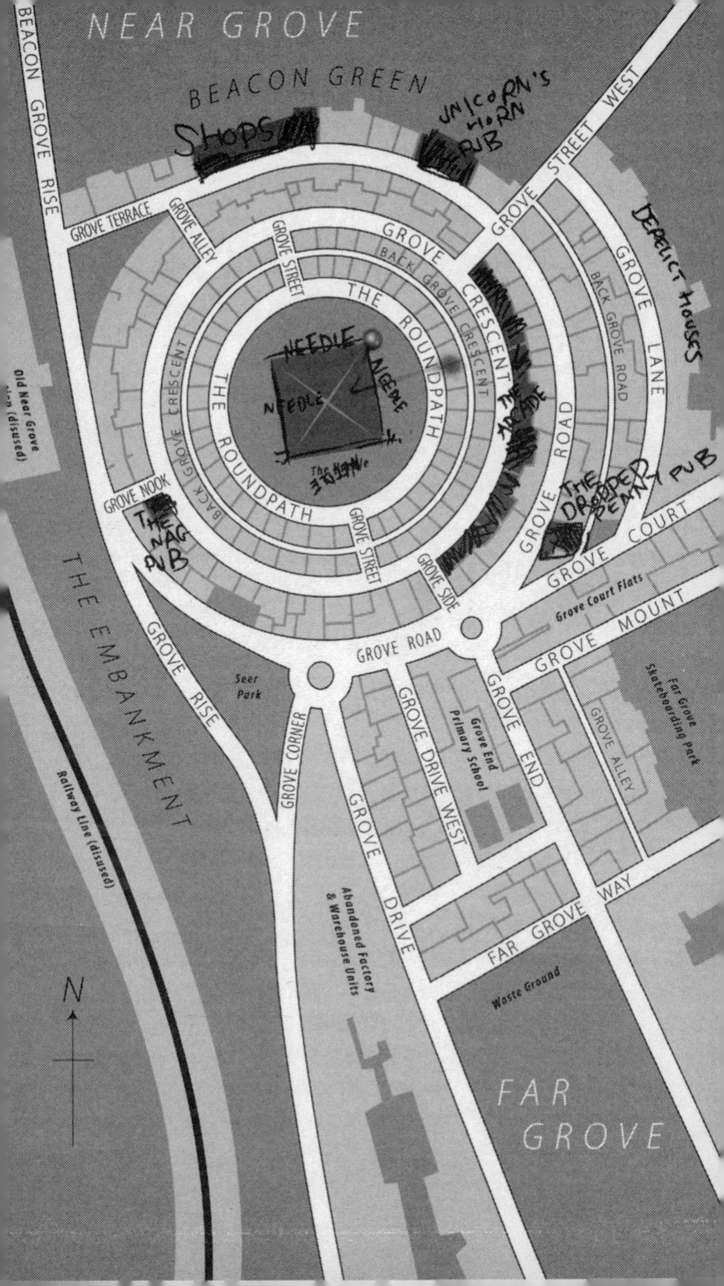
NEAR GROVE
BEACON GREEN
BEACON GROVE RISE
SHOPS
UNICORN'S HORN PUB
GROVE TERRACE
GROVE ALLEY
GROVE STREET
GROVE CRESCENT
BACK GROVE CRESCENT
THE ROUNDPATH
GROVE STREET WEST
DERELICT HOUSES
GROVE LANE
BACK GROVE ROAD
GROVE ROAD
NEEDLE
NEEDLE
NEEDLE
THE ARCADE
THE DROPPED PENNY PUB
Old Near Grove
(disused)
GROVE NOOK
BACK GROVE CRESCENT
THE NAG PUB
THE ROUNDPATH
GROVE STREET
GROVE SIDE
GROVE COURT
Grove Court Flats
GROVE MOUNT
GROVE ROAD
THE EMBANKMENT
GROVE RISE
Seer Park
GROVE CORNER
GROVE DRIVE
GROVE DRIVE WEST
Grove End Primary School
GROVE END
GROVE ALLEY
Far Grove Skateboarding Park
Railway Line (disused)
Abandoned Factory & Warehouse Units
FAR GROVE WAY
Waste Ground
N
FAR GROVE

One of the widespread beliefs is that hummingbirds, in some way, are messengers between worlds. As such they help shamans keep nature and spirit in balance.

Source: www.hummingbirdworld.com

PART ONE

SHADES AND SHADOWS

"I don't like it here. The closer you get to the centre, the weirder it feels."

– Hailey Fraser

CHAPTER ONE

HER NAME WAS Hailey. She was just fourteen years old.

And she was afraid.

No, that wasn't quite right. Hailey wasn't afraid, not exactly; she was sad and confused and worried about her mother, and all she really wanted was to be left alone. Just for a few minutes, maybe even as much as half an hour. She needed some time on her own, during which she could think about things and set the facts in order. The world always seemed a little less harsh when the facts were put in place, with everything lined up in neat little rows where she could see them properly. Like her books on their shelves or her stuffed toys sitting against the skirting board at home.

It was Hailey's mother who was afraid. Even Hailey could see that. Her mother, she knew, was terrified.

Things had been tense around the flat lately – even Hailey, with her limited ability to empathise, was aware of this tension. Her mother chewed her fingernails all the time, and she lost her temper much easier than ever before – easier and more regularly. She was drinking a lot – cheap wine in big bottles from the local off-license – and Hailey could sometimes hear her crying at night through the thin walls of their crummy little flat in the Grove. In the morning she would pretend that she'd slept well and everything was fine, but Hailey knew that there were tear stains on her mother's pillows.

Hailey walked slowly through the narrow streets, ignoring the youths who were perched on garden walls and loitering at the corners smoking cheap cigarettes and drinking cider from plastic bottles. She paid no attention to the fat man who always seemed to be watching her from a parked car near the shopping arcade, and blanked the old woman who stood on her front step shaking her fist at the sky and shouting at the birds.

Such sights were normal in the Grove – the Concrete Grove. Hailey had learned this. The people who lived on the estate were somehow different from the ones she had known before, in her old life, when her mother had a job and money wasn't a problem.

These people, the ones she now lived among, were closer to the bottom of the pile than anyone else she'd met. That's how her mother termed it: the bottom of the pile. As if society was just a big pyramid of people, squirming and shouting and fighting for position, and she and Hailey had slipped through the gaps to end up somewhere near its base. Sometimes, late at night, when she was unable to sleep, she could almost feel the pressure of all those bodies above her, pushing and shoving and nipping and punching... looking for a way to climb.

She quickened her pace and reached the north end of Grove Road, where the Bailey brothers lived. The twin boys, both fifteen and in the year above Hailey in classes, were possibly the worst bullies at her school. A month ago they'd put little Lloyd Jones in hospital, slashing his back with a straight razor taken from their father's things. Hailey recalled the police visiting the school, when not one of the other pupils had dared say anything against the brothers – which meant, of course, that they had got away with their crime because there were no witnesses. They remained unpunished, even though everyone knew they'd done it. Even the headmaster knew, but he was just as scared of the Bailey family as everyone else in the area.

Was every school like this, or just the one she went to? She didn't remember her old school being so violent or filled with such aggressive pupils, but it was so long ago now – a full *eighteen* months – that she could barely recall anything about the place, other than it had seemed so clean and bright and stress-free in comparison to her current educational establishment.

She was glad that school was over for the day, and that she could roam around on her own just to get the horrible prison air of the place out of her lungs. At her old school, she'd been happy to stay behind and help the teacher tidy the class, or play outside the gates with her friends before heading home for dinner. These days all she wanted was to be away from school, yet still she could feel its awful shadow at her back.

She was now nearing the centre of the estate, where the Needle was located. She'd bypassed the shopping arcade, where the worst trouble-makers tended to gather like a herd of bored animals, and was now approaching the middle of the set of concentric streets that made up the main body of the Grove. A number of the flats and houses around this central area were empty, their doors and windows boarded. Others were occupied either by the kind of people you didn't want to meet or tenants who rarely stepped outdoors before nightfall. It was a creepy place, even in broad daylight, yet she was often drawn here by its sense of emptiness.

A border of old timber hoardings and security fencing surrounded the derelict tower block, but everybody knew a way in. Hailey's point of access was through a shallow channel someone had once dug under the fence close to the old red-brick electricity sub-station at the front of the building. She couldn't remember who'd shown her this route inside the perimeter, only that it had been pointed out to her late one Sunday evening, when dusk was falling and the sound of motorbike engines churning up and down the surrounding streets had filled the air.

Hailey got down on her belly and wriggled through the gap, trying her best not to ladder her thick black tights on any hanging wire or splinters. Her mother would kill her if she ruined another pair; the tiny clothes budget for this month was long gone.

The sky seemed to darken around her as she slid under the barrier, as if her entrance had triggered a dimmer switch in the heavens. She knew this was a silly thought, that it was too early in the afternoon to grow so dark, but there was something nice about pretending to be so important that the sky would create an atmosphere just for her.

Somewhere in the depths of the estate a dog began to bark; a burglar alarm went off, the wailing tone bound to be ignored and left to peter out of its own accord. A police helicopter hummed through the sky above her, so she stayed where she was, belly pressed into the dirt, until it passed by. But this was just another game. Nobody cared that Hailey was here; nobody was concerned about her whereabouts. Not even her mother.

After several seconds had passed, and sensing that she would not be seen, Hailey jerked upright and scurried across the cracked and stained concrete forecourt towards the waiting Needle. She stared at the empty building as she approached, peering at its boarded upper windows and security-shuttered doorways. Several of the caged windows on the ground floor had been partially exposed by vandals tearing off the timber and paint-daubed metal sheets and breaking the glass beneath. These openings bled darkness; they provided small, square glimpses of something black, unhealthy and rotten. If she allowed herself, Hailey could imagine things moving in there. Strange things. Dark things. Things that lived in such forgotten places.

What was she doing here? Why did the decrepit building have such a hold on her? She always came to the same place when she was feeling uneasy or simply craved solitude. Despite its central location on the estate, and the fact that there were so many ways in, children rarely played here. The place, Hailey's few friends had often told her, was haunted;

and once, a long time ago, a bunch of children had even been harmed by the spirits who dwelled within its crumbling concrete walls. Depending on who she spoke to, these children had either been scarred for life or murdered. The story changed with each telling, the way a fairytale might.

Hailey kept walking. The Needle ignored her, just like everyone else.

She stopped, confused. Why was she thinking of the old building in terms of a personality?

Hailey stared at the grubby concrete, trying to understand her feelings towards the place. She should be too afraid to set foot here, especially alone, but for some reason the resolutely upright Needle seemed to offer her some kind of solace.

Yes, that was the word: *solace*. She'd encountered it in English class. It meant comfort or consolation. That, she thought, sounded just about right.

She started to move again, towards the tower block. Broken glass crunched underfoot; her left ankle twisted slightly as she stepped into a shallow depression in the ground; her right foot kicked something hard and it rolled away from her across the uneven surface. But she didn't look down. She kept on staring ahead, watching the Needle as it loomed closer. Its tall grey rendered walls were as cold and dry as reptile skin; the boards across its windows were closed eyelids; the patches of weeds and wild grass at its base were as welcoming as a doormat at the threshold of a lovely home.

The conflicting emotions rushing through her – fear of the dark and empty spaces within the building's shell; a sense of feeling welcomed or, more precisely, bidden – made her feel slightly sick, as if she'd eaten something bad.

The main doors to the tower block were sealed with security shutters, so Hailey continued round to the rear, where there was a way in through a small ground floor window where the metal sheeting had been pulled aside. The window panel had been removed long ago, before the access point had been shored up, so whoever had then torn away the corrugated metal had been able to slip inside without having to shatter the glass.

Hailey peeled back the thin metal square, struggling to fold it away from the wall. The metal groaned as she moved it, and then finally it seemed to relent under the pressure and bent back to reveal the window aperture beneath.

The opening was roughly the size of the screen of the portable television Hailey had in her room at home. She was a slim girl – didn't eat much, and wasn't even keen on the sweets and sugary treats the other kids seemed to love – so she was always able to squeeze through without much of a problem.

She leaned in and forced the metal sheet further back with her shoulder, turning her body so that she could scrabble up the wall and begin to climb through. She wriggled her body into the gap, aware of the metal sheet digging into her side as she moved into the space. Then, with a final shrugging motion and a kick of her legs, she was through and tumbling onto the floor at the other side of the wall.

Dust rose in a cloud around her; the noise she'd made echoed through the concrete shell. Hailey sat on the ground and blinked into the darkness. It always seemed too gloomy in here – much more than she would have expected from the outside. It was as if natural daylight was afraid to enter, and the darkness held inside the Needle acted as a sort of barrier, protecting whatever else lived here from the light.

Now there was another unwelcome thought. Why did she keep doing this, trying to scare herself? It was like some kind of challenge. She was throwing down the gauntlet, daring herself to venture further inside the building. Maybe the bullies were right, and she really was as weird as they said.

A sound came to her from up ahead: a brief scraping noise, like a stick being dragged along the wall. She peered into the darkness, waiting for the interior to resolve in her vision. She saw the empty space, the walls and black rectangles of doorways. Her ears thrummed. She was in a hallway – she knew that much from past visits – but for some reason she never knew which way to turn. Was it left or right up ahead?

Standing, she moved across to the wall, reaching out to touch it, to confirm that it was there, as solid and immobile as ever. The sound did not repeat. Silence grew and swelled and threatened to become something even worse than noise. Hailey closed her eyes tightly for a couple of seconds, and then opened them again. This time the room was clearer; she could see deeper into the building.

A few metres ahead, the hallway became a T junction. Hailey paused for a moment to think, and then remembered that the left turn led to more rooms and the right one would take her to the reception area at the front of the building, which was usually littered with empty beer cans and bottles, used condoms and dirty syringes left behind by nocturnal visitors. Everyone who came here used the reception area: it was large and uncluttered, and the walls were covered with graffiti that probably dated back to the time when the Needle had been emptied and sealed.

Hailey moved forward, and when she reached the junction she turned left. Her ears felt under pressure, like when she went swimming in the deep end at the local pool. Doorways seemed to lean forward, blocks of blackness taunting her, challenging her to enter. She walked along the hallway, stepping over mounds and heaps of garbage – despite keeping the main area clear of debris everyone seemed to dump their rubbish here. She passed an old sleeping bag, holes torn in the fabric and the white guts seeping out. An old armchair sat against the wall, the stain across its back and arms resembling the bloodied outline of an unusually thin human figure.

Something moved behind her. Hailey refused to turn and look. There was nobody there; the building was empty. It was just a cat or a rat, or even a bird that had gained entry through an upper window, rooting around in the garbage.

The last doorway was closer now. It was the room she always used. The doorway had no door; even the hinges had been removed. She could never say why she came to this room, only that it was small and nondescript and relatively untouched. The other rooms she'd been inside were either blackened by fire, smelled of old sweat and urine, or were filled with random objects – black plastic bags filled with water-damaged porn magazines, broken crates and pallets, wheelie bins, shopping trolleys, and even a surprising number of discarded children's toys.

It was amazing what some people would dump in places like this...

When she reached the final doorway she stopped at the threshold. For the first time she felt a strange sense of apprehension, a feeling that she shouldn't be here, not now. She waited, and the feeling faded. Perhaps it was just a result of the increased tension at home, or something stirred up by that noise she'd heard earlier.

But no, that wasn't it. There was something... something else. Then, at last, she realised what was troubling her. Since entering the building she had been aware of a sort of vibration in the air, a soft thrumming sound that she had at first put down to distant construction machinery or heavy traffic. But there were no building works nearby, and the nearest main road was a couple of miles away. That police helicopter she'd spotted earlier? No. That would be long gone by now.

So what was it, that small sound, that weird throbbing in the still, dead air?

Not hesitating any longer, Hailey stepped through the doorway. The thrumming sound inside her head was threatening to leak out.

The room looked the same as it always did, but there was something different about the space as she entered. That sound was stronger here, inside the room. It sounded like bees, buzzing around a hive. Hailey was puzzled. Was there a wasps' nest in here, or perhaps a swarm of flies clustering around a pile of shit?

Part of her screamed that she should leave, but another, calmer part of her made her legs move and forced her deeper into the room. It was dark. The two windows were covered. The buzzing grew louder, as if responding to her presence.

At the end of the room was a cupboard – a built-in wardrobe. The doors remained intact, and the cubby hole was always empty, as if nobody had even noticed it, or if they had seen the cupboard they had not been interested enough to look inside. The buzzing seemed to be coming from within, behind the closed doors. It wasn't only in her head after all, and the realisation filled her with relief.

Hailey moved forward, towards the wardrobe. The buzzing sound intensified.

She stood before the doors. They were tall and narrow, with stainless steel handles. She reached out and grasped one of those handles, her fingers tightening around it. *Don't*, she thought. *Leave it alone*. But that other part of her – the calm part – whispered to her that she should open the doors.

Her hand made a fist around the small handle. Then it turned, pulled, and the door eased noiselessly open.

At first Hailey didn't know what she was seeing. There was a dense cloud inside the wardrobe, low down near the floor on the right hand side. The cloud seemed to be moving, vibrating. The buzzing sound was louder now – it filled her ears, flowing inside her head. The sound was that of their wings: quicker than thought, lighter than dreams.

She was looking at a swarm of giant insects. Flies. Bees. Hornets. No, that wasn't right. They were too big, too quick... too beautiful.

They weren't insects, they were birds.

Hummingbirds.

Hailey had only ever seen hummingbirds on television, on nature programmes, and they had always fascinated her. As far as she knew they lived in America, and places like Ecuador and Mexico. There certainly weren't any in England. So what were these ones doing in a dingy cupboard in a derelict tower block in Northumberland?

They were gorgeous. Their plumage was radiant – green, red, yellow and gold. The colours bled and mingled as she watched, lighting the darkness and forming a shimmering mirage of sad beauty in the bottom corner of that wardrobe.

There were a lot of them in there. Each one was tiny, the size of a baby's hand, and they were clustered in the corner as if they were all feeding from the nectar of a single bunch of flowers. Hailey watched them in silence, feeling a sense of awe creep along her arms, then climb to her neck, where it rose higher and flushed her cheeks.

"Beautiful," she whispered.

And that one word was enough to break the spell.

The flock of birds seemed to undulate, shifting as if their natural rhythm had been disturbed or even broken. They turned to Hailey as one, their little black eyes peering at her from the corner, their sharp little red beaks glinting in the shadows. Then, as if dancing, they flowed out from their hiding place, breaking apart their formation to hover before her, creating a brightly-hued screen between her and the interior of the wardrobe.

Spellbound, Hailey reached out a hand... her fingers opened, then closed. She tried to grab one – just one – of the hovering miracles, but they all flowed away from her, breaking ranks and forming an opening. She looked through the gap they had made and into the cupboard. And she saw what it was they had been eating, and why their beaks were so red, like they'd been carved from ruby.

The dead dog was folded into the corner of the wardrobe, its legs broken and twisted, its head crushed. The fur of the dog's jaw, and along its neck, was red, tattered, and the corpse had been punctured thousands of times. By countless tiny little beaks. Red beaks. Like rubies.

Hailey tried to scream but the hummingbirds were stealing her air, sucking it from her throat. She backed away, flailing out at the suddenly obscene creatures. Their wings moved faster than she could see; the buzzing sound was louder than anything she had ever heard. She knew that she would fall before it even happened: the image flashed through her mind, clear as a frame from a film.

Walking backwards, panicked and unable to take a breath, she felt her legs tangle and then she went down, hitting the concrete floor hard. She cried out in pain and shock and fear, and the hummingbirds swooped backwards, allowing a small space to open up between her and them. She drew breath; her cheeks swelled; her throat opened. Finally, and with great relief, she opened her mouth and screamed.

The birds backed away as one hovering mass: their colours were like spilled paints, their motion was nightmarish. Where Hailey had first perceived beauty, she now witnessed horror of a kind that she barely even understood.

She scrabbled on the floor, turning around and rising to her feet, pushing away and heading for the door.

Then she saw what the birds were moving away from.

Her scream had not caused them to flee. It was something else. A thing so alien, so unlike anything she had ever imagined, that it took on a strange kind of beauty – a beauty tinged with horror and darkness, and with tears and blood and sweat. Hailey's belly began to cramp; she felt moisture between her legs.

"What?" she said, and it was the only thing worth saying, the only question she could have asked. She tried to move back the way she'd come, towards the birds, but was caught between two extremes. Her legs skidded on the smooth concrete floor, her skirt riding up to show her dirty, slashed tights. The floor was cold on her exposed flesh. The backs of her legs turned to stone.

Hailey glanced down at the exposed parts of her legs: her scuffed knees, the smooth patches of thigh visible through her ripped tights. Then she looked back at the small, ragged shape that was blocking her escape.

Something vague, dusty and tattered shifted in the shadows near the doorway. Then, as if responding to her whispered question, it began to chuckle.

Others joined the creature, spilling from the joints in the walls and ceiling, squeezing through the plug points and light-fittings. Then, clustered together in a dense and leering pack, they came streaming towards her, aiming for a point directly between her open legs.

CHAPTER TWO

TOM RAN AS if the hounds of hell were snapping at his heels.

It was an old phrase – one his mother had been known to use whenever she needed to get a move on, if she was late for work or an appointment she needed to keep. *The hounds of hell.* Tom hadn't heard those words in years, never mind used them, so when they came into his head now, as he sprinted between lampposts on a street two miles away from home, he felt a twinge of grief somewhere deep down inside, like a guitar string snapping.

Tom's mother had died when he was twenty-one. She had never seen him finish university and get his first proper job, or even had the opportunity to meet his wife, Helen.

He ran faster, closing in on the crooked No Entry sign he was using as a marker.

Fartlek – it was Danish for 'speed play'.

The training method was one of Tom's favourites; it helped rid him of the formless anger he often felt burning up his insides. The technique involved sprinting for prolonged periods between two fixed points – usually street lights or concrete bollards – and it helped improve speed and stamina. In Tom's case, he would run at a steady pace for ten minutes, and then vary this by increasing his pace for a set distance. He only ever used the method when he was feeling particularly low. Today was one of those times.

Helen was having a rough time this week. She had developed minor abrasions that might turn into bedsores along one side of her back, and he was forced to roll her every hour or so to prevent this from happening. She screamed in pain whenever he moved her on the sheets.

Tom wished that she would just make an effort, try to get out of bed, before it was too late. She hadn't left the bedroom for over two years now, and he was losing patience. The woman he had fallen in love with, had worshipped with his mind and his body, was now nothing but a shell. The doctors had told him that physically there was no reason she should not at least be attempting to move around the house, even if she remained in the wheelchair instead of transferring to the sofa or a dining chair. No, her problem was a mental one – she was terrified of shifting her arse from the mattress, just in case she injured herself.

He reached the No Entry sign and allowed himself to slow to a jogging speed. He'd run six miles – two more miles than he had planned – so could afford the luxury of letting his muscles relax a little.

Tom's breathing was soon under control. He knew that fitness was all about recovery time, and his fitness was at a pretty high level. If nothing else, Helen's injuries had helped him get in shape. The shame was, of course, that those same injuries had also ruined her life. Both their lives, if he was honest.

He moved steadily along the street and turned left, cutting through a narrow ginnel and into the heart of Far Grove. He didn't like coming out here even in the early evening, hated straying this close to the place everyone called the Concrete Grove. It was a rough part of town, a Bad Area. Petty crime and anti-social behaviour were the norms, and Tom was not a man who believed in putting oneself in danger.

He increased his pace again, preparing to take the next side street and leave the Grove behind. Even on the outskirts, he could sense the hatred, the poverty, the basic lack of respect, for which the area was known. Even if this negative image was media-created, it was rooted in some kind of truth: the bad always outweighed the good in areas like this one.

The housing estate had been designed to form a series of concentric circles, each one bearing the word Grove in its title: Grove Street, Grove Avenue, Grove Terrace… one after the other, all the names similar and monotonous, just like the bland flats and houses and the sallow faces he saw whenever he did stray here.

Darkness was staining the sky; he'd been gone too long. Helen would start to worry.

Let her, he thought. *I'm sick of worrying about her all the time.*

He felt immediately guilty, almost as if he had landed her a physical blow. He knew it wasn't her fault, not really. Ten years ago she had been in an accident with a man who was in all but name her lover. They had been on their way to a country hotel to consummate the relationship, travelling too fast in the rain. The road surface was poor and the tyres had lost their grip on a turn. A simple thing, a small accident, but one whose repercussions could be felt like shock waves even now.

Tom no longer felt a sense of betrayal regarding Helen's illicit tryst, but still he could only think of the man who had been driving the car as That Man. He had become a symbol more than a human being, and his death in the accident was only fitting.

The accident had left Helen emotionally as well as physically damaged, and Tom realised that there was a possibility she might not ever again be the person he had married. No, that wasn't right. She would *never* be the same, it was a certainty. Too much time had passed with too little improvement. He was stuck with her like this forever, or at least until she decided that enough was enough and stopped wanting to carry on with what was left of her life.

As Tom approached a row of asbestos garages – surely the council should have demolished them, in the name of Health and Safety? – he glanced across the road to examine the grass verge opposite. There was a metre wide strip of what should have been green but was actually brown, with a footpath on the other side. Lying on the ailing grass and curled up into a tight ball he saw what looked like a large rag doll, or perhaps a Guy – but it was nowhere near Bonfire night, so the shape couldn't be an effigy of Guy Fawkes, England's most beloved terrorist...

Once again, Tom slowed his pace. He jogged to a point where he was level with the doll, or heap of clothes, or rolled up carpet... then he realised that he was looking at a person. A small, crumpled person. A child, in fact.

He looked both ways along the street and saw no sign of anyone else in the vicinity. Even the lights in the houses were off. A handful of the doors and windows – even this far out of the heart of the estate – were covered with wood or metal security shutters, and the rest, those still occupied, were shut up tight for the evening.

The sky was growing darker. A couple of birds flew overhead, one of them letting out a sharp squawking noise as it glided over a low house roof. He heard a faint buzzing sound, like flies swarming nearby.

Tom crossed the road, slowly, carefully. He had heard stories of people pretending to be injured so that they could mug an unwitting Samaritan. Granted, these possibly apocryphal tales had been reported in the seedier redtop newspapers, but still it paid to be cautious. These days, caution was the byword. You couldn't just rush into these kinds of situations acting like the big hero, not anymore. That way you risked being beaten or stabbed. Only a few weeks ago there had been an incident where a man coming to the aid of a young woman being abused by her boyfriend outside a pub had been turned on by the couple and beaten so badly that his skull had been fractured in five places.

"Hello." His voice was low. Small. He felt ashamed at how frightened it made him sound. "Hello there. Can I help?"

The body – the child – did not stir.

"Are you okay?"

As he moved closer, Tom realised that it was a girl, probably in her mid-teens. She was wearing a grey school blazer and a crumpled black skirt. Her black tights were dirty and torn; one of the ripped tight-legs had rolled down to the ankle. There was a smear of mud on one exposed knee.

"I'm not going to hurt you." He wasn't even sure why he'd said that, but it had seemed right, a small reassurance. If the girl had been mugged or raped then it stood to reason that she must be scared, and she might even be pretending that she was unconscious until he went away. "I can help."

He was now standing roughly two metres away from the girl. He could see the knots in her dirty brown hair and the pale skin of her cheek. Her small hands were clutched into fists, her arms drawn inside and held tightly against her chest.

Tom moved closer and went down onto his haunches, feeling his knees creak a little. Sweat dripped from his brow and into his eyes. He wiped it away with the back of one hand.

The girl moved, just an inch. She turned her head slightly, her nostrils flaring, one eyelid fluttering.

"My name's Tom Stains. I was running... I saw you here. Can I help you?" He felt idiotic, stuck there and not knowing what to say. All he could do was repeat the same tired lines, like an actor in a bad television play.

The girl's eyes flickered open. They were blue. Like cornflowers. The blood rushed back into her cheeks, colouring them a warm shade of pink. She opened her mouth, worked her jaw and tried to sit up.

"Let me." Tom went over and grabbed her by the arm, trying to help her to her feet. She looked up and smiled. Her lips were dry; the skin was chapped. He was amazed that he was able to make out such intimate details.

"Thanks," she said. Her voice was dry and croaky. She lurched upright, holding on to him for support. Her grip was tight, her fingers digging into his biceps. "Sorry."

"Don't worry. Let's just get you on your feet." Tom was painfully aware of his bare legs, his ridiculous running shorts and the T-shirt with the silly logo that said "If Lost, Return to the Beer Tent." For some reason he wanted to impress this teenage girl, to make her feel safe. She invoked a strange paternal instinct that took him by surprise as well as a faint erotic charge: a curious set of feelings that he had not realised he was capable of experiencing.

"I'm okay," she said, still leaning against him. He prayed that he didn't get an erection, and deliberately ignored the sight of her thighs, visible through the rips in her tights.

Still sweating, but now for a different reason, Tom led the girl over to a low garden wall. She sat down, finally relinquishing her grip on his upper arm, and rubbed her face with her hands. She had a long, graceful neck. The top three buttons of her blouse were undone.

Stop, thought Tom. *Just stop it.*

"Are you... are you injured?" He kept his distance, still feeling silly in his shorts and T-shirt.

The girl looked down at herself, seeming to

inspect her body for signs of damage. "No. I don't think so."

"What happened? Were you attacked? Mugged? Did they take anything?" Tom licked his lips. His throat was dry.

"I dunno. I think I just passed out, like. Fainted. You know?"

Tom nodded. But he didn't know; he didn't have the slightest clue as to why a healthy young girl might faint. "Are you ill, or something? Is that why you passed out?"

The girl shook her head. "I don't know why it happened. It just did. I was walking around near the Needle, next thing I know I'm waking up here." She smiled, but it looked forced, as if she were trying to convince him of something.

"The Needle? That's all the way over there, isn't it?" Tom turned his head due north, raised a hand to point but dropped it before it even reached waist level. Everybody knew where the tower block was; it was visible from just about everywhere on the estate.

"I know. Weird, eh?" She smiled again. "What did you say your name was?"

"Tom. Tom Stains. I've been running..." He glanced down at his legs, lifting his arms away from his body in an almost apologetic manner.

"Yeah. Whatever." She glanced along the street, dismissing him.

"What's your name? I should take you home; get you back safe and sound to your parents." God, he sounded like an old man.

"I'm Hailey. I live a few streets away. I'll be fine." She pushed away from the wall, but stumbled a little. Steadying herself, she grinned. "Or maybe not."

"Come on, Hailey, let's get you home. I'm sure your parents will be worried." He took a step towards her but did not touch her. It wasn't appropriate, not now. She could walk by herself, unaided, and if he grabbed her she might get the wrong idea – or *he* might.

"Mum. It's just me and Mum. But, yes, she will be worried. She worries about me all the time round here. It's not like where we used to live." She turned and began to walk along the street, her strides slow and uncertain.

"I see." Tom fell into step alongside her, ready to catch her if she stumbled but not willing to offer his arm unless she asked. "Just you and your mother, eh?" Something turned inside him, like a key in a lock or a tumbler falling into place: some hidden mechanism within the chambers of his heart. Tom didn't believe in fate or destiny, he clung to no god. But there was something about these events, a sense that the picture was not what it seemed. Beneath the surface, under the façade of reality, something was happening, changes were taking place.

Unbeliever that he was, Tom was confused to think that the steps he was taking now were in fact the beginning of some kind of journey. The destination was unclear, the aim unknowable, but he had willingly taken a turn off the beaten track and allowed himself to be led astray.

Somehow these thoughts failed to trouble him. In fact, he felt more alive than he had in years. Tom couldn't remember the last time he had embarked upon anything that might be considered an adventure.

CHAPTER THREE

NIGHT WAS FALLING in slow shades as they walked along Grove End, past the dark hulk of the primary school, and headed towards the Grove Court flats. The long nights were drawing in. It would soon be Christmas. Tom hated Christmas.

He was so aware of Hailey strolling along at his side that he could think of nothing else, not even the things he hated. He knew that Helen would be expecting him home to prepare dinner, but he could barely even picture her face. All he could see was the girl.

Tom realised that after the initial near-sexual thrill he'd experienced his feelings towards Hailey had faded to something more like fatherly concern. The girl was in some kind of trouble, that much was certain. He didn't believe her story about fainting and not knowing how she came to be lying unconscious at the side of the road, half a mile away from where she'd been roaming.

"Just down here," she said, as if she were deliberately trying to break into his thoughts. She turned, smiled, and then faced forward again. Her strides were now long and even. She seemed much more in control than when he'd first found her. Perhaps he should just leave her here, close to home, and be on his way?

No. If she had been accosted, as he suspected, that would be a foolish thing to do. She was a young girl and it was growing dark. He was duty-bound to accompany her at least to her front door.

There was also the voice at the back of his mind, the soft, purring one that suggested if the girl was this pretty, then her mother must be beautiful. There was no father around, and she might be so grateful that she invited him in for coffee...

Tom laughed softly.

"What's wrong?" Hailey glared at him, her blue eyes flashing in the growing dimness. "What you laughing at?"

"I'm sorry," he said. "It was nothing. Just a silly thought I had, that's all." He smiled at her and hoped that she couldn't see through his mask.

Hailey coughed, and then glanced slowly around, as if she were looking for someone. "I don't like it here. The closer you get to the centre, the weirder it feels. Don't you feel it? It's like something in the air – a gas, or something."

Tom was confused. He didn't know what she wanted him to say. "This is a run-down area. There are people here who you don't want to meet after dark. That's all."

Several lights had come on in the front rooms of houses and flats. Television light shuddered like a submarine's lamps through thin curtains. Tom knew what the girl meant. This was a strange place, especially after dark. That was why he didn't like coming here, why he wished he could run the other way... any way, just not deeper into the estate.

They turned right onto Grove Mount and then crossed the road. There were two cars parked alongside each other at the mini roundabout at the end of the street, young drivers leaning out of the side windows to make some kind of exchange. Tom thought it was probably a drugs deal, but it could be something worse. He'd heard rumours of all kinds of things changing hands down here, and lethal weapons being given to kids who were stupid and desperate enough to use them.

"Which number is yours?" He tore his gaze away from the illicit transaction – although, part of him reasoned, it couldn't be that illicit if it was being carried out in plain view. Another, more cynical voice replied: *it's more a case of nobody giving a damn.* The air was turning cold, and his legs prickled with gooseflesh.

"Number eleven," said Hailey, slowing down. "Just here, the one on the corner." She approached the squat block of flats – a two-storey building with a grass verge outside its spiked metal railings.

"You'll be fine from here. I'd better get back... my wife will be wondering where I am." He pulled back, away from her, taking a few backward steps across the footpath.

"No, come in and meet my mum. She'll want to thank you for helping me." Her smile was impossible to ignore; he felt his own come to life in response, as if it were a bloom flowering in sunlight. "Just for a minute."

Tom felt his legs move towards her, dragging his resistant body behind. He had the feeling that he might regret this, but still he followed her through the gate and along a narrow concrete path. He didn't try too hard to leave her and go home.

"It's here somewhere…" Hailey fished inside her blazer pocket and produced a set of keys. She opened the main door to the flats and walked inside, clearly expecting him to follow.

Not knowing what else to do, Tom paused for a moment to glance both ways along the street, and then he quietly stepped inside the building. The external darkness gave way to a smoother, duskier darkness inside the building. Hailey didn't bother to turn on the lights as she ghosted across the ground floor. She opened a door and turned towards Tom, smiling. "Come on up." Then she walked through the doorway and Tom was forced to hurry before it closed.

They climbed the stairs without speaking, their footsteps echoing on the tiled treads. Tom felt apprehensive. Would her mother really welcome him or would she think that he was some kind of pervert in his daft shorts and sweat-stained T-shirt? "Maybe I…" But he didn't finish. Hailey had reached the landing and was opening another door; this one let out light as it swung wide, and Tom could do nothing but follow.

The hallway was clean but narrow. At one end there was a glass fire door – presumably this led out onto one of the tiny balconies Tom had seen from the street. He stayed a few steps behind Hailey, wishing he'd just turned and walked back down the stairs. But it was too late now; he'd gone too far to risk looking like a fool. *An even bigger fool*, he thought as he glanced again at his bare legs.

As he watched, someone walked quickly past the other side of the glass door. Then, abruptly, they returned and crossed in the opposite direction. He waited for them to do an about-face and repeat the pass, but nothing moved. For some reason he felt a prickle of fear across his back; his muscles tensed, an involuntary reaction.

Then one of the doors in the hallway opened.

"Hailey! Where have you been?" The woman standing in the doorway was beautiful. Tom stared at her, wishing that he wasn't there, dressed like an idiot, but he was also glad that he'd accompanied the girl home. It was worth the hassle just to catch sight of this woman, to see her leaning out into the landing and clutching her shirt collar shut across her pale throat.

"This is Tom. He brought me home." Hailey's voice had lowered an octave, her whole manner changing and becoming surly, that of a stereotypical teenager.

"Hello... listen, I'm sorry." Why the hell was he apologising? He'd done nothing wrong. "I found her out in the street, near Far Grove. She'd fainted. I just brought her home. So she'd be safe." He was backing away, raising his hands and probably looking like he was trying to escape. He might as well be wearing a T-shirt with 'Guilty' printed across the chest, rather than the message about the Beer Tent.

The woman turned to Hailey, her brow furrowed with worry. "Did it happen again? Did you black out?" She pushed fallen hair out of her face with a thin hand. Her hair was so black that it looked blue beneath the cheap hallway lighting. Her hand was like a small animal, snuffling along her neat hairline.

"It's okay. I'm fine. He helped me." Hailey turned to face Tom, pouting. She suddenly seemed much younger than she had before.

Tom smiled. He didn't know what to say.

"I suppose I should thank you." The woman stepped out of the flat. Her feet were bare. She was wearing an ankle-length skirt along with a white blouse – the outfit made her look vaguely bohemian. "I didn't mean to be so unwelcoming. People round here… well, you know. Some of them are a bit grim." When she smiled her dark eyes blazed. Her cheeks flushed red.

"I didn't do anything. Just brought her home. I thought she might've been mugged." He was poised for flight. Just one wrong move on her part and he felt like he might flee. What was wrong with him? Was she so alluring that he was afraid of her?

Yes. Yes, he was. She was terrifying.

"Please. Come in. Have a drink. Let me thank you properly." She stood aside, and he caught a glimpse inside the flat. It was small, poky really. Bland white paper on the walls. Cheap carpet on the floor. "You must think I'm terrible. Fancy a beer before you go running off again?" She gestured with her head, raising one eyebrow as she looked at his shorts.

"Oh. Yeah, I was out for a run. I don't usually wander around the streets in this get-up. Not after dark, anyway." This exchange finally broke the tension; he felt calmer now, in control of his emotions.

"Drink?" She made a drinking motion with her left hand. He noticed that she wasn't wearing a wedding ring.

"That would be lovely," he said, and took a step forward. A single step that felt like he had recommenced the journey started outside, when he'd decided to escort Hailey home. "If you don't mind, that is."

"If I minded, I wouldn't have asked. By the way, my name's Lana. Lana Fraser." She held out a hand. Her fingers were extraordinarily long – he hadn't noticed before, but they seemed distorted above the top knuckle. He reached out and shook her hand, feeling those weird fingers. They were cold to the touch.

Tom walked into the flat. Hailey was already inside, vanishing into a room – presumably her bedroom – on the right hand side of an entrance area that was too small to be called a hallway. Another door up ahead – this one open – led into what must be the living room.

"Go on in. Make yourself at home." Her voice was close to his back. He imagined that he could feel her breath on his neck, but that was silly. He knew that she was standing a few paces away, closing the door, locking it behind them. "I'll just a moment."

The living room was small, but cosy. There wasn't a lot of furniture, just a TV, a slightly battered two-seater leather sofa, two mismatched armchairs, a coffee table, a bureau shoved against the wall and a bookcase stacked with hardbacks. Tom made for the latter, crossing the rug that lay over the laminated floor. He had always been an avid reader, and loved to check out people's book collections.

He could hear voices in the other room, the one Hailey had entered. They were raised, but not shouting. A concerned mother checking that her daughter was okay.

He ran his fingertips along the worn spines of Lana's books, noting the fact that these were well-thumbed copies.

"Tea, coffee, or a nice cold beer?"

He turned, surprised for a moment that she had managed to sneak up on him so quickly. "Oh, I think a beer would hit the spot."

"I think I'll join you," said Lana, heading for the open-plan kitchen that took up one whole side of the room.

The cooking and living/dining areas were separated by a series of floor-to-ceiling wooden shelves and a narrow breakfast bar, which helped give the impression of two rooms where there was really only one. Tom watched Lana moving behind the shelves, catching sight of her through ornaments and knick-knacks as she bent to the fridge and then crossed to the sink. Then he turned back to the bookcase. He spotted a couple of Graham Greene novels immediately, and nodded his approval. The books were in no particular order that he could make out – unless it was a purely personal system – and each one was a hardback edition, either with or without a dust jacket. Steinbeck stood next to John Irving; Tom Sharp rubbed shoulders with Dickens; Shakespeare snuggled up next to Stephen King.

"Are you a reader too?"

He turned, clutching a battered copy of Norman Mailer's *Tough Guys Don't Dance*. It was one of his favourite novels. "Yes, I am. I love books, always have done."

"Good," said Lana, handing him a glass of pale beer. "That's something we have in common from the start, and I think that potential friends should start off from a shared interest." Her smile was radiant... it was also cheeky; he felt as if she were teasing him.

"So we're going to be friends, are we?" He took a sip of his drink. It was ice-cold. He closed his eyes briefly, savouring the taste.

"I think it's the least we should do, don't you? Seeing as you were kind enough to help my daughter."

"Is she okay? I mean... unharmed?"

A flicker of something dark passed across Lana's already dark eyes. She shook her head; a vague gesture that Tom failed to read. "She's been having these mini blackouts. They don't last long, just a few minutes. The doctor says it's nothing to worry about, just stress from the move and some stuff that went on back where we used to live." She waved her hand, dismissing the subject. "Yes, she's fine. Thank you for being so concerned." She smiled to show him that the comment was genuine, but her eyes remained shaded.

"Shall we sit?" She moved across the small room, heading for the sofa, then changed her mind and lowered her thin body into one of the armchairs. Tom followed her, and sat on the sofa. He had almost finished his beer. "Refill?"

"Only if you are," he said.

She nodded, stood, took his glass. Their fingers touched again, and this time it felt strange, like a tiny electrical current had passed between them. She stared at him with those dark, dark eyes, a puzzled expression on her face.

When she returned from the kitchen she was carrying a tray. Upon it were their refilled glasses, and two more cans of beer. "One for the road," she said, winking.

"So," said Tom, a panicked feeling welling in his chest. "You say you haven't lived here long?" This woman was confusing him. There was a mutual attraction here, he could feel it, but it seemed that they were both trying to ignore the connection.

"Do you live here, in the Grove?"

Tom shook his head. "No. I... not that there's anything wrong with living here, of course." He felt his cheeks burning. He was talking himself into a corner. "I mean... shit. Sorry."

She laughed. "Don't worry. It *is* shit here. I'm not fooling myself otherwise. Hailey and I used to live in Newcastle. It was South Gosforth, to be exact, right next to the Metro station. We had a nice home, I had a good job. Then a couple of years ago it all went tits-up when my husband bailed on us and his debtors. We lost the house and we had to come here. It was the only place the council would give us; according to their stupid little points system we didn't have a high enough rating for anywhere decent." She took a long swig of her drink, closed her eyes and swallowed.

"I'm sorry. I shouldn't have been so nosy." He rubbed his palms on his thighs, then realised that the action made him look like some kind of madman. He stopped, held up his hands. Then he picked up his glass and drained it. "Listen, I should go."

Lana nodded. She licked beer foam from her lips. "Is the wife waiting for you at home?"

For some reason he could not identify Tom felt guilty. "That's right. She's… she's not well. There was an accident several years ago and she relies on me." Why did he feel the need to justify himself? Was it because, really, he didn't want to leave? He wanted to stay here and drink into the night with this woman, trading histories, telling stories, laughing and bonding and becoming friends – perhaps even more than friends.

He stood, tugging at the hem of his shorts, trying to cover the goose pimples that had appeared above his knees. "I should… you know. I should leave." He felt dizzy, like the world was spinning faster beneath his feet. He tried to hold on, had to hold tight. If he didn't, he thought that he might fall off the edge of the planet.

"Thanks again," said Lana, following him as she walked to the door. "Listen, I didn't mean to come on too strong then. It's just that I don't have any friends here, and I think I get a bit needy. Just ignore me." She reached out, as if she were about to touch his arm, but then let her hand drop away.

"It's fine. I can be your friend." Jesus, did he really just say that? "How fucking corny," he added, pausing by the door.

"Just a bit," said Lana, smiling now, looking happier than she had done only seconds earlier. "But it was a nice thing to say." She turned her head slightly to one side, and he caught sight of a faint scar along her jawline.

When he left the flat he had to fight not to look over his shoulder, just to catch another glimpse of her as she closed the door. He heard the locks slide into place, and paused to listen for her footsteps. But of course he couldn't hear them; there was no way her bare feet could be heard through the door. Yet he told himself that she was standing on the other side, thinking about him.

Tom descended the concrete stairs, and left the building. He glanced at his watch and was shocked to find that it was now almost 9 PM. The street lights were on. Voices drifted towards him – kids' voices, filled with intent. The song of distant sirens accompanied him as he jogged back along Grove End, along the side of the school and towards Far Grove. He felt like he was leaving something behind, something that might just prove to be worthwhile. Never before in his life had he experienced feelings like these: it was terrifying, but it was also liberating. Had he ever felt this kind of thrill when he and Helen had first met? He thought back, to the time when they'd swapped phone numbers in the university canteen, and realised that what he had felt then had been but an echo of this, and not a very strong one.

The voices receded, far behind him. Laughter. Running footsteps.

In the silence that rushed in to replace the sounds, Tom became aware that he was being followed. He turned his head to glance over his shoulder and saw a quick, light movement as something shot through a gap in the school fence and padded across the yard. He felt his feet slowing; his hands clenched into fists. *Run*, he thought. *Just keep going*. But his body refused to obey. It felt like all the blood was rushing out of his feet. The beer he'd consumed pooled in his lower stomach.

Despite this physical reluctance, he pushed onwards, aware that whatever had entered the school was now moving back in his direction. It drew level with him, keeping pace behind the high metal railings. He saw its dark, glistening flanks as it ran. The shape darted between pools of sodium light, and for a moment he thought that it was a child loping along on all fours. Then, gasping with relief, he saw that it was a short-haired dog. Of course it was. The relief was displaced once again by fear when he remembered that there had been sightings of packs of stray dogs in the area – he even recalled a story about someone being attacked one night by a mangy mongrel.

Tom tried to look away, to look straight ahead, but he was unable to take his eyes from the beast that ran alongside him, loping between patches of lamplight. The road was narrow here; the creature was so close that he could have reached out and touched it through the gaps between railings. There was moisture in his eyes; he felt like weeping.

Then the dog turned its bristly head to face him. And Tom felt an emotion that at first he could not explain. Never before in his life had he experienced real fear – the kind of fear that makes you realise that you are always a single moment away from death. One thought filled his mind, casting everything else in shadow: the dog's face was human.

It was a hound with the features of a person, a male. A boy.

In the split second during which the thing looked his way, Tom made out its wide green eyes, its strangely hairless cheeks, its flaring nostrils and thin, curling lips. He was struck with a sort of nostalgic horror as the face of a young boy smiled at him from the body of a dog. Nothing he could have imagined would have scared him as much. He had not been this afraid since childhood.

And then it was away, bounding further into the school grounds, towards the dark classrooms. He tried to tell himself that what he had seen could not be real. That it was impossible. After all, he'd experienced but a single, snatched glimpse and not a prolonged look at the thing. He even managed to fool himself for a while, as he peeled away from the school railings and ran along in the middle of the road. Then, when finally he reached the brighter area where the road bisected Far Grove Way, he admitted all over again that what he had seen had been something from a nightmare, a nightmare that he should have remembered from long ago.

Even if his eyes had deceived him, it must have been his brain trying to tell him something, to warn him that he was close to making a big mistake. He shouldn't be here, in this godforsaken wasteland of the Concrete Grove. In fact he should never come here again.

Helen was waiting for him back home. Behind him, at Lana's flat, there could be only trouble. It was time to go home to his wife, and return to the life he had chosen many times, whenever he had been called upon to make the decision.

Running hard now, quickening his pace towards a full sprint, he tried to rid his mind of the shame and the guilt and the slow-burning rush of illicit pleasure. But no matter how fast he ran, and how far he went, Tom knew that he could never outrun himself.

CHAPTER FOUR

TOM WAS COLD when he arrived home. The temperature had dropped outside, and the skin of his legs was taut and goose-pimpled. He fumbled for his key in the tiny pocket at the rear of his shorts, his fingers unable to get a firm grasp on the Velcro flap. It took him a lot longer than it should, but at last he grasped the key and slipped it into the lock. The downstairs lights were off. Shadows swarmed around his feet, cast by the light that bled down the stairwell from his office.

"Tom?" Helen's croaky voice drifted towards him from the ground floor. "Is that you, Tom?"

Who the fuck else would it be? He thought. Then he said: "Yes, it's me. Sorry I'm late." He closed the door and walked along the hallway, flicking on the kitchen lights as he entered the room. The spotlights seemed to snap on too quickly, too brightly, and he closed his eyes against the glare.

The breakfast dishes were still in the sink. This morning, feeling lazy and careless, he hadn't even bothered to load the dishwasher.

"Tom?" Her wavering tone annoyed him, made the hairs on the back of his neck bristle like those of a cat just about to pounce. He closed his eyes again, silently counted to ten.

"Tom!" Impatient now, he could hear her manoeuvring her body in the bed in the other room.

Her excessive weight made the timber frame creak.

"Just a minute, love. I'll bring you some soup." She always liked soup on a week night. Even when she was fit and healthy, in the days before the accident, she had enjoyed a bowl of cream of tomato or oxtail after coming in from work.

Tom moved quickly, opening the can and pouring its contents into a saucepan on the stove. He stirred the soup as it warmed up, and once it began to bubble slightly at the edges, he buttered two slices of bread. When the soup was ready he ladled it into a large bowl, and then placed the bowl and a plate containing the bread on a plastic tray. He added a spoon and a napkin, and then left the kitchen and walked through the house to her room.

Helen had occupied the reception room since she'd come home from hospital. At first it had been a matter of sleeping in there so that Tom could get some rest. The pain had kept her awake; she didn't want to cause him any sleepless nights. Now, much to his relief, she stayed in there because she was too lazy to move. He couldn't stand the thought of her joining him upstairs in the master bedroom – even if their sex life had not died along with her ability to walk, the idea of her massive body beside him was enough to bring a sour taste to the back of his throat. And she was so big these days that he stood no chance of carrying her up the stairs.

He pushed open the door and stepped inside. The room was dim – she rarely let him open the curtains, and the light she used to read by was fitted with an energy-saving bulb that never cast much light.

"Sorry I'm late, Helen. There was this girl, just a young lass, really. She'd fainted in the street and I had to stop and help her."

Helen put down her book on the bed. She turned and peered at him over the lenses of her tiny reading glasses. Her jowls shuddered. "Really? Was she okay?"

He nodded. "Yes, she was fine. Just a bit shaken. I took her home to her... her parents. They said she suffers from fainting spells, some kind of seizures. But she was fine when I left." He smiled. Why wasn't he telling her everything? Parents? He felt guilty for hiding the fact that Hailey had only a mother – and an attractive one at that – but something held him back, made him give a sanitised account of events. Was it guilt? But why? It wasn't as if he had done anything wrong or improper. He'd thought about it, yes, but thinking a thing and acting upon those thoughts were entirely different situations.

"Here," he said, moving towards the bed with the tray balanced on his open palms. "I made your soup."

"You never forget, do you? Never let me down?" Her smile was big and loose, like a mother smiling at her child. "I'm glad I have you to look after me, Tom. God knows what I'd do without you, you know."

He set down the tray on her meaty thighs. "Why do you say that? Of course you have me. Why wouldn't you?" Again, he felt that his own guilt was making him labour the point. She often did this, a sort of passive-aggressive emotional blackmail. He usually ignored it... but now, this evening, what had happened earlier was making him defensive. "Just eat your soup. I have crusty bread; it's your favourite."

Her small, spongy hand grasped the spoon and she shuffled up against the headboard, trying to settle into a more comfortable position. When she raised the spoon to her mouth some of the tomato soup spilled down the front of her nightdress. For a moment, Tom thought it looked like blood. She tipped the spoon and drank the soup, closing her eyes to savour the taste.

Tom felt like picking up the bowl and pouring the scalding contents over her head, onto her face... and then he felt ashamed, disgusted with himself for resenting Helen in this way. It wasn't her fault she'd been partially paralysed, not really. Yes, she had chosen to be there, with That Man, but nothing in life was ever so clear cut that you could fairly apportion blame. Nobody was innocent; everyone was guilty of something. It would be unfair of him to place the whole of the blame onto Helen's shoulders.

Maybe so, he thought. *But it's her fault that she won't even get her fat arse out of bed.*

Again, he felt a deep sense of shame; a depth charge of emotion detonated in his stomach. The accident – why did they all keep calling it that, even now, *especially* now? – had left deep mental trauma, like a trench in her soul. Helen was afraid to go out, and she was equally as frightened to remain inside. Her whole life was lived in a state of fear now, and there was very little anyone could do to change that. All Tom could do, all he could really manage, was to collect her prescription drugs once a week and feed and care for her every day, offering her support when she needed it. Washing her armpits, emptying her colostomy bag. Keeping her human. Whatever their marriage had once been, it wasn't the same now. Everything had changed that day ten years ago, when That Man had crashed the car in which she was a passenger and she'd lost all feeling from the waist down. That day, that terrible, terrible day, was effectively when their love had died.

Oh, they still shared something like love, but it wasn't the same kind they'd known before. The feelings had changed, mutated, as they were battered and torn in the accident, and then they had re-emerged as a form of duty.

Tom watched her eat, trying to take pleasure from the fact that she was still alive. At least she still lived. But he knew in his heart that living was something she no longer really did: all she was capable of was existence.

When she was done he took the tray and left her bedside. He turned back at the door, looking at her, but she was concentrating on her book. It was a paperback mystery, the kind she couldn't get enough of these days. It puzzled him that although she was terrified of everything outside the front door, she enjoyed reading about murder and mayhem. Perhaps the fictional horror helped keep her real-life fears at bay.

"I'm going to work for a while. Shout for me if you need anything else."

She did not look up from her book. "Thanks, I will." Her eyes blinked behind her small reading glasses and she licked her colourless lips. She had not even noticed the soup stains on her nightdress. She was so utterly unconcerned with how she looked these days that it had passed her by.

She used to be beautiful, he thought. *So very beautiful. Like Lana Fraser.*

He left the room and closed the door, leaning back against the thin wooden panels and feeling moisture gather in his eyes. He looked at the tray, at the dirty, red-smeared bowl and the crumbs on the plate, and he realised that he'd always fucking hated tomato soup.

The memory of what he had seen on his way home – the dog with a boy's face – came back to him. If he was seeing things, imagining monsters, nobody could blame him. His life was a slow implosion of duty and regret. Tom knew that he was going under, that things were getting to him in a way they never had before, and perhaps his strange vision was a result of his conflicted emotions.

Wouldn't any man who was forced to wipe his wife's arse after she took a shit in a plastic bowl, and then struggle with her spongy, shapeless form to pull up her pants experience some form of breakdown? Not to mention the fact that once she had deteriorated enough to have the bag and tubes fitted, it was up to him to keep them washed and sterilised. Didn't that justify some kind of emotional upheaval?

Now that he was home, and away from that grotty estate, he could rationalise what had happened. The thing he thought he had seen out there in the darkness could not possibly exist. His mind had conjured a demon to represent his inner turmoil – that's what the psychology books and websites he occasionally read would say, anyway, and he was inclined to agree with them.

But still he could not shake the fear he had felt when he thought that he was being stalked – or, to be more precise, when he felt hunted. It was like nothing he had ever experienced before. It was real, and the terror had been so strong, so overpowering, that it had felt like a twisted kind of happiness.

Jesus, was he so messed up that he now equated fear with a feel-good factor? He laughed softly, but even to his own ears it sounded forced, as if he were trying to convince an unseen listener that he was taking none of this seriously.

The truth was, of course, that he was unable to do anything else.

He went back through to the kitchen and loaded the dishwasher, wiping down the work surfaces before slipping the washing tablet into its slot and pressing the buttons to set the machine away. The dishwasher thrummed softly, a soft voice singing in a foreign language. He closed his eyes. The sound was almost soothing.

Closing the door on his way out of the kitchen, Tom made his way upstairs to what he still occasionally liked to call his study, a room that had once been the guest room, where their friends had stayed after entertaining dinner parties and drunken conversations. The room had served as his office for ten years now, since Helen had come out of hospital to be cared for at home.

Ten years. It felt to him like a lifetime, a span of time that he could barely make sense of. How had it become so long so very quickly?

He booted up his computer and waited for the programs to load. He knew that he should start work immediately, but felt restless. There was no way he could settle down this evening, not without something to calm him. Internet porn? Meeting Lana had certainly stirred his libido. But no, it didn't feel right. Maybe he'd hit one of the regular forums and chat for a while with his faceless friends – other lonely carers reaching out across cyberspace to try and make their own lives seem less empty.

The computer screen flared into life.

Tom ran his fingers over the mouse, trying to make sense of his need.

Lana. Lana Fraser.

What's your story, Lana Fraser?

Tom opened the browser and without thinking about what he was doing he typed her name into the search engine. The name was not uncommon. The search summoned a lot of unrelated hits, but halfway down the first page he saw the one he wanted. His eyes were drawn right to it, as if he were meant to see the details.

It was a link to an article in a local newspaper, dated eighteen months ago:

… Mrs. Fraser has lost her home… murderer… wife and daughter… prominent businessman killed himself…

Tom clicked his cursor on the link and was taken to the relevant page. He read the article, feeling sad and horny and shameful. There was a photograph of a much younger version of Lana, black and white, clearly taken some time ago. She was wearing a dark suit. Her hair was pulled back into a tight ponytail. She looked glamorous and sharp as a blade.

He had no recollection of the story, but must have read about it at the time. Her husband had murdered three people – shady businessmen with organised crime connections – and tried to make the killings look like gangland assassinations. They were revenge killings, brought about because of an investment that had gone sour. When his crime was uncovered, and he became aware that the police had marked him as their top suspect, Timothy Fraser, aged thirty-eight, had taken a small-calibre handgun and shot himself in the face. He lived on in hospital for a week, in a coma and under police guard, and then he died.

Lana had lost everything: her home, her money, her lifestyle. It had all been taken by administrators to cover the cost of the bankruptcy and pay back her dead husband's debtors.

Tom needed a drink. He pulled open the top drawer of his desk and took out the whisky bottle and tumbler he kept there. He poured a large measure, knocked it back in one. Then he poured another, smaller amount into the glass and returned the bottle to the drawer.

"Lana Fraser," he said, his lips burning slightly. "I think we might both be in need of a friend." He took a sip and closed his eyes, then threw back his head to enjoy the swallowing motion as the harsh liquid flowed down his throat to light up his insides like a flame.

CHAPTER FIVE

LANA SAT IN the chair by the window and watched the fire in the sky. She wasn't sure what was happening out there, or where exactly the source of the reflected flames was located, but at least it wasn't right outside her door. That, at least, was a comfort.

These days she took her comforts where she could, and they were always small. So small, in fact, that she was often unable to pinpoint them amid the general chaos of her existence.

The flames burned on, beautiful and pitiless, as if a great furnace door had been opened.

Only last week Lana had been sitting in the same position, sipping a similar glass of Chardonnay to the one she now held, when some kids had let off a firework in the street outside. The rocket had arced up into the sky and then turned slowly towards her window, striking the glass. The crack was still there: it was paper thin, barely even noticeable, but she saw it every time she looked through the window. She'd called the council, trying to get a workman to come out and replace the pane, but her request had been met with a wall of apathy.

"Little bastards," she said, gripping her wineglass, not knowing if she meant the culprits or the council workers. The fire in the sky shimmered, as if in response, and then it dimmed before giving off another surge of brightness.

Kids, it was always kids. Places like these, council estates inhabited by the people society had shoved to the bottom of the pile, were full of ill-mannered kids out to cause trouble. Some of the parents didn't care, many of the ones who did simply lacked the skills to manage, and the schools were unable to cope. The rest got lost in the shuffle.

It was just the way of things; there was nothing anyone could do about it. The situation had gone too far, the rot was set too deep, and the country had long ago accepted this kind of anti-social behaviour as the norm at a certain level of society. The level she and Hailey now occupied.

It seemed like there was a constant stream of bad behaviour on the estate: lighting fires, vandalising private and public property, killing house pets, bullying the incapacitated. It never stopped. There was no end in sight.

It all amounted to just another night in the Concrete Grove.

Hailey was in bed, dreaming of whatever she craved for these days – no doubt pining in her sleep for everything they had lost. Her bedroom door was closed, perhaps even locked. She had never locked her room at the old house in South Gosforth. Back then, there had been few secrets between mother and daughter. But now, in this new life, it sometimes seemed like secrets were all they had, the only things that kept them close. They shared nothing but the fact that they hid things from each other. The glue that bonded them was impure, toxic.

The details of what had happened to Timothy constituted one of those secrets. At first Lana had even tried to keep it from Hailey altogether, but once the newspapers and the local TV news started reporting the story, that soon became impossible. So she was forced to tell the child at least part of the truth – the fact that her father had been broken by life and chose a dark way out. The effort to keep the secret from everyone else – to remain tight-lipped around the estate in which they now lived – had finally brought them together again. The bond they shared was not the same as the one they'd had before, but it was all they could hope for under the circumstances. Quite frankly, Lana suspected that it was now the closest thing to love they would ever know.

She sipped her wine and wondered whether she could possibly summon any more tears, or if her well had finally run dry. Then, disgusted with herself, with her stupid self-pity, she emptied the glass and refilled it. She was getting drunk. Her eyes were heavy and her mind was blurred, as if layered in cotton wool. She could no longer trust her emotions, or her instincts.

But that was good: she liked being drunk. It made the lies seem more like truths.

That man. The one from earlier this evening. What was his name? Tom? He was nice. She smiled at the memory of his nervous grin, his loose limbs, dumb T-shirt and silly running shorts. Why was she thinking of him now, at her lowest ebb? Was it because, for some reason, when she had spoken to him she had felt less alone?

"Fuck," she said, enjoying the way the word tasted of wine and stolen kisses. "Get a grip, woman."

Now that she had time to think about him, Tom seemed even more attractive than he had when he'd brought Hailey home. After Hailey had gone to bed, Lana finally had the time to consider what she had felt as he stood there, bare-legged and shaking in her doorway. Clearly he found her attractive too – Lana was experienced enough to recognise the signs. But it was more than that, deeper. There was a connection between them, a quiet spark that had simultaneously slowed down and speeded up the short time they'd spent together. He was older than her, but that might even be part of the appeal: a figure of authority to cling to in the night, when her demons came loping towards her out of the dark.

Lana struggled to understand the thoughts in her head. The wine, the night, the worry over Hailey and those weird fainting spells, it was all setting her off balance, confusing her to the point where she no longer felt that she could trust herself to do the right thing.

But what was the right thing? And how would she recognise it? There were no rules here, no written bylaws she could follow. Everything was fluid: even emotions were up for barter.

She took another mouthful of wine, held it, and then swallowed. The taste was good: bone-dry and woody, just how she liked it.

When the telephone rang she took a few seconds to register its quiet buzzing. Frowning, she glanced over at the handset where it rested on the windowsill. She stood and walked to the window, once again looking at the fiery darkness hanging above the distant silhouette of Far Grove.

Sirens drew close as she reached out to pick up the phone, as if the sound had been triggered by her motion.

"Hello." Her voice was bounced back at her through the earpiece – a fluke of acoustics, or a fault on the line. "Hello," she said again, and this time she was answered by a thick, heavy silence.

Feeling her heart swell in her chest, Lana waited. She knew who it was. There could be only one man who would call her so late, and project such a sense of menace down the line.

The line hummed. It sounded like distant wings, hundreds of them, beating so fast that it filled her ears with a single note.

"Do you have it?" His voice was like rocks splitting, concrete breaking under immense pressure.

There was no point in pretending, in playing dumb. "No. Not yet." She closed her eyes. "But I will."

She pretended that she could hear the sound of her own heart beating, and if she waited long enough it would rise in volume and drown out his words, silencing his threats.

"I want it tomorrow." Again, that gritty voice: pure verbal hatred. "I'll send a couple of the chaps round."

Lana still could not open her eyes. If she did, she thought she might see him standing there, grinning, his hair slick with gel and his eyes blazing. "It's too soon. I don't have it. Please... just give me a few more days. A week." She loathed the pleading tone in her voice, the fact that she was reduced to begging from scum like this, whining like a dog for scraps from the table.

"Tomorrow." That humming. The sound was audible behind his voice. "The chaps'll call on you. Be there or it'll only be worse for you." Then he hung up.

Lana stood there, bathed in distant firelight, her forehead sweating and her hand gripping the telephone receiver. She was unable to put the phone down. Her fingers refused to budge, to open and relax their grip.

"No," she said, and the word was like an exhaled breath. It made as little impact on the world as a sigh. "I don't have it."

Finally, after what seemed like a long time, she was able to relinquish her grip on the handset. She put it back on the windowsill, carefully, delicately. She still had her eyes closed. Her lips were trembling. Darkness danced behind her eyelids. The world was unstable, as if someone had untied her from her moorings and she was beginning to drift, to move away from everything that had ever seemed safe. The darkness behind her eyes beckoned.

"Mum?" Hailey's voice, behind her and filled with concern.

Lana opened her eyes and the fiery darkness flooded in... then, gradually, it receded, letting in the light. The sirens were louder.

"Mum? Are you okay?"

She turned round and faced her daughter. Hailey was standing in the doorway, the light from her bedroom forming a bright pool at her feet. She was wearing an oversized nightgown and clutching the ear of a ragged teddy bear – the one her father had given her, and which they had both, for some reason, christened Well-do. It was a private joke, one of the few things father and daughter had ever really shared.

"Hi, honey. Can't you sleep?"

Hailey shook her head. She was fourteen years old, yet she often seemed a lot younger. Right now, standing there with her weight on one hip and Well-do in her hand, she looked about ten, maybe even younger than that.

"What's wrong, Hay? Bad dreams?" Lana started to move across the room, towards her daughter, but Hailey flinched long before she even made it to her side. "What is it, honey? Tell me about it."

Then, at last, she saw it: the dark stain at the crotch of Hailey's nightdress, the way she was standing turned fractionally to one side to hide the damp patch. "Oh, Hailey. Oh, baby, come here…" She went down onto her knees and hugged her daughter close, ignoring the smell of urine and the way that Hailey shuddered at her touch. "It's okay. Just an accident, that's all." She felt her eyes begin to prickle and blinked away the threat of tears. "Let's get you cleaned up."

So for the second time that night Lana comforted her daughter, treating her as if she were an infant. She ran a hot bath and watched in silence as Hailey undressed, trying to hide her thin body in the steamy bathroom. Lana stared at her slight arms and legs, at her small mound of a tummy. She was aware of a strange sensation in her chest, like the slicing motion made by a thin blade, and she looked away, unsure of what it was she was feeling.

There was a soft splashing noise as Hailey climbed into the bath; a louder one as she sat down in the water and moved her hands through the bubbles.

"Everything's going to be fine." Lana heard herself say the words, but she couldn't believe them. The lie came easily, like a gift, and she accepted it with good grace. Sometimes it was easier to let people hear what they wanted, and this was certainly one of those times. "*We're* going to be fine." But they weren't; of course they weren't. They were in a lot of trouble and nothing she could do or say could alter the facts: she owed money to the biggest bastard in town, and he wanted it back, one pointless payment at a time.

Lana ran the sponge across her daughter's narrow shoulders, letting the hot water spill across her pale skin, turning it pink. Hailey said nothing. She just sat there in the bath, letting the water soak her, staring at the same spot on the tiles. She didn't even blink.

What is it? Lana squeezed the sponge, stared at the soapy water on soft flesh. *What's come between us?*

A lot more than the murders and Timothy's suicide had created a vast gap between them, pushing them and keeping them apart. There was something else – an unknown quantity – and Lana did not know what she was meant to do to fix the problem. She was not armed with all the facts; whatever Hailey was going through, she was keeping it to herself.

For some reason, perhaps even fear, the girl would not come to her mother for help.

"Speak to me, honey." Lana whispered through tight lips, her jaw aching from the tension. "Tell me what it is."

But Hailey kept staring at the wall, at the stained white tiles, her eyes unfocused yet seeing something beyond the room, the flat, the entire estate. Whatever it was she was looking at, Lana felt that it was changing her daughter, transforming her into a stranger. Making her different. Turning her inside out.

The room was filled with steam, obscuring her vision, and Lana felt that she should open the window but she didn't want to leave Hailey's side. Something kept her there, near the body that had begun life curled up within her, the construct of skin and hair and bone she had built for nine months inside her womb.

Lana was afraid for her daughter, but she didn't know why.

Hailey had not wet the bed since she was two years old, and even then it had been an accident. Even her father's death had not caused this kind of physical reaction, just the expected crying and outbursts of rage.

So what, Lana thought, was so terrifying that Hailey was suddenly fainting in the street and pissing herself in her sleep? What the hell was scaring her this much?

The steam moved sinuously, as if it were hiding shapes within its cloudy mass. At last Lana was able to move away, and she walked to the window and opened it, letting in the cool night air. The steam shifted, breaking apart like a hacked sheet. There was nothing behind it, no monster hid within the folds of dissipating steam. Nobody was in the bathroom apart from the two women, mother and daughter, and the unmistakable presence of their shared fear.

"Please," said Lana, once again hating the fact that she was forced to plead.

Hailey said nothing. She twitched her head to the side, one corner of her mouth turning up in an expression that was not quite a smile but something else, something unreadable. "It's nothing," she said, and her voice was like that of a small child, not much more than a baby. "I promise, Mum. There's nothing wrong. Nothing at all."

Lana stood by the window, the cold air kissing her neck, the sirens wailing in the night. In that moment, with the song of the estate ringing in her ears, she knew that Hailey was lying.

CHAPTER SIX

WHEN LANA WOKE she felt a strange sense of panicked urgency, as if she should be doing something important but couldn't remember what it was that required her attention. She blinked at the daylight, opening her mouth to run her dry tongue across her even drier lips. She felt the beginnings of a headache flaring up behind her eyes.

The radio was playing at a low volume on the dressing table. There was make-up scattered across the table's surface, on the seat of the chair and on the floor. Eyeliner pencils, tubes of lipstick and other beauty paraphernalia had been thrown down carelessly. She didn't remember much, just a vague notion of applying make-up, washing it off, and reapplying it differently. She had a mental picture of her face in the mirror, eyes blackened by mascara, lipstick smears across her mouth.

She sat up slowly, not wanting to encourage the headache. An empty wine bottle rolled off the bed and onto the floor, hitting the carpet with a soft thud. She'd taken alcohol to bed again. That was never a good idea, and she knew that it was happening too often for comfort. Her father had died from drink – his heart had failed under the pressure of too many years of chronic alcohol abuse. She didn't want to go the same way, leaving behind a blotchy, wine-sodden corpse for her daughter to bury in a cheap coffin.

Lana glanced over to the open bedroom door. She usually closed it at night – a leftover fear from her childhood, when she couldn't sleep with an open door – but now it was wide to the wall. Daylight slanted through the gaps between vertical blinds, forming lines across the carpet which stretched to the doorway. Lana watched the bright tramlines, light-headed and slightly nauseous.

She reached out and turned off the radio.

There was a noise from somewhere inside the flat. It sounded like something heavy falling to the floor, or perhaps a door slamming. Was Hailey up and about, getting ready for school? Lana slid out of bed and put on her dressing gown. She caught sight of her reflection in the wall-mounted mirror and was relieved to see that last night's horror-show make-up had been cleaned away. Her cheeks were bare, shiny. They looked sunken. Her eyes were too wide, and as flat as old-fashioned copper pennies. She tried to swallow but it hurt her throat. Her skin was clammy.

She left the room and walked along the short hallway, towards Hailey's room. "You up yet, honey?"

There was no reply.

"Hailey? Come on, let's get up and get you ready for school. No messing about, now." She stood outside Hailey's room, one hand on the door handle. She squeezed the handle but didn't turn it. Something held her back, an echo of fear. She didn't understand why she felt so afraid, but terror filled her like water, drowning her from the inside. Lana felt like she was about to choke on it, to stop breathing.

She turned the door handle and pushed open the door. Breathing steady now, she entered the room. Some identikit boy band stared down from a poster on the wall. Hailey's books were all lined up neatly on their shelves. Stuffed toys glared at her from the floor. Her television was on, the picture stuck on a DVD menu: images of dancing animals dressed in human clothes.

The bed had been made, the quilt smoothed down on the mattress and the corners – weren't they called 'hospital corners'? – tucked down tight. "Hailey, where are you?"

She listened to the silence, waiting for a tell-tale sound, but none came. Hailey, if she was still indoors, was keeping quiet. Lana glanced at the alarm clock on the nightstand. It was 7:30. Hailey didn't usually leave for school until well after 8 o'clock, so she must still be here. The girl didn't have many friends she could go and meet up with before classes, and there was nowhere else she could have gone this early.

She turned and padded quickly back out into the hallway. The bathroom door, at the far end near the front of the flat, was closed. She moved towards it, wondering if Hailey was having a bath – the shower had worked only sporadically for almost two months, and no-one from the council had been out to fix it. This failure to fix things was a recurring pattern, both in the home and in Lana's life in general.

She paused for a moment at the door, and then knocked. A sudden burst of daylight shone in her eyes, reaching her through the lounge window; it was hot and bright, making her wince. Then the light faded, and when she looked at the window the day outside was dull and hazy.

"Are you in there, Hailey? What's wrong? Are you ill?"

There was a long pause, and then Hailey finally answered: "Not feeling well, mum. Just a bit sick, that's all."

Lana tried the handle but the door was locked. "Come on, let me in. Do you need something? Is it your period?"

Again, Hailey said nothing. Lana knew that the girl was embarrassed to talk about these things, but it was an important part of life, and one that required discussion, particularly if Hailey was having problems.

"Listen to me. I used to suffer really badly with cramps. They were so bad that I used to vomit. Is that what's up with you? Is it cramps?"

"Yes." Then she heard the sound of the toilet flushing, followed by what might have been Hailey putting things back in the bathroom cabinet. Was that a bottle of pills she could hear rattling?

The lock clicked; the door opened. Hailey stood there in her white school blouse and pleated black skirt. The tail of her blouse was hanging out of her waistband, and she looked small and frail. Her eyes were huge, with dark circles beneath them. There was a splatter of vomit on her chin.

"Wipe your mouth," said Lana, picking up a tissue and using it to wipe Hailey's face, doing a mother's job before Hailey even had the chance to pull away and look in the mirror. "It's okay, honey. I can do this." She smoothed down her daughter's hair with her fingers, noticing how dry it felt. The skin of Hailey's forehead was hard and flaky; her T-zone felt like fine emery paper.

"Thanks," said Hailey, taking a step back, partway into the bathroom. Her eyes were squinted, as if the light hurt them. She licked her lips and her tongue looked dark, almost purple.

"What is it? Aren't you feeling well? Maybe you should stay off school today."

Hailey shook her head. "We have a maths test. If I miss it I'll have to sit it again some evening after school. I'd rather go in. I'm fine." She pushed the hair out of her eyes with her thin, white fingers.

"I've never seen you look so pale... it's like you're anaemic. Maybe I should make an appointment with the doctor." Lana wanted to hold the girl, but felt that it might scare her. When exactly had they moved so far apart?

"No. Really. I said I was fine. I am, really. I'm okay. Just a bit tired."

Lana moved away from the door. "Aren't you sleeping?"

Hailey shook her head. "Not too well. Not here, in this place." She walked past Lana, being careful not to touch her.

Lana felt like crying. "I'm sorry. I never wanted it to be like this. I had plans for us, big plans." She stood where she was, bathed in the glow from the bathroom light, feeling its fragile warmth on the side of her face. "I thought things might be better once we settled in."

Hailey wasn't listening. She crossed the lounge and went into the kitchen area, where she sat down at the breakfast bar, staring at an empty bowl. Her eyes looked odd, as if she were blind.

"Let me get you something." Lana followed her daughter, opened a cupboard, and poured some cornflakes into Hailey's bowl. Then she opened the fridge. "Fuck," she said, feeling useless. "There's no milk. I forgot to buy milk." The omission felt like a metaphor, a symbol of how bad a mother she was. "How could I forget to buy the fucking milk?" She felt hysteria building, as if she were about to laugh or scream – she wasn't sure which, and even when it came the sound would be difficult to identify.

Slowly, carefully, she closed the fridge door. Then she closed her eyes and gritted her teeth.

"Don't worry about it," said Hailey, standing and pushing the stool across the cheaply tiled floor. "I'll get something on the way to school."

Lana was unable to open her eyes. She was entranced by the dancing darkness behind the lids. "Do you have money?"

Hailey laughed, but it was a bitter sound. "Yes. I have money." Then she went to the front door, opened it, and slammed it behind her as she left.

Lana straightened up and opened her eyes. She saw bright little points of light in her field of vision; dancing moonbeams, trapped in her kitchen in broad daylight. The bright spots faded, going out like distant flames blown by a wind, and then vanished altogether.

Acting on impulse, she returned to the bathroom, lifting the toilet lid and staring down into the bowl.

Stringy vomit floated like pale kelp in the water, clinging to the side of the bowl where it had not quite been flushed away. There were tiny red flecks in the matter, as if Hailey had also brought up a small amount of blood. She could be mistaken, but it looked as if that was what had happened... unless she was suffering from the hangover and the weird morning light, and the redness was simply the result of tired eyes. She reached out and pressed the flush, watched the water as it swirled and cleaned away the stains.

A rogue thought entered her head, and she was unable to push it away: *what if it isn't vomit?* But the thought of Hailey issuing that pale, clotted material from elsewhere was one she couldn't countenance. It was too much; too terrible to hold inside her mind.

Back in the kitchen she made instant coffee and sat at the breakfast bar wondering how she could get her life back on track. Things had gone so wrong by now that it seemed impossible to put them right. Everything was difficult; the world was at best uncaring and at worst actively against her. Nothing went right, not now: everything she tried seemed to fail, and her attempts to fix their situation usually brought more pain into their lives.

At first she didn't hear the knocking at her door, but after a short while the sound grew louder and drew her attention. Lana put down her cup and walked across the room to the door. Monty Bright's phone call was fresh in her mind. She thought about putting the security chain in place, but then decided against it. If Bright wanted to get to her, he could pick and choose his moment. A cheap door chain would not hold him back.

She opened the door.

The man standing in the corridor was big, possibly the largest human being she had ever seen. He stood well over six feet tall and his girth was proportional to his height. A large round shaven head sat on a neck that resembled a joint of uncooked beef – wide, raw and spilling over the collar of his white shirt – and when he smiled a gold tooth glinted somewhere at the back of his mouth.

"Morning, darling." His voice was squeaky, quavering, like a tardy teenager's late-breaking tones.

He was wearing a tight black leather bomber jacket and dark blue jeans. The clothes were so big that Lana assumed they must be custom-made, and were probably expensive to buy.

Lana took a single step back, into the narrow hallway. She didn't mean to retreat; it was an instinctive reaction to the presence of the giant at her door, the monster who was even now following her inside. Only when he moved did she catch sight of the other two men behind him. They were not as big as the first, but they were big enough; tough enough.

"I hope we aren't disturbing you, Miss Fraser." The last one in closed the door behind him. The flat felt tiny, as if it were a doll's house.

"I haven't got the money." She stood against the wall just inside the lounge, giving them the run of the place. She decided that subservience might be the safest course of action. "I told Monty yesterday, when he called me. I don't have anything this week."

The smallest man, the one closest to the door, stepped forward and gave her a fast back-handed slap across the face. Just before her head started buzzing, Lana noticed that he was wearing black leather gloves. She didn't realise that her head had shot backwards and hit the wall until the pain started: a hot, beating place at the back of her skull. She felt tears rolling down her cheeks, and she was ashamed. The last thing she wanted to do was show these bastards how much they scared her.

"Just keep your fucking mouth shut until we tell you to speak, Miss Fraser." It was the one who'd hit her: he was standing right in front of her, his scarred face only inches from her own. He ran a hand along her bare arm; the black leather felt wrong, like diseased skin.

She nodded, trying to smile.

"That's better," said Leather Glove Man. "It's always easier when you people let us control the situation."

"Get a fucking move on, Terry," said the large one. He was examining the room, picking up books and putting them down again, running his fingers over her ornaments and framed photographs. "Ooh, nice." He picked up a photo of Hailey in a swimsuit. "I like it when they get those little pointy titties. Like buds, they are." He brought the photograph to his face and licked the glass frame.

Lana closed her eyes. The third man, who had moved further into the room, began to giggle.

"Dirty bastard," he said; his voice was nasal and unpleasant. "You'd shag anything, wouldn't you?"

"If it bleeds it breeds," said the big man. "And I do like it when they bleed..."

Lana opened her eyes. "Listen, I can give you some other stuff, just to buy some time. I have jewellery. Some of it's still worth a lot of money – it's from before, when we were better off." She moved away from the wall but Terry pushed her back against the plaster, his leather-clad hand pressed against her chest, between her breasts. He looked right into her eyes and smiled.

"Come on," she said, feigning weakness while all the time she wanted to tear out his throat with her teeth. "Be reasonable."

"Reasonable," said the big man. "And what's reasonable about borrowing money and not paying it back? Monty's a *reasonable* man; all he wants is what's due to him. Nothing more, nothing less. He wants what he's owed." The gold tooth glinted. Leather Glove Man's hand at her chest pushed harder, shoving her back against the plasterboard wall.

Lana was trapped. She knew it, and the men in her flat knew it. This was a game, a routine, and they were all aware of the rules. They would intimidate her for a little while, maybe even rough her up a bit more, and then they would take whatever they wanted in lieu of money owed.

Her right cheek was burning. The pain where she'd hit the wall with her head was a gentle throbbing, subsiding as she spoke to the men.

The big man stepped forward. His leather jacket creaked and his footsteps were loud and heavy, like sacks of wet earth being dropped onto the floor. "You know why we're here." He pushed Terry out of the way, bringing up his hand to stroke her cheek. "We're going to take your stuff and go away. Then we'll come back again, but for the money next time. This is a warning. We won't hurt you, not today. But next time we're going to have to break some fingers, or maybe even a pretty little hand. Not an arm or a leg – that'll come after. It gets worse each time." His meaty fingers slithered across her face, cupping her chin. He squeezed, forcing open her mouth. "We might even take something else... something that you won't want to give freely. You have a very pretty mouth." He blinked rapidly, as if there was something in his eyes. "So does your daughter."

Lana was breathing heavily, as if her heart was approaching a cardiac arrest. It was panic, building in her chest and spreading outwards, like a fire. She fought to control her rage: lashing out would make things worse, and probably result in even greater violence.

Just a warning, she thought. *That's all*.

"There's a message, too. From Monty. You want to hear it?"

Lana nodded. He was still gripping her chin, keeping her jaws locked open. Her mouth was wet. Saliva filled the back of her throat, but she was unable to swallow.

"If you want to pay off the debt in another way, come and see him at the gym. He's always willing to negotiate, and you're a very attractive woman, Miss Fraser." He paused, cocked his head to one side like a dog. "You don't mind me saying that, do you?" He pushed his knee between her legs, forcing them apart.

"No," she said, her breath coming in short, sharp stabs. "No, not at all."

The big man pressed his broad kneecap into her groin. Her legs began to tremble.

"Thank you, Miss Fraser," he said, pulling away from her. "Now we'll just take a few things and be on our way."

Lana felt her body crumple like a discarded suit. Her legs buckled and she slid down the wall, rubbing at her chin. Her face ached; her legs felt like partially disassembled plastic toys, unable to hold her upright. She sat on the floor and watched the three men as they moved around the flat, mentally cataloguing her belongings. When Terry, the one with the leather gloves and the quick hands, entered Hailey's room she fought the urge to scream.

It took them less than thirty minutes to clear her out. They knew what they were doing and the type of goods they were looking for. They only took the stuff that was worth something in terms of resale value; everything else they either left behind or destroyed for fun. The last thing they carried down the stairs to load onto the back of their van was the television. Hailey would be distraught if she couldn't watch her shows: lacking close friends or any kind of regular social life, she used her video games and the TV as her main sources of distraction.

But at least they'd left her books. Thugs like these were not renowned for their love of literature, and

Hailey had a shelf filled with classics and science-fiction novels, books that had belonged to her father. Hardy, Wells, Vonnegut; the girl loved her books, and would have been distraught if she'd lost them.

The men said little more before they left: just a few words, a couple of vulgar promises that washed over her, not even touching her where it mattered. The big man grabbed his crotch in his massive hand and blew her a kiss on his way out the door. "Next time we'll have some proper fun," he said, before thrusting his hips like a piston. "Some proper *fucking* fun..."

Lana remained where she was on the floor, squatting like some primitive warrior woman delivering a baby in the dirt. She was no longer shaking. It was comfortable down there, near the dusty skirting board. She stayed there for a long time even after they left, thinking about her options, trying to work out what to do about the situation. Once again, she had failed her daughter. The choices she had made led only to despair.

Soon all she could think of was Hailey's face when she walked through the door after school to find the flat emptied of their belongings.

Hailey's poor, sad face and a single word, one she'd always been afraid of, even when it had entered her life two years ago. A word that stayed there, lodged inside her head, even when she stood up, crossed the room and closed the door. Her hands, when she looked at them, were as steady as those of a stone sculpture.

The word in her mind brought horror, it promised terror and a release from financial bondage: the word was *revenge*. But it was something she shied away from, terrified. Violence was an option she could only ever consider once everything else had failed. She'd learned that, at least, from her desperate murderer of a husband.

THE THREE MEN walked outside and headed towards their car, the largest of the group hanging back from his colleagues. He stopped, looked up, and then looked back at the Grove Court flats, feeling a strange tingling sensation at the back of his neck, as if he were being watched.

"Boater! You coming?"

He kept staring at the grey-walled building, his eyes scanning the façade. Finally they came to rest upon the window of the flat they'd just left – Lana Fraser's place. What was drawing his gaze? Why was he staring so hard, so intently, at that window? Was it that he was desperate to get another glimpse of the woman inside? Yes, she was beautiful, but he'd seen better. In truth, he'd had better. Despite his size, and the fact that he was not a handsome man, the power associated with his position as one of Monty Bright's pack-dogs ensured that he never went hungry for physical pleasure.

No, it wasn't just her beauty. There was something more – an inexplicable desire, a craving. It exhausted him to think about her, and the obscene act he'd put on inside the flat had caused him to lose his grip on the day. All he wanted now was to go home and rest.

"Come on, man! For fuck's sake, we have work to do. That junkie needs sorting out, for one thing. Monty doesn't want him coming down from his high before he can go to work on the skinny bastard's arse."

Francis Boater fought hard to drag his eyes from the window. He strained, forcing the muscles in his neck to turn his head. Then, when he was once again facing in the direction he was meant to be heading, he pushed his reluctant feet across the pavement.

"I'm coming," he said, but what he really wanted was to get away, to go back to the flat and tell that woman that everything would be fine. These thoughts were new to him; never before had he felt even a glimmer of tenderness. Not way back when his mother used to treat him like a house pet, or during any of the subsequent desperate relationships he'd fallen into. This feeling – it was so large, so much bigger than him, that he felt like falling to his knees and crying, or pummelling the nearest face into mush.

Yes, that was it – that felt so much better. A normal reaction: the lust for violence. Francis Boater would be nothing, just an empty shell, if it were not for the violence at his core. It was what drove him, what made him real.

He joined the others at the car, those alien thoughts banished for now. Banished but not forgotten.

CHAPTER SEVEN

HAILEY KNEW SOMETHING was wrong before she even entered the main door of the Grove Court flats. She stood outside the building, clutching her book bag, and looked up at the balcony of the flat she and her mother shared. The window looked smeared, as if someone had rubbed dirt across the glass. The concrete balcony jutted out from the façade like an afterthought, its crooked rail looking as loose and dangerous as ever.

She thought about the Needle, and what had happened to her there. She had no real memory of the events, just a vague image of hummingbirds and something small and lithe and dusty darting towards her from the shadows. Then she'd blacked out and found herself lying on a grass verge a mile away, on the border of the estate, with that man – was his name Tom? – leaning over her, his face knitted with concern.

She pulled the strap of her book bag over her shoulder and pushed on through the door, into the building. At the bottom of the stairs she felt an involuntary internal shudder pass through her as she glanced up the concrete stairwell. Hailey didn't like enclosed spaces, and the stairs always smelled of stale piss and sweat. Kids often sat around on the steps at night, drinking beer and smoking spliffs, urinating up the walls and shouting into the empty spaces.

She began to climb the stairs, clinging to the handrail and moving as quickly as she could without fear of stumbling. By the time she reached the next floor, she was breathing heavily. Her stomach rolled, once, as if she were carrying something fluid in there, and she belched. Tasting egg in her mouth, she opened the fire door and moved slowly across the landing, heading for the door to their flat.

Outside the door she took out her key and adjusted the bag on her shoulder. Her stomach felt bloated, gaseous. She rubbed the area above her belly button, experiencing mild discomfort. Then she slipped the key into the lock, jiggled it, and turned. The door latch popped and she kicked the door open a couple of inches, jamming her foot between door and frame to stop it from closing again – the lock mechanism was automatic, and she didn't want to have to fiddle with the key again.

"Mum." She walked into the hallway, pushing the door shut behind her. The latch clicked into place. She threw her keys onto the telephone table, let her book bag fall to the floor, and shrugged off her jacket. Her arms felt cold; she hugged herself, rubbing at them, wondering if she was coming down with something. There was some kind of bug going around at school, and she could easily have picked it up from one of the other kids.

"Mum! You in? I'm home... what's for dinner?" She walked along the short hallway, turning the corner into the living room, and was surprised to see her mother sitting on the floor and cradling her head in her hands. The side of her neck was red, livid, and the lights were out. The sky outside the window was growing dark, signalling the early approach of evening.

Then she noticed that most of the furniture was gone.

"I'm sorry, honey. They took it all." Her mother's voice was muffled, as if she were afraid to make herself properly heard. "All of it."

Hailey remained where she was, standing in the doorway. "Did they take the TV? *My* TV?" She clenched her hands, making little fists, and began to press them into the flesh of her thighs. Her stomach churned, the innards rolling like an internal tide, back and forth, in and out, stirring along with her mood.

"Yes. I'm sorry. They took anything they could sell. I didn't have the money. I couldn't get it. I tried." She removed her hands from her face and looked up. Her cheeks were pale against the red rawness of her throat, and her eyes were dark. "I really did try. I even rang around a few old friends of your father's, turned on the sob story... but the fuckers didn't even want to know." She stood, sliding her spine up the wall as she straightened her legs. "Not one of those sorry bastards would even offer us a few quid, just to keep the wolf from the door." She smiled, but it was not a pretty sight. It looked more like she was baring her teeth, trying to snarl like an animal. "And that's what they are: wolves. Or maybe sharks." She smiled again, and Hailey looked down at the tops of her shabby trainers.

"It's okay, Mum. We'll survive. It's just stuff... belongings. We can replace them." She didn't mean what she said, but she knew it would comfort her mother. Hailey felt nothing, she was beyond feelings. Whatever had happened to her at the Needle had exacerbated a transformation that was already well under way. Gradually, over the past few months, she had been shedding the capacity to empathise, to experience emotions in the way she saw others do. It felt like she was removing herself from the society in which she was trapped. Like a snake, she was shucking off her skin, layer by layer, to reveal a new being beneath.

Quite where these thoughts had come from, she was unsure. They were brand new, alien. She had never before even considered notions like these, and it was terrifying and enlightening. Somewhere deep within Hailey, it appeared that there was the potential to be someone else, to become something new. Whenever she focused on her own mind, picturing what might be hiding there, she heard the distant buzzing of hummingbirds' wings and smelled dust and rot and the essence of memory.

She saw things behind her eyes when she closed them, late at night when she was chasing sleep. Strange things, dead things: hideous yet beautiful things that shouldn't be there, not in this world. She knew they were dead because they were twisted, decayed, and they did not move. Not, at least, until she saw them. And then they moved slowly and gracefully, as if underwater, and they turned their shadowed eyes upon her... seeing her, marking her out, noting her as one of them.

That was when their true beauty dawned upon her, and she realised that instead of horror these things promised freedom; they offered salvation, but only if she were brave enough to reach out and take it. That was what her transformation – this unbecoming of the self – was all about. Hailey might be 'educationally slow', as her teachers put it, she could even be emotionally underdeveloped, but she was bright enough to know that something was trying to reach her, to communicate with her. She also knew that whatever it was, this being, this presence, its source was the Concrete Grove.

For the first time since moving to the area, Hailey began to feel like she might, in fact, have come home.

"Don't cry, Mum. We'll be strong together."

Her mother stepped across the carpet; her bare feet were soft and silent on the thin weave. She fell into Hailey's arms.

"It's okay. Don't worry." Roles had reversed. Hailey now felt like the parent, the protector. She was not quite sure how this had happened, or when it had begun, but her definition of reality had shifted to accommodate the changes going on inside her. She held her mother close, stroking her sweaty hair, and kissed her cold, pale cheek. "We can get through this. I love you." The words tasted sweet, like all lies, and she repeated them out of greed rather than affection. "I love you, Mum."

Her mother's body went slack against her, the tension leaving her limbs and the looseness of relief taking its place. Hailey didn't know how she sensed these things, but it made her feel strong, and more intelligent than ever before.

Was this part of the change? Was it making her brain expand, filling it with new knowledge? She smiled. "There, there," she whispered. "Nobody's going to hurt us."

Later, when they parted, they tidied the flat, brushing up the broken ornaments and toys, putting away the things the men had thrown down onto the floor. They changed the bedding and washed the kitchen work surfaces. Hailey watched her mother carefully, noting the changes in her – just as she had mentally absorbed the ones occurring to her own inner being.

It felt like the end of something... and the beginning of something else.

"Come here," she said, when the cleaning was done. "I have something to show you. You need to feel it, though."

"What is it? You seem different... what have you done?" Her mother stepped closer, one hand reaching out to hang in the air between them.

"I've done nothing, Mum. Honest. But I am different, and so are you. We both are. There's something here, in the Grove, and it wants to help us. It's taken me a long time to figure this out, but whatever's here, in this place, it can help solve our problems."

Her mother shook her head. Her eyes shone in the lamplight. "No, honey. You're imagining things. I know everything's bad right now, but I promise I can make it better. I have... I have an idea. A plan. I just need to work things out in my head before I do anything."

"Look, Mum. Can you see?" Hailey raised her shirt, pulling it up over her now swollen belly.

More changes had taken place in the last couple of hours, and the pain was gone. Now, in the dimness, she felt radiant, as if she were supplying all the light they needed.

"Hailey... oh, my God. Hailey, what is this?" Her mother's hands flapped towards her face, like larger pink versions of those hummingbirds, whose wings Hailey could even now hear inside her head. "*What is this?*"

"It's help," said Hailey, bowing her head to take in the sight. Her belly was swelling even now, as they watched. It looked like a balloon being slowly pumped full of air. She stared at the skin in wonderment as it rose and bulged, pushing forward and straining at the waistband of her cheap school skirt. The skin was taut and translucent, like a stretched rubber sheet. There was something inside, and it danced with the rhythm of her blood. A shape pulsed against the whitening flesh of her stomach, not trying to get out but simply making itself known, saying hello to the women it had sensed on the other side of the flimsy sheet.

"Hailey, this isn't right! It's not normal! Are you pregnant?"

Hailey giggled. "Pregnant? No, not really. That's not what I'd call it."

Her mother began to make a sound, low in the throat, which was something half way between sobbing and laughter. "But what..." She could not finish her thought. Her eyes had gone shiny, clear, as if she were seeing something clearly for the first time in her life.

"I'm not pregnant exactly, but I am carrying something. It isn't a new life, it's an old one. Ancient. The seed of a place that I think can only be reached through pain and heartbreak; a place where the corpses of dead dreams are stored." Hailey heard the words coming from her lips, but she knew they were not her own. The thing inside her, the being that was writhing and coiling and thriving within her womb, was speaking through her, using her thoughts to commune with the other side of the flesh barrier.

"They are the Slitten. And they can help us. But only if we ask them to."

Her mother was down on her knees and cupping the air in front of Hailey's distended stomach. "If we ask?"

Hailey nodded, but she was not sure. Nothing was certain. "I think so." At last she had her words back; the Slitten had returned her voice. "That's what they told me, from inside here." She flicked her belly with her forefinger. It made a sound like a tom-tom drum.

"No," said her mother, standing now and shaking her head. "This is crazy. It isn't real." She turned away, flexing her fingers and stamping her feet, powerless to express her anger and frustration. "It's fucking stupid."

Darkness bled back into the room, filling the corners and shading the walls. The lamps seemed weaker than before, as if some of their power had been leeched away. The brightness Hailey had felt previously now dimmed, faded, went out. Her belly deflated quickly, flattening against its occupant. She looked down, still holding the hem of her shirt.

"See? We were hallucinating." Her mother stood across the other side of the room, near the kitchen. She was lost in shadow, her dark form blurring at the edges. Only her eyes shone. "It's the stress. We're both tired… exhausted, really. We need to sleep and stop talking like this." She did not move. Her outline bled away, as if unseen hands tore at her, picking her apart.

Hailey tucked her shirt into the waistband of her skirt. Her hands were shaking.

"Go to bed," said her mother, opening the fridge. Light flared, spilling across the floor. She took out a wine bottle, slamming it down onto the bench. "Go to bed, now."

Hailey turned away, the palm of one hand held against her flat, flat stomach. She was crying, but she dared not make a sound.

She retired to her bed without any more fuss, keeping her movements slow and easy to avoid any kind of disturbance.

The Slitten needed their rest, too.

CHAPTER EIGHT

TOM WOKE IN darkness. He knew that he'd been disturbed, but he was unsure what might have caused it. Perhaps Helen had shouted, or the telephone had rung, stirring him from restless slumber. He waited for the sound to come again, and when it failed to appear he wondered if his own conflicted thoughts had roused him, his fears tumbling like performing clowns around his skull as he slept.

He sat up and looked around the room. Nothing had changed; it remained as always. He didn't know why he'd expected any difference, and the thought confused him, making him doubt that he was fully awake. He slipped out of bed and went to the window, opened the curtains a few inches. The street was quiet and empty; not even a single car moved along its length. A slight breeze stirred the privet hedges along the garden fronts; litter prowled the edges of the gutter outside the house opposite.

Tom turned away from the window and went out onto the landing. Shadows pooled in the corners, like dark water. Yellow light, refracted from the streetlamps through the landing window, hung in the air like an incandescent fog. He walked along the landing, passing the open door to the upstairs bathroom. From the corner of his eye he spotted something, but when he spun around to look at it directly there was nothing there. He could have sworn that there was a man – or at least a man-shaped shadow – sitting on the edge of the bath with his hands held up to his face. But, no: more tricks of his tired mind, his aching eyes.

He walked slowly down the stairs, being careful not to make a noise. Helen slept well, but she was easily disturbed. Her ears, even as she rested, were attuned to even the subtlest of movements within the house. He turned at the bottom of the stairs and headed for the kitchen. Then he stopped. Backtracking, he turned again and went to Helen's room. Her door was ajar – she always demanded that he leave it that way. She was too afraid to have it fully closed yet nervous enough that she would not rest if it was wide to the wall. She wanted to be able to hear him as he wandered about the house. She said his movements comforted her.

He played his fingers along the doorframe, and then traced a line across the middle of the door, grasping the handle. He pushed gently and stepped inside. His bare feet sank into the carpet – this was the only room where they'd spent a bit of money, because Helen was always in there, never leaving, even to use the toilet.

She was a huge mound on the bed, her bulk only partially covered by the heavy winter quilt she insisted upon using whatever the season. He often wondered how someone so fat could always be so cold. Then, ashamed and saddened, he would try to forget that he'd ever thought about her in that way.

She was his wife, and he loved her. At least he used to love her, before she became like this. He did, he loved her, with all of his heart. But he also hated her, and wished that she would die.

Gritting his teeth against these familiar thoughts, Tom approached the bed. Helen was snoring lightly, the air wheezing through her nose. Her lips shone in the darkness, coated with drool. Her hair – never styled these days, rarely even washed unless he did it for her – lay like rat tails on the pillow. She was flat on her back, with one arm raised above her head, as if grasping for the headboard.

A sea cow – a manatee: that was how he often pictured her. He'd watched a documentary a few years ago about the creatures, and the image had seemed appropriate. His sea cow wife: all fat and lazy and defeated.

"Helen," he whispered. "I think I love you. I *do* still love you. I don't know what I feel." He often did this, late at night or into the early hours, when sleep was his enemy and he felt as restless as a thief. He came down here, to her sick room, and he spoke to her in low tones, telling her how he felt or how he thought he felt, sometimes even how he knew he was supposed to feel but didn't, couldn't, or just wouldn't.

"You make my life a living hell, but I'm glad that I'm here for you, to take care of you. Yet I wish... I wish you would pass away quietly in your sleep." He leaned in close as he spoke, his lips mere inches from her slack, flabby cheek. "I do. I wish you would just go away." He closed his eyes. "When I open them again will you be gone?"

No, she was still there, on the bed, snoring and sweating and filling his life with regrets. His very own pet sea cow.

Tom did not even realise that he had raised his hand, curled it into a fist. He looked to his left, staring at the fist as it hovered in the air. He thought about bringing it down, as hard as he could, and repeatedly smashing her in the face. The distance between thought and action narrowed; it would be so easy to beat her to death.

"But messy," he said. "Far too messy."

He grabbed the other pillow, from the side of the bed where her head was not resting. He held it in both hands, feeling its soft weight, and scrunching it into a shapeless wad of material. He moved the pillow down, close to her face. There was an inch between pillow and skin; a tiny fraction that she filled with her stinking breath.

He could kill her in minutes. It would not be easy – he'd read somewhere that it was difficult to suffocate someone, that it took longer than you might think – but it would be clean and almost merciful. She would wake in confusion, gasping for air, and by the time she knew what was happening she would be on her way down, into the darkness.

Yes, he could do it. It was feasible that he could murder his wife. Especially if he continued to think of her as an animal, a wounded sea cow…

He replaced the pillow on the bed, turned stiffly away, his bare feet shuffling across the carpet.

No. he couldn't do it; of course he couldn't. He never would.

"Tom?"

He stopped dead, shocked that she was awake. Had she been awake all along, waiting with her eyes closed? Waiting to see what he would do?

"I wouldn't blame you, Tom. Not really." Her voice was slurred, as if she were drunk, but she was not talking in her sleep. She was aware; she knew what had been on his mind, and that he had fought against it.

"Go back to sleep," he said, without turning around. "It's late."

"I won't wake up next time. If you do it, I'll consider it a mercy." She was fading again, diving deep, going under. "A mercy..."

Tom stayed where he was, unable to move. He did not start moving again until he heard Helen begin to snore, and even then he moved slowly, carefully, afraid that she might be faking it, giving him an opportunity to go back to the side of the bed and pick up the pillow.

He closed the door behind him. Shut it tight, just the way Helen didn't like it.

"Mercy," he whispered, wondering exactly what that was, what it meant. Could mercy be quantified, weighed and measured like sacks of grain? And if so, how much did he have inside him? *Not much*, he thought. *Not nearly enough.*

He passed the bottom of the stairs and glanced up the stairwell. There was the suggestion of something having just moved away, sloping across the landing to stand round the corner, near the entrance to his room. He stood there for a few seconds, trying to regain his balance, to get a grip on his sense of reality. Everything was slipping away, becoming fluid, and he felt like he was drawing close to the brink of some kind of mental abyss.

He had never felt so alone.

That woman – Lana – appeared in his mind. Her dark eyes, gypsy-dark hair, beautiful half smile. Why was he so drawn to her that he would think of her now, in his darkest hour? Just what was it about the woman that made her haunt him in this way?

The telephone at the bottom of the stairs began to vibrate. It didn't ring, not fully: just a gentle thrumming sound, like an electric razor. He moved across the floor, picked up the receiver and placed it against his ear.

"Hello."

All he heard on the line was a series of electronic ghosts: clicks, hisses, distant connections being made. Then, growing closer, as if it were travelling along the miles of overhead lines and underground cables, he began to make out a sound that reminded him of childhood.

When he was a boy, before the madness of adulthood drew him in, he would ride for miles on his bicycle. He and his friends, adventurers to a man, would set off in the early morning and not return home until well after dark, their prolonged absence causing mayhem in the family home. Sometimes they would take wooden lolly sticks and place them so that they stuck in the rear spokes of the bikes, and when they pedalled the noise was like fingers snapping at a hundred miles an hour, or the fast, harsh music of Spanish castanets.

This was the sound he heard now, on the other end of the line. It drew closer and closer, getting louder and louder, until all he could think of was those friends and the long bike rides they enjoyed. It was like a calling – an echo from summers now long dead – and part of him wanted to answer. He listened to the clicking noise, allowing it to reach inside him and grasp his heart, but once it had him he began to doubt its authenticity. It seemed false, faked: a sound fabricated to lure him elsewhere.

He thought of Helen lying in bed, her face blue, vomit on her chin. He thought of punching her saggy sea cow face until the bones broke and the flesh tore beneath his knuckles. The clicking sound seemed to encourage these thoughts, to embellish them and make them even more vivid in his mind.

"No," he said, pulling the phone away from his ear. "This isn't right."

As if on cue, the clicking sound began to fade, leaving him behind. Part of him wanted to follow it, to get on his bike and pedal after the sound through summer lanes and across sunlit fields. But the part of him that mattered – the strong part, the undefeated fragment of his humanity – held back.

The clicking sound diminished, absorbed into the digital static, the black-hiss voices undulating through the ether. For a moment he could have sworn that he heard a snatch of laughter, followed by the mumbled word *"Soon."*

Tom put down the phone and grabbed his coat from the hanger at the bottom of the stairs. Still barefoot, he took his keys from the pocket and unlocked the door. Stepping out into the cool night air, he took a breath and allowed his legs to carry him to the car. He reversed out of the drive, spun the car in the road, and set off to the place he had been thinking about all day.

He drove to the Concrete Grove.

Passing through Far Grove, he saw a police car parked outside an all-night kebab shop. One uniformed officer was holding a young man across the counter, cuffing his wrists, while his partner radioed a report in to the station. The boy's eyes locked onto Tom's as he drove by; the boy smiled at him, and went limp.

The waste ground adjacent Far Grove Way was burning. Someone had set light to a sofa, and black smoke and yellow sparks rose from it like ugly phantoms, dissipating into the black night sky. Tom slowed down as he passed the blaze, staring at it through the side window. There was nobody around. The fire continued as if the fuel had been laid out and ignited for his eyes alone.

A fox crossed the road as he put his foot down on the accelerator, its eyes blazing red as they caught the light from his headlamps. It was an example of his mental instability that he thought the fox, too, was smiling – just like the boy in the kebab shop. He felt like everything was turning its gaze towards him, waiting to see what he would do, how he would respond to this situation. The area, and everything within it, was ripe with expectancy.

Paranoia, he thought. *I'm fucking paranoid.* It was a feeling he knew all too well.

He cruised along Grove End, past the terraced houses on one side and the primary school on the other. He stared between the school railings, hoping that he would not catch sight of that strange human-faced dog. He knew the beast was a fantasy, a fiction, yet still he was afraid of seeing it again... and part of him desired just that: a single glimpse of a thing that could not be, another look at the numinous, just to prove that there was something else beyond the life he was leading now.

He parked the car at the end of the street, beside the mini roundabout. Sirens wailed far off, like banshees, and he heard the sound of breaking glass. A dog barked, disturbed by the sound, and he listened to its rhythmic cadence.

He watched Lana's window, wondering if she was in there, sleeping, or possibly out for the evening. There was no way of knowing whether or not she was home, but he felt that she was safe in her bed. More than a feeling, in fact, it was a certainty. No doubt she slept lightly, like most people who lived in troubled neighbourhoods, and all of her dreams would be bad ones.

It came to him like a light going on inside his head: he could help her, if he liked. He could possibly even save her. He didn't know what kind of trouble she was in, or how serious it was, but if she would only let him he could help her out of the mess.

If he'd been asked, he couldn't say how he knew this: he simply did. Sitting here, in the car, outside her building, he felt closer to her than he ever had to another human being – closer even than he had ever felt to his wife. He gripped the wheel with his hands and stared out through the windscreen. Then, overcome with an emotion he could not name, he lowered his head and began to weep. His hands still gripped the wheel, tighter, tighter, until his fingers ached.

"What am I doing here?" he said, looking out at the sky, the depthless dark beyond the fine grey skins of clouds. There came no response – just as always. Even if the universe knew the answers, it was not telling. It would never willingly divulge its secrets to the likes of him.

Tom waited there until the sun turned the sky in the east a light shade of red, like blood smeared along the blade-edge of the horizon. Then, his face still wet with tears, he started the car and set off towards home, the place where he now realised his heart had never truly belonged.

CHAPTER NINE

BANJO SAT IN the chair, shivering. He wasn't cold; it was warm inside the room, despite being located underground, in a section of the huge cellar directly beneath the gym. No, it was not because of the temperature that his body was jerking and spasming repeatedly, like a series of tiny orgasms. It was because of fear.

Banjo was tied into the wooden dining chair. His hands had been pulled back, around the back of the chair, and secured with plastic ties, like the kind some people used to keep their expensive wheel trims on their posh cars. He'd also seen police detectives in the American cop shows he loved to watch when he was stoned use similar ties to cuff prisoners, rather than using traditional steel handcuffs.

He struggled to get his body under control, tensing his muscles and taking a deep breath – which was difficult in itself because of the PVC ball gag someone had stuffed into his mouth and belted tightly at the back of his head. On top of all the drugs he'd ingested, the situation was enough to make him think that he was finally losing his mind.

The room was dim. There was one light – a small lamp in one corner, which stood on a low wooden table. The lamp was missing its shade, and the low wattage bulb cast a meagre illumination. Shadows crawled around the walls, grouping in the corners. When Banjo looked up, straining his neck because of the ball gag straps, it looked as if the ceiling was covered in a wet black substance. He knew his eyes were creating narcotic-phantoms, but it was a disturbing image just the same.

The attempt to calm down was failing. Fear filled him, turning him into a repository for terrors he could not have imagined only days before. Why had he done it? There had been no real reason for his crime, and everyone knew what a bastard Monty Bright was, how he dished out his own brand of punishment to keep the Grove under his control. So why the fuck had Banjo taken the loan shark's money?

He remembered everything so clearly, all the little details. It had been cold, crisp, and the stars were unusually bright, like little isolated lamps across the sky. He'd had the idea weeks before, when he was smoking spliffs and dropping cheap acid with an old girlfriend. They were bemoaning the fact that they were always skint, couldn't ever afford to do anything interesting or buy any decent drugs, and Banjo had decided right then that he needed to do something to alter the course of his life, even if it was for just a weekend.

He thought it would be easy to pose as one of Bright's collectors, and target some unsuspecting biddy who owed a payment on her loan. He even knew who to choose: old Mrs. Waits, from Grove Rise. Everyone knew she'd come into a bit of money, that when some distant cousin had died he had left her a few grand in his will. The old bird was so dotty she'd probably forget that he'd been to visit, and think nothing of paying twice... Alzheimer's or something. Her memory was shot to shit.

But things hadn't quite worked out the way he'd planned.

Yes, he'd gone round there, wearing his long leather coat, with his game face on, and acting like some TV tough-guy, and Mrs. Waits had given him the cash – five-hundred quid, right in his hand. When he'd walked out of her house, heading for the Unicorn to enjoy a couple of pints, score some quality coke and reflect on the success of his mission, he had even felt good about things. For once in his life, Banjo had made something work. He had bettered his situation.

Then, several days later, when the real collectors had gone round to see Mrs. Waits – the guy who always wore those leather gloves and the big fat one with a chip on his shoulder – the old bat had been able to give a good description of Banjo, and, when pressed, had even known his name. Turned out the estate gossips were wrong and she didn't have Alzheimer's after all. She was just old and slow, but her mind remained sharp.

That was the fatal flaw in Banjo's plan. He had not even realised that the woman knew him, and her supposed mental condition had made him lax. He knew who *she* was, of course, but as far as he knew he was unknown to her.

As far as he knew.

In reality, of course, it turned out that she recognised him from years ago, when he'd worked in the FastFilm video rental shop on the Arcade, his first job after leaving school. His *only* job after leaving school, if he was honest: working a nine-to-five had never appealed to Banjo.

He'd considered leaving the Grove then, fleeing the area and perhaps heading south, to London. That's what they always did in the movies – all the ones he'd watched free of charge in the back of the rental place where he'd once worked, his face bathed in the light of their reflected glory. But in those movies they always seemed to have more than five-hundred quid in their back pocket, and even if they didn't, they always managed to pick up some additional pocket change along the way to fund their adventures.

Again, the reality was miles away from fiction; the truth, life's truth, was never quite as promising as the truth of VHS.

The room was bare. The walls were covered in timber panelling, and the varnish was peeling. His mind was racing; his body was rushing from the drugs. The floor was concrete, hard and cold and uneven. The only furniture in the room, apart from the chair into which he was tied, was the coffee table with the lamp on it. There was nothing else, just two doors, facing each other from opposite walls.

The bloke with the leather gloves – what was his name? – had given Banjo a few slaps, back and front-handed, as if he were hitting a woman. The violence had been demeaning more than painful, although the blows had stung at the time. Now all he felt was a slight hot sensation across his cheeks, which moved around as his drug-rush developed. His eyes watered. The ball gag was drying out the inside of his mouth.

The lamp flickered. There was a slow, dragging sound from behind one of the doors. Nothing else. Just silence. Had he imagined it, or was somebody there?

Banjo had no idea how much time had passed, or whether it was night or day. They'd come for him at around two in the morning at least a couple of days ago, kicking down the door of the squat he'd been using as a bolt-hole and a shooting gallery to use the smack he'd spent a large portion of that five-hundred quid on. They dragged him outside, where they pushed him into the back of a car. He knew where they were taking him; everybody on the Grove was aware that Bright had rooms beneath the gym on Grove Lane, and he used them not just for storage but for other, less conventional functions. Even the police had knowledge of Bright's underground lair, but they just left him alone to go about his business. As far as they were concerned, he kept the Grove under control.

There were rumours that he had bodies buried down here, in the foundations, under the concrete floor, even inside the walls. Banjo couldn't be sure how much truth was in these stories, and had always doubted them, but right now, strapped into the chair, they had never seemed so real.

The lamp flickered again. He saw colours bursting behind the sudden glare.

Banjo closed his eyes to stop them watering. He tried to swallow but his throat was dry and his tongue felt as big as a side of beef in his mouth. His rush continued, gifting him a strange sense of ease. They'd been pumping him full of drugs – pure, uncut

– since he got here. It felt like he hadn't been clean and sober for weeks.

Footsteps approached from the other side of the door – which door, again he couldn't be sure.

Somebody knocked, three times.

That was an odd thing to do, knocking on the door, as if whoever stood out there was a visitor and Banjo were not being held captive. He waited, listened, and the knocking came again. Three times, like a charm.

Then there was the sound of a key being inserted into the lock, moved around in the barrel; and finally the locked clicked. The door swung open without a sound. Banjo strained to turn his head and peer around at the door, to see who was coming in and hopefully appeal to their sense of pity. He flexed his hands behind him, making fists and opening them again, and tried to move his legs against the chair, maybe tip the whole thing over.

Darkness surged towards him, clashing with the drugs in his system. He knew that he wouldn't come down from this sweet high for hours, and somewhere at the back of his mind he realised that by then it might be too late to make a difference.

"Be still." The man who drifted towards him was not tall. He was broad, and his familiar face hung in the dimness like a ghostly apparition. There was nothing overtly threatening about the way he looked. Yet he was terrifying.

"Calm down or I'll kill you right now."

Banjo stopped struggling. The man's voice – low, even, rather bland – acted like a physical restraint, even more so than the plastic ties which bound him to the chair.

"That's better." He walked around to stand before Banjo, his movements slow and deliberate. He was wearing a short black bomber jacket zipped up to the throat and dark denim jeans. His black hair was slicked back against his skull with some kind of product, as if he were stuck in the 1980s or had seen the film *Wall Street* too many times. To Banjo, in his messed-up state, that hair looked painted on, like some kind of lacquer. It glistened like a beetle's carapace in the dimness. Banjo wanted to laugh.

"Now we can talk, like a couple of good old fellows. Yes?" His lips didn't move much when he spoke: his teeth remained clenched, like those of a ventriloquist throwing his voice.

Banjo nodded his head, kept nodding it. The drugs they'd been feeding him had taken control of his actions. He couldn't stop even if he tried.

"Stop that. You might hurt yourself." Monty Bright smiled, and it was like every last bit of light in the room rushed towards his mouth, smearing against his small, white teeth.

Banjo stopped nodding. It was strange how this man's energy seemed to cut through even the tremors of the drugs to make Banjo do as he wished.

"You took something from me, son. You robbed me, and that isn't nice. I now find myself in a position – one I've been in many times before – where I'm forced to make an example of you." His voice remained low. There was nothing particularly aggressive about his tone, but Banjo sensed his violence, even saw it moving snakelike behind the mask he wore. Bright didn't waste words; everything he said had a purpose, and that purpose was usually dark.

Banjo felt tears rolling down his cheeks.

"Poor boy," said Bright, taking a couple of small steps forward so that he was directly in front of his captive. "Wasting tears on this life... your life. It wasn't much, you know. Your life. Not really. You were ejected, bloody and screaming, from your mother's gaping cunt, and then you were raised like an animal, a sacrifice for whatever dark gods rule places like this." He smiled again: quick, tight, like a wound opening up on his face for one brief moment. The lamplight quivered. "You fucked a few girls, smoked a few drugs, and made a few casual friends. You wasted your time at a shitty state school, learning nothing and dropping out before you'd even dropped in. Then you were ejected again, from a different cunt this time, to stand bloody and screaming before the jaws of society."

Banjo could do nothing for crying. The ball gag was making him choke; his throat ached. He was sobbing now: deep, heartfelt, half-choked muffled sobs that shook his entire body. He felt no grief; something else, an entirely unnameable emotion, stirred within his depths.

"It's such a fucking waste – a waste of *everything*, son. Do you see that?" Monty Bright bent forward. He smelled of an enclosed room after heavy rain, a dark corner where water seeps in to cause rot. "But let's not waste these tears." His tongue, long and rough and pointed, slid between his thin lips and he licked Banjo's cheek, lapping up his tears like honey. This perverse and intimate act lasted only a couple of seconds, but it made such a great impact on Banjo that he felt his heart break. Here was a man

– a strong, powerful man – who thought so much of Banjo's regrets that he would feed on his tears. It should be horrendous, a concept so inhuman that it was monstrous, yet Banjo felt nothing but love.

He loved Monty Bright like a father.

Banjo smiled around the ball gag, tasting plastic. The drugs raced through him, changing him, making him malleable to the consciousness of this other.

Bright nodded, reached up, and removed the gag. "Are you ready to redeem yourself, to make sure that the rest of your life isn't wasted?" Then, producing a small knife, he cut the plastic ties, freeing Banjo's arms and legs.

"Yes," said Banjo, still smiling, his voice raw in his dried-out throat. "Yes, I'm ready." He rubbed his arms, trying to get the blood flowing. His legs felt like wooden stilts, stiff and unresponsive.

Bright took him by the hand – no man had ever done that before – and led him across the room, to the other door. Banjo's legs grew stronger, the muscles remembering how to walk. Soon he was moving more easily, his body becoming more responsive and the drugs in his system flowing freely now that he was unbound.

Banjo felt like he was floating, tethered to the ground only by the grip of his captor's hand.

The door he stood before was old, scarred, and weathered, as if it had been kept outside for decades rather than inside this room. The ancient paint was peeling like scabs; the heavy grain of the wood looked like burst veins and capillaries.

"Step inside and become something else, something more than human wastage." Monty Bright stepped back, prodding Banjo gently in the small of the back. Bright didn't touch the handle, but the door began to open. It moved smoothly, without a sound, and Banjo stared at the ribbon of darkness that grew between door and frame, becoming a black wedge.

"Go on, now. Let's get this done, son. Let's get this show on the road. The fucking road to nowhere." Bright's voice, along with his accompanying laughter, sounded as if it was reaching him from a great distance.

Banjo stepped into the welcoming darkness and felt the last vestiges of his old fear leave him as the door closed behind him. He thought of his mother, and the way she had wasted her life on drink, her own drug of choice; he remembered his father, turning away and leaving them all behind; he recalled fondly the touch of his baby sister's hand, the night she had died of pneumonia in hospital. None of these memories upset him – they were like pictures on television, scenes from the videos he used to love. He was free of them now; this room he had walked into, and the drugs, had cut him off from harm.

Banjo walked to the centre of the room, his eyesight now growing accustomed to the darkness. The ground was soft, like mud, and the walls seemed to writhe at the corner of his vision. Soon he realised that he was surrounded.

He stood at the centre of a number of televisions. Each of them was an old model – some of them must have dated back to the early days of the technology. Big dusty screens stared blindly in his direction; dead cables trailed behind bulky sets; large buttons and dials were like mutations on the shells of these machines.

At one level he was aware that there must be something here, for him to see, but at another level, where he stood apart from the scene, he knew that he was so wasted that he could be looking at a bunch of cardboard boxes and moulding the image to suit his mood.

Banjo kneeled on the soft ground. He was not sure why, it just felt right, like an act of communion. His entire life had been spent in thrall to these things as they pumped out images and lifestyle choices, so why not worship them now, in a dark underground room that felt so much like a church?

He bowed his head just as the screens came to life.

One after another, in quick succession around him, forming a crude circle of brightness, the screens flared, bathing him in their holy light. Dust swam before his eyes, giving the illusion that he was underwater. The television sets throbbed, a cathode-ray heartbeat, and he watched as pictures began to form from the static. It was like birth: difficult, painful. The forms bucked and writhed, twitched and jerked, and the screens bulged outwards as the figures took shape.

Drug-demons: nightmares snatched from inside his head. He watched them with a sense of wonder.

They were small and they were naked. Their skin was the colour of static; their eyes the grey of the dusty concrete that had surrounded him his entire life. They emerged like grubs from the television sets, their substance formed of the material of the screens as well as the nebulous static and the ghost of the heroin in Banjo's blood. They left behind their empty TV shells as they rolled away, their legs lengthening in sudden thrusts. The fronts of the television sets looked like a series of kicked-in faces. The things that had hatched from these wounds lay curled on the ground before them, twitching occasionally; sleeping dogs dreaming of the chase.

Then, simultaneously, they sprung up from the ground and stood erect, uncurling swiftly and almost mechanically. They stood before their televisual eggs, rocking back and forth, torsos without arms, long, back-folded insect legs lacking a midriff, flat, featureless heads unsupported by anything even resembling a neck.

Their concrete-grey eyes were big and square and blank. Their mouths were just stretched ragged holes, lacking teeth or gums. They were tubes, those mouths, and Banjo didn't want to see where they ended. He raised his hands to these new gods, these entities sired by the great glass tit of television, and opened his mouth to pray or question or perhaps just to scream. His drugs high had reached a new plateau: never before had his dreams become flesh.

They were upon him within seconds, flowing through the space like a rogue signal, moving in the syncopated jinks and jerks caused by a faulty transmission. Banjo felt his cheeks expand as his mouth was filled with their flexible tubes. He tasted burnt copper and charred wires. He felt pregnant with emptiness. Then, without warning, the effects of the drugs abated. Banjo's fear resurfaced, finding a way back inside the crowded schedule of his TV-learned emotions, and he felt the channel inside his head change forever.

CHAPTER TEN

IT WAS EARLY morning and Tom was running again.

He had no idea why he was here, skirting the edge of the Grove, but he knew that he had come to some kind of decision. He ran at a steady pace – jogging really – and tried to give himself time to think about what he was doing. Last night had been a tipping point, where he had been forced to confront a truth he had hidden for years. He did not like the man he was becoming – betrayal was not something that came easy to him – but this constant mask-wearing was taking its toll and he was rotting away inside.

Tom had not loved Helen for so long now that he could not even remember when his feelings towards her had changed. Even before she had been injured by That Man, his emotions had confused him. They had grown apart steadily, without any major problems causing clean fractures in their relationship, and the result of this gradually increasing distance was that when she went into hospital he was almost relieved to be alone.

His shame at these feelings had forced him to bury the truth, to smother it under layers of forced emotion: duty, empathy, a sense of needing to do the right thing by his wife. Her injuries – her lower-body paralysis and resultant emotional neediness

– had served to distract him, and also given him a reason to carry on pretending that he still loved her. Even though she had transformed into the likeness of an aquatic mammal before his eyes.

He thought of this now, as he padded along the pavement. On the surface, he had no idea where he was heading. But underneath, where his real emotions lay, he knew that he was running towards Lana Fraser, and the promise of salvation he had glimpsed so briefly behind her dark eyes.

Last night, as he'd sat in his car watching her flat, wishing that he could spot her silhouette at the window, he had crossed some kind of invisible border. He felt that he had travelled far, and under false pretences, to reach this place, and now that he had arrived he could no longer wear the lies in which he wrapped himself like a second skin. He had shed that skin and beneath its rotting layer had been a brand new being, a man who accepted his own needs and the fact that they had not been met for such a long time.

Before he knew it he was running along Grove Drive, past the tract of waste ground where derelict factories stood like the repositories of nightmares. Small fires burnt across the bare earth, smouldering and sending up black plumes into the pale blue sky. Someone was incinerating old tyres. A thin man walked between his private pyres, prodding them with a long stick. Tom paused by the fence, staring through the railings, and watched the figure as he traipsed back and forth, tending the sputtering flames.

The black smoke broke apart and rose in tendrils, like skinny arms reaching towards a liar's heaven.

Tom felt strange, as if he were being given a glimpse of another world. The figure was too thin to be human, and the long stick was actually an extension of his arm. He moved slowly and dragged his left leg behind him.

Tom's eyes began to water, but it was not from the thick, acrid smoke. The land beyond the fence was grey; there was no vegetation growing through the flattened soil. In the distance, beyond one of the fires, a small dog sniffed at a heap of rags on the ground. Tom was certain that it was the dog he had seen before – the one with the human face. He had even dreamed about the same creature many years ago, when he was a small boy.

His father had been a distant man, cold and abusive in the way that he withheld his affection. Tom's mother was also emotionally cold, as if she were afraid to show how she really felt. At night, when he found it difficult to sleep, Tom would imagine a dog with a boy's face wandering around the house, raking in the kitchen bin, sniffing at the cupboards, and padding softly upstairs to investigate the top floor of the house. The dog would never enter his room: it just sat there, outside his bedroom door, either guarding him or waiting for him to come out so that it could attack.

It was worse on the nights when his parents had sex.

Tom could hear them through the thin walls: his father's repeated obscenities, his mother's tears; and terrible animal sounds, culminating in a series of muted thuds as his father repeatedly punched either the headboard or his mother's body as he climaxed inside her. Then silence, which was slowly filled by yet more of his mother's weeping. After a short while she would go out onto the landing, walk to the bathroom, and lock herself inside. Tom always fell asleep before she left the bathroom, so he never knew how long she remained in there, or what she did behind the locked door. He had always imagined that she must be tending to her bruised body.

Those nights, above all else, were the worst. They were the times when Tom was faced with the reality of his parent's flaws, and no matter how hard he tried he could not block out the sounds. On mornings following these events, his mother would move slowly around the kitchen, wincing in pain with each step she took. She never said a word; she took it all in silence.

Tom stopped dreaming of the dog when he was eleven years old. It appeared in his dreams only once more after that, on the night his mother died. It was as if her death had finally exorcised some kind of crude ghost, a shoddy spirit that only ever came to him because he craved his mother's love.

He had forgotten about the dog until he saw the vision yesterday evening in the Grove. He knew it was not real – it couldn't possibly exist in the waking world. But what scared him more than seeing it was the thought that something had reached inside him and pulled out that childhood dream, putting flesh on its bones.

The man tending the fires looked normal again: just a thin figure with a pointed stick. Tom smiled, feeling sad and empty as he pulled back from old memories.

Then he resumed running, heading towards Lana's Fraser's flat and the precious new memory of her face, her eyes, and her ambiguous smile.

Turning right onto Grove Road, he saw a car parked at the kerb. The vehicle was a Vauxhall Nova, the paintwork scratched, the wings battered from a collision, and the rear bumper hanging askew. Two boys in baseball caps sat in the car. The windows were rolled down. Another boy – this one younger, barely in his teens – was leaning against the side of the car and poking his head through the open driver's side window. Tom slowed his pace to a walk. He was breathing heavily but still felt as if he had a few miles left to go. He watched the boys as they talked, and then caught sight of a small brown-paper package changing hands. The boy on the pavement straightened up, slammed his palm against the roof of the car, and then turned away, setting off in the direction of the Needle, whose pyramid-shaped roof and upper storeys could be seen from almost everywhere on the estate.

The car's engine revved loudly. The rear wheels spun on the road surface, and then the car shot off, taking the right turn into Grove End at such great speed that the rear end skidded across the carriageway.

Tom knew that drugs were big business on the estate. He would have to be a fool not to recognise that he had just witnessed yet another deal, but rather than frighten him it filled him with an intense feeling of sadness. These kids, they were wasting their lives before they'd even begun. If they were dealing in that stuff now, what would they be doing in five, ten years' time? Gun crime was a recent problem and it was only going to get worse. Things here still weren't as bad as they were in the States, but surely that kind of gang-driven chaos wasn't too far away... a decade, maybe even less?

Tom was glad that he and Helen had never been able to have children. Then, feeling guilty once more, he thought about Hailey, Lana Fraser's girl. What kind of future did she have to look forward to, trapped on this godforsaken estate? Nobody seemed to care – not the local council, the central government, or the media. The latter were more than happy to demonise the people on estates like this, but they refused to examine the real problems at the root of this kind of behaviour. These sink estates were forgotten zones, dead spots in the nation's psyche. The public would rather envisage them as the playgrounds of devils than the places where those who had lost everything ended up.

Facts were always difficult to consume; fiction made for a much less complex diet. Tom had learned, and accepted, a long time ago that most people were content to be spoon-fed a simpler gruel. It was easier to keep down, and to forget you had even eaten.

Tom stood on the pavement outside the Grove Court flats, undecided whether he should ring the buzzer or continue running. Part of him wanted to escape, to get away from the emotional holocaust he sensed might be the result of any further association with Lana and her daughter. Yet another part of him – this one stirring, as if roused from a lengthy sleep – reached out towards her, needing her by his side.

"Tom?" Her voice came from behind him. For a moment he was too stunned even to move. "It is Tom, isn't it? From yesterday?"

He didn't realise that he was holding his breath until he remembered to let it out. His chest deflated; his throat ached. He turned around.

She was standing on the pavement a few yards away, clutching a blue plastic carrier bag in her left hand. She was wearing a faded denim jacket, buttoned half way up with the neck left open, and her legs were bare beneath a red knee-length skirt. On her feet she wore a pair of battered running shoes. Her hair was loose, messy, and it framed her face like the fur of a hood. Her eyes were lowered, as if she were unable to meet his gaze.

"Hi," he said, feeling small and weak and needy. "Sorry."

"For what?" She smiled, tilting her head to one side. She showed him her small white teeth: they were perfect, like lovely ivory sculptures of teeth rather than the real thing. "Why are you sorry?"

"For being here, I guess. I'm not some kind of stalker. Honest. I was... well, would you believe I was just passing?" It sounded pathetic. He felt ashamed.

She laughed, then, her eyes widening, those flawless teeth flashing in the morning light. And all at once he knew that it was okay, that everything was fine. She didn't think he was pestering her; she enjoyed the attention. "Come on up," she said. "I was going to make coffee." She held up the carrier bag, indicating that she had been shopping for provisions.

Tom followed her in silence. He did not want to speak, not yet, even to accept her invitation, in case she changed her mind.

Upstairs he stood at the window as she unpacked her shopping in the kitchen. He stared out at the view: the circular array of streets clustered around the Needle, and the imposing sight of the crippled concrete tower itself. The windows on the lower floors were covered with wooden boards and metal shutters, but those higher up the building, where nobody could gain access, were mostly unsecured. Some of the frames still held panes of glass, others had only shards, like curved and pointed teeth, where kids had shattered them with stones.

The glass of the pyramidal roof was in bad shape. It was unbroken, but birds had desecrated the panes with their droppings to mix with the other general filth. It looked to Tom like there was a swarm of flies gathered around the pointed tip of the skylight, but surely flies would be invisible to the naked eye at such a distance? They were too small to be sparrows or pigeons, and he didn't know of any birds that were capable of hovering in such a manner. They were almost motionless: just a faint blurring of their wings against the sky.

There was a lot of graffiti on the walls at the lowest levels, where kids had sprayed obscenities and depictions of sexual acts. A few names had been added in a cruder style, almost as an afterthought. Further up, on the south wall, the word 'Clickity' had been daubed in dull red paint. Isolated in such a way, it was incongruous, entirely random, yet Tom felt that it must hold meaning to someone. He recalled something he'd often seen on the side of a footbridge over the A1 motorway when he used to travel south regularly for work: *Cigarette Burns*. He'd often wondered what that meant – was it the name of a band, a record label, or something more sinister? He hadn't thought about the piece of graffito in years...

"How do you take it?"

"Sorry?" He turned stiffly.

"Your coffee. How do you take it?" Lana was leaning across the kitchen counter. She arched her black eyebrows. Her cheeks were pale, almost white at the edges, but small circles of red had appeared at their centres.

"White. One sugar."

She nodded and slid back into the kitchen.

"What happened here? Where's all your stuff – the furniture. Where did it go?"

She appeared from the kitchen holding a mug in each hand. The coffee steamed, sending out bitter ghosts. "I owe money to someone and couldn't pay this month's instalment. So they sent somebody round to take our stuff instead." Her smile was rueful, yet behind her eyes he could see what he could only describe as restrained terror. Lana was scared, and trying hard not to show it.

"Who is he, this man? A loan shark?"

She nodded. "His name is Monty Bright."

"I don't know the name. Then again, why would I? I don't know anyone round here." He took a mug from her hand and sipped the hot coffee.

"I got myself in a bit of trouble. Hailey and me, we needed things. *She* needed things. She's a teenage girl, how could I deny her?" She drank from her mug, lowering her head but not taking her eyes from him. "I was stupid."

"I'm not going to judge you, Lana. I know nothing about your situation. I do know that you don't belong here. I'll be honest; I did some research on the internet. If that offends you, I'll leave and you never have to see me again."

Her dark eyes flashed with anger for a second, but then she smiled. Putting down her cup on the windowsill, she walked towards him, stopping only inches away. "That's fine. I gave up my right to privacy when the newspapers started sniffing around Timothy. That's my husband, the one who killed those people."

"You don't need to explain anything." Tom licked his lips. "I'll take you at face value if you do the same for me."

Lana turned away, picked up her cup, and stood with her back against the wall. She lifted one leg, placing the sole of her foot against the wall, and blew on her coffee. "Hot," she said, unnecessarily. Then she took another sip.

"Do you owe this man – this Monty Bright – a lot of money? I mean, if it's a small sum I might be able to help." He was testing her, pressing her buttons, seeing how far she would go. Trying to figure out exactly what she wanted from him.

"I don't want your money, Tom. I want your friendship."

"I suppose that's something we both need," said Tom. "My wife... she's lost to me. She's a paraplegic. I've tried my best, but there's nothing there. Just a shell of what we used to have. All I am is her carer; she doesn't need a lover these days, just somebody to keep her clean and feed her medicine." He smiled, but it was as bitter as the coffee.

"My turn." Lana did not move from her spot on the carpet. "I borrowed three grand from Bright. Now, with his fucking criminal rate of interest, I owe him twenty grand. It's like a game to him: he enjoys having people in his debt. I think it's his drug, the way he gets his kicks. Fuck knows, he doesn't need the cash. He's loaded." She shook her head. Fingers of black hair came free and plucked at her cheeks.

"What is this," said Tom, "*Quid pro quo?* Tit for tat?"

Lana laughed, throwing back her head. Rogue sunlight caught in her hair and was held there, amid the thick black tresses. "We're a couple of fuck-ups, aren't we? Real class acts."

They had moved together across the room without Tom realising. One minute there was space between them, the next they were almost touching. Holding his mug in one hand, he raised the other to waist level. Lana did the same, opening her fingers and reaching for him. Their hands met, the fingers entwining, forming a knot that he felt might never be broken.

"Is *this* what we want?" His voice cracked. "I mean, do we really need more problems than we both already have?"

Lana sighed. "I don't know. What do you think?"

But the decision was taken from them; it had already been made. When they kissed, it came as a surprise. Tom knew it was happening, but it shocked him just the same, like a tiny electrical charge. Her tongue was warm and smooth. He licked her perfect teeth; she snapped her jaws together, pretending to bite.

They did not move apart for a long time, and when finally they did, the damage was already done.

PART TWO

PEOPLE UNDER THE INFLUENCE

"Self-delusion is often just another coping mechanism."

– Lana Fraser

CHAPTER ELEVEN

HAILEY WENT TO her room early that evening. She was tired, washed-out. Her stomach felt oddly empty, as if she hadn't eaten for days, and her throat was parched. No matter how much water she drank – and she had consumed at least a litre of the stuff since returning home from school – she still felt thirsty.

She lay low down on her bed with her arms by her side. Her bare feet hung over the edge of the mattress. There was a breeze coming in through the open window and it felt good against her body. She was naked. She didn't know why she had not put on her pyjamas, but it had something to do with a vague yearning to feel the air on her skin, allowing it to breathe.

Tomorrow was Saturday. Apparently Tom was coming to take them out for the day, to Hadrian's Wall. Her mum had seen him earlier today, and they had discussed the outing. She said that Tom wanted them all to be together. In fact he had insisted that Hailey come along.

Hailey knew that Tom was married, and that his wife was ill. Her mother had let it slip, and then tried to lie her way out of the situation.

Tom wanted to fuck her mum. It was obvious. The way he looked at her, with hungry eyes and his lips slightly parted. He'd looked at Hailey the same way, when she had first met him. He probably wanted to fuck her, too.

She wondered about his wife: whether he still slept with her, or if her condition denied him a sex life. Maybe he was sick of masturbating, and saw her mother as a viable receptacle for his desires.

Hailey smiled. These thoughts – illicit, virtually obscene – were new to her. Never before had she considered such things. She'd kissed a couple of boys, one at a school party who had been all hands, and the other on her way home from school just for the hell of it, but still she failed to see the appeal of tasting the spit and enduring the clumsy touch of a classmate. Some of the girls in her class talked about giving blow jobs and hand jobs, and one or two of them claimed to have gone all the way with their boyfriends. Hailey suspected that most of them were lying, just to give the impression that they were grown up, women of the world instead of blinkered little girls from the estates.

She smiled, reached down and stroked her flat belly. It pulsed softly. She liked the sensation: it was erotic, how she imagined the touch of a grown man's hand in the same place might feel – a man rather than a silly schoolboy. Somewhere deep inside of her a door had opened, and the woman she would soon be was peeking out, taking stock, getting things in order before she stepped across the threshold.

It started to rain. She turned to face the window, the gap where the curtains had not been fully closed. Street lights. Rain. Shimmering on the glass. The sight was like a promise of beauty, but one from which she was separated, as if by physical barrier.

She closed her eyes and fell into sleep as if it were a hole in the ground. One second she was awake, the next she was dreaming.

SHE IS STANDING before the Needle, still naked. The ground is wet beneath her bare feet but the rain has stopped. Lights move beyond the unbarred upper storey windows of the tower block; unstable figures move within the spots of illumination, waving their hands like stage magicians.

She walks towards the building, feeling the cold air as it caresses her skin. Her legs feel long, lithe, and her nipples stiffen because of the chill. She enters the building through the front door, but is not aware of doing so. She simply takes another step and she is inside, standing in the foyer. The concrete floor has cracked open in several places, and thick, gnarly roots poke through the gaps. Large patches of wall inside the foyer are covered in thick swathes of bark; it feels like she is standing inside a hollowed-out tree.

The sound of humming is everywhere. She looks up and around, at the branches forming a lattice across the shattered concrete ceiling and the rough bark that covers the walls. Hummingbirds have made strange conical nests. She moves towards one of the walls, reaches out and touches the bark. It is hard, rough. One of the nests is within reach, so she runs her fingers over it. The nest is made of human hair and what look like finger bones – she can make out the gristly knuckle joints. A tiny blue hummingbird flies out of the hole at the narrow end of the cone, and then it hovers before her face. Its wings move faster than she can see; there is just a blue-grey blur, a glorious vision of rapid movement. The hummingbird's eyes are black. Its beak is ruby red.

"Hello," says Hailey, moving her hand, trying to catch the bird on her palm. "I won't hurt you."

The bird flies backwards, gliding like a smaller dream within the larger dream she inhabits. It opens its red beak and unfurls a long, thin tongue or proboscis. Like a soft, hollow tube, the tongue unrolls, growing longer and longer, until eventually it reaches the floor, its end scraping in the dust. More hummingbirds join the first, flying from other nests, some of which are located high overhead. The walls no longer contain any trace of concrete; they are all dark brown, an armoured layer of bark. The floor has turned to vegetation. The roots crawl and writhe, like snakes, around Hailey's feet. Weird insects burrow beneath this mulch, their bodies displacing the earth and making small heaving tracks across the ground.

"Where am I?" It seems like such a huge question. The answer must be equally as large, perhaps so big that the universe cannot contain it.

The birds form a circle around her, like the flipside of a Disney cartoon, where the magic animals arrive to help the princess. But these birds, she knows deep inside, are not here to offer her aid. They are trying to warn her, or perhaps to scare her away. They are the harbingers of something else – something large and old and terrible. Like the small fishes that feed on a shark's back, these things co-exist alongside the monstrous, and by doing so have become like tiny monsters themselves. Their beauty is not joyous; it is terrifying. It is the beauty of decay and degradation, the empty grandeur of destruction.

Hailey does not know where this knowledge comes from. It is just sitting in her head, waiting to be accessed.

"You're old, aren't you? So very old." Her voice echoes within the tree-chamber. When she glances away from the birds, once again inspecting her surroundings, she sees that she is now standing at the centre of a small grove of tall oak trees. She knows they are oaks because she recognises them from school, when she and her classmates did a nature project and had to draw the leaves of different species of tree – oak, maple, pine, willow. The oak tree was her favourite: there is something mysterious and majestic about the oak. It is one of the bones of England.

The trees lean in towards her, as if attempting to pass on some secret knowledge. They grow as she watches, dwarfing her, becoming the likeness of what they used to be, thousands of years ago, when this land belonged to nature and contained some kind of indigenous power. But man came along and dug up the land, shattered and fragmented whatever power was buried here, and poisoned it.

"Is this home? Is it where we belong?" She isn't sure if she means her family or everyone else, perhaps she is referring to all of humanity. "Is it where we started? Where we'll end up?"

The trees shudder, as if her words have made an impact. Then, slowly, they draw back, moving away. Leaves fall like solidified tears upon the ground. They turn dark as they tumble, crisping as if they are being dried out in an oven. The fat roots slither across them, folding over the fallen debris, crushing it and turning it to compost. Great slabs of concrete erupt through the mat of knotted roots and branches, noisily reclaiming the space, raping it and making it unfit for anything but human habitation. The only animal corrupt enough to live here is man.

Suddenly Hailey understands everything. Then, just as quickly, she realises that she understands nothing. She begins to cry but doesn't know who – or what – the tears are for. The trees diminish, shrinking, shedding their leaves, going to ground. The hummingbirds take frenzied flight above her head, performing wild, graceless loop-the-loops and almost crashing into each other in their haste. The sound of their wings is that of a million little heartbeats; their vibrant colours are like paint splashes in the air.

Far off, somewhere deep within this ravaged primeval forest, a beast cries out in the throes of either hunger or despair.

CHAPTER TWELVE

LANA USED TO look forward to the weekends. She remembered a time when everything in her world was stable, and she worked part-time at a solicitor's office in Newcastle. She was the best legal secretary in the firm, commanding a higher salary and better benefits than her peers, and the senior partners thought a lot of her.

Then Timothy had gone spectacularly off the rails. He had invested all their money in a long-distance haulage business that was actually part of an elaborate front for human trafficking, and the world she had so carefully created began to fall apart. It took less than a year for her loving husband to turn from a responsible family man, a respectable investor (or so she'd thought, before he threw in with gangsters) and property developer, into a murderer and a suicide.

It had taken such a short time to fall a great distance. But was the distance really so great? In all honesty, was the difference between family man and vengeful, paranoiac killer so huge? Sometimes, when she remembered him caressing her, whispering his desperate plans for their future into her ear, she thought there was hardly any difference at all.

Weekends these days were much the same as the rest of the week, apart from the fact that Hailey did not have to go to school. Hailey usually stayed in bed until just before noon, watching her DVDs and reading her books and magazines. But now she could no longer do that – her television was gone, the DVDs were useless without a player, and only the books remained.

Today they were both up and ready before nine o'clock. Lana was dressed in jeans and hiking boots, with a good fleecy jacket she'd bought years ago, in more affluent times. Hailey was wearing a pair of battered charity-shop Nikes, her best skinny jeans, and a man's padded coat that looked so big on her frame Lana suspected she'd either stolen it or been given it by a mystery boyfriend.

Tom had said that he would pick them up at ten, and even though Hailey showed no interest at all in the planned day trip Lana felt as excited as a schoolgirl preparing for a first date. She knew that she was using this as a distraction from her troubles, that Tom's unexpected arrival on the scene had offered her a smokescreen behind which to hide everything else. But she didn't care; she was happy – albeit a muted sort of happiness – and she would allow nothing to spoil that feeling. Even if it was just for a day.

Self-delusion, she thought, *is often just another coping mechanism.*

She heard a car horn blaring outside, and when she rushed over to the window she saw Tom's car parked in the bus lay-by across the street. She waved but he didn't see her. He was staring straight ahead at a figure that had just stumbled through a narrow ginnel along Grove Lane and was making its way slowly and awkwardly across the road in front of the block of flats in which she lived.

"What is it, Mum? Who's that?"

Lana stared at the figure. "I'm not sure, honey. But he looks drunk."

"Or stoned," said Hailey.

"Yeah. Maybe."

Lana felt a formless fear moving at her core. This was the kind of thing she hated most: social terrors in the early morning, or the middle of the day. At night she could almost accept this kind of behaviour, or at least convince herself that she could deal with the threat by locking it out. But during the hours of daylight, when the world was meant to be bright and without shadows, the sight of a junkie staggering about in the road was akin to a personal insult.

"Come on," she said. "Let's get down there before that idiot causes a commotion. Tom's waiting. We don't want him to have any hassle." What she really meant was that she didn't want him changing his mind and driving away.

Their footsteps sounded hollow as they hurried down the stairwell, and they both moved with a sense of urgency, as if something were pursuing them. Lana felt fingers of terror brush along her spine, and was prompted to look back over her shoulder. Dusty shadows quivered down the stairs. She looked away, feeling absurd that she should be so afraid.

Lana burst through the doors, tightening her grip on the cooler bag she'd slung over one shoulder. The other hand clasped her handbag, and she wished it contained something she could use as a weapon. Mace. A pair of nail scissors.

The man was now standing in front of Tom's car, weaving on the spot like a listing galleon. His hands were raised and grasping, as if he were trying to grab handfuls of fresh air.

"I know him," said Hailey, slowing down as they crossed the road and approached the mini roundabout. "It's that junkie – what's his name again?"

Lana reached out and grabbed her daughter's hand, dragging her towards the car. Tom had seen them. He opened the driver's door and set one foot outside. "Everything okay?" His voice was quiet; the slight breeze took it and lifted it above the rooftops, carrying it away like a scrap of litter.

Lana nodded. "Hurry, now."

"Banjo!" Hailey stopped dead in her tracks. Her hand slipped from Lana's grip.

"What are you saying?" Lana spun on her heels, keeping one eye on the unsteady fool who was still standing directly in front of Tom's car, staring into the windscreen but clearly seeing nothing outside the theatre of his own head.

"That's his name: Banjo. He always hangs around here. Went missing a few days ago – I remember somebody was asking around for him, wanting to know if anyone had seen him. He's just a harmless druggie dude."

"Come on. Let's just go." Lana tugged the girl across the road, to the car. Tom was now fully out of the vehicle. He was torn between watching the junkie and greeting the two women.

"Who the hell's this?" He half smiled, half grimaced.

"Just some local druggie," said Lana. "Let's get in the car."

Tom nodded. "Nice to see you, too." The smile grew, making his face look younger, cleaner, nicer.

Lana shook her head. "Sorry. This place. It spoils everything."

Tom opened the rear door and then walked around the back of the car to open the passenger door. He stood, balanced in a moment where he was not quite sure who would sit where.

"Fuck!"

Lana turned towards the front of the car, the direction in which the expletive had come from. Banjo was now weaving so violently that he looked like he might fall down at any minute. His feet remained fixed on the ground but he was now bending forward at the waist, as if performing a weird little dance. He was thin, snake-hipped, and able to manage a wide range of movement. It looked strange, like the beginning of some drug-fuelled urban dance recital. His fingers moved like pincers. He had long, dirty nails. They looked sharp as knives.

"*Fuck!*" He screamed the word this time, white foam flecking his lips. "Gerroff me!" His face was pale, bloodless, and his lips had peeled back from his teeth to give him a feral expression. "*Fnugh!*" Speech was deserting him; his throat was convulsing too violently to produce language. Lana watched in fascination as his Adam's apple bobbed like a ping-pong ball caught in a python's gut.

"Oh, shit. Get in the car." She glanced at Hailey, who by now had moved around to the other side of the vehicle. She was closer to Banjo than any of them. "Get in, Hailey. Get in now."

"Wait a second, Mum. We should call an ambulance, or something."

Banjo leapt, pushing himself forward like a giant cat attacking its prey. His lower body slammed into the bodywork, and he rolled along the car's left wing. This gave Hailey enough time to back-pedal, and Tom moved his body between her and the gibbering junkie. He stood firm, hands clenched into tight fists.

"Hailey!" Lana ran to her daughter, pulling her away from the car. She fumbled inside her purse for her mobile phone and thumbed the emergency number.

"Just stay back," said Tom. "Keep the fuck away." He took a single step backwards, stumbling slightly.

Banjo was wailing now, like a baby demanding food. His mouth was lathered in foam; his eyes were weeping blood. His hands were still raised in front of his face, and he turned his palms inward, twisting his thin fingers into hooks. Then, still moaning wordlessly, he began to claw at his cheeks with those long, guitar-picking fingernails.

"Oh my God. Do something. Shit, do something!" Hailey's voice had risen to such a high pitch that it sounded like she was singing.

Lana screamed into the phone: "Grove Court! There's a man killing himself, send help, now!" The operator tried to calm her with words she could barely even hear, and she just yelled her request over and over again in the hope that it would be answered. "Send someone now!"

Everything seemed to freeze apart from Banjo, and what he was doing. The others just stood there and stared, incapable of anything but watching the horror as it happened.

Banjo's fingernails had gone in deep. Lana saw flashes of white tooth or skull amid the red, and the man's cheeks already hung from his face in fine tatters, like thin slices of Parma ham. He had stopped crying and worked now in silence, raking the loosened flesh away from muscle, the thick muscle away from bone.

The man slumped to his knees, his hands still working furiously at his ruined face, as if controlled by an external force. His fingers pushed through into his oral cavity; Lana could see them wriggling in there when he opened his mouth in a gurgling scream. He tore away the flesh, hooking his bottom lip between finger and thumb and tugging it like a fattened maggot from a feast of rotten fruit. By the time the sirens were audible, wailing across the estate like a bunch of harpies, he had taken off half of his face.

Lana didn't think it was possible to cause this much damage to your own body without losing consciousness, but somehow the fucked-up drug-head had managed it.

When the ambulance pulled up at the kerb and ejected two paramedics from its rear doors, Banjo was slumped against the side of the car and still pulling away the flesh directly under his chin. Blood decorated his shirt like a bad dye job. His legs twitched against the tarmac, his shoes slapped the kerb. His features were obscured by the dangling raw-meat mask he now wore. He had stopped screaming and worked in a strange, almost formal silence.

CHAPTER THIRTEEN

THEIR TRIP WAS delayed, but they were determined
to continue with their plans. The ambulance crew
took away the injured and sedated man, strapping
him to a gurney, and they were told to wait until the
police arrived. There was not much to say when the
officers questioned them, just a précised version of
the facts, and they were asked to call in at the local
station as soon as it was convenient to give a formal
statement.

Nobody seemed to care that much about Banjo; the
emergency personnel went about their business in a
calm, detached manner. He was just another junkie
who'd lost his mind, overdosing on cheap smack,
and turned his emotions inward to cut himself.

The area was full of people just like him, and the
police seemed unimpressed even by the manner in
which Banjo had done himself harm. They'd seen
it all before. It was part of the job, another aspect
of their day-to-day existence: self-harming junkies,
street drugs, and common-or-garden madness. Just
one aspect in a grim parade of extremity, the same
as every other event they were trained to deal with.

"Are you sure you still want to do this?" Tom
glanced into the rear-view mirror as he drove out of
the estate. He knew what he wanted to hear, but didn't
want to prompt a reply she was reluctant to give.

Lana sat with her arms around Hailey's shoulders, but the girl remained oddly unmoved by the experience. "What do you think, honey? Shall we still go, or would you prefer to go home?"

Hailey shook her head. "We'll go. What have we got to go back for? There'll be blood on the road and questions and gossip from the neighbours. I'd rather stick to our plans."

"Only if you're sure, baby." Lana stroked her daughter's hair. Her eyes remained locked on Tom's in the mirror. Her lips formed a tight line across the bottom of her face, as if underlining the event.

"He was just a drugged-up loser, Mum. Who cares?"

Lana's hand stopped moving on Hailey's scalp. "Okay, honey." She stared at Tom.

Tom nodded. "So we continue, then: to Hadrian's Wall. It might do us all a bit of good, actually, just to get away from all that madness back there."

"Can we have music on? Please?" Hailey was sitting up straight. She'd folded her arms across her chest and moved away from her mother, pressing her body against the inside of the door. She seemed to have forgotten about the horror they had witnessed.

"Yeah. Sure we can." Tom reached out and turned on the radio. He noted that his hands were shaking, even as he turned the dial. The radio was tuned to a local station; they were playing a pop tune he vaguely recognised from a television commercial. He wasn't sure what kind of product the ad was selling, but he knew most of the words to the song's hideously catchy chorus.

"That's good. Thanks." Hailey smiled as she looked out of the side window. Her eyes looked empty, bereft of anything but the reflection of daylight.

He drove west, towards Hexham, taking the A69 – a road which followed the route of Hadrian's Wall. Green fields were pocked with strange pools of light and shadow. Small tumbledown stone walls barricaded dirty sheep and kept them from the roadside. The occasional fell walker waved as they drove by, raising red-cagouled arms to indicate some kind of bond they did not share. Tom drove in silence until they reached the signs for a place called Greenhead, where he turned off the main road and followed the signs for the Hadrian's Wall Path.

Tom parked the car on a patch of gravel. The sky was turning dark, clouds were bloated and shuffling. A few other people – pensioners, on a day out – were milling around, putting on or taking off their walking boots, sorting out rucksacks and packed lunches.

"I brought a picnic," said Lana. She was buttoning her coat against the chill.

Tom nodded. "That's nice. I'm sorry, the weather's turning bad, and that thing back at the estate... It seems like something doesn't want us to have a good time today."

Hailey was walking away, towards a low fence. She sat down on the top bar and stared back along the road.

Lana moved towards Tom, placing her hand on his arm. "*I* want us to have a good time," she said. "What happened earlier doesn't matter. It's what we did yesterday that really counts."

Tom placed his hand over hers. She was warm, and her long, thin fingers moved against his, rubbing his thumb. "I want us to enjoy this, too," he said. "All of it." The sky churned above them. A large bird – black, and with a huge wing span – flew over their heads, cawing loudly. It was like an omen, but Tom refused to let its message inside his head.

"Come on, let's go for that walk." She squeezed his hand, and he felt brittle, like calcified bone. If he stopped for even a moment to think about all of this, he might snap into a million pieces, his skeleton shattering and the broken bones spilling across the hills and dales.

They walked together to the spot where Hailey was sitting, her legs tucked up under her bottom and her hands pressed flat against the wooden fence. "Come on, we're going to work up an appetite." Lana brushed her fingers across Hailey's cheek, and the girl flinched away before getting to her feet and following them across the flat, wet grass.

They crossed the fence using a wooden stile, and headed up a long, gradual rise. The gravel path soon became a hard-packed dirt trail, and the bushes and trees thinned out the higher they climbed. Scrawny lone trees stood like sentinels, surrounded only by flat stretches of grass. Old rock falls had created shallow caves, and the roots of old trees clasped the stone walls of these strange natural constructions.

Soon they reached the tip of the hill, and went through a gate to follow part of a bridle path. As they turned to follow the tip of the rise, the partial remnants of the great Roman wall came into view.

The uneven stone spine of the wall stretched away from them, dipping into small valleys and then rising to rocky peaks. The route was no longer steep, but it did undulate dramatically, so that the wall itself resembled the sculpture of some great stone serpent. Tom recalled with passing fondness the legend of the Lambton Worm, and the old folk song they used to sing at school when he was a small boy:

But the worm got fat an' grewed an' grewed,
An' grewed an aaful size;
He'd greet big teeth, a greet big gob,
An greet big goggly eyes

This particular worm, the one whose back they were following across the ancient landscape, hoping that it might lead them to a glimpse of something better than they already had, was made of stone. But no, that wasn't right. It wasn't the wall that would lead them to better things, it was their own ambition, and the strength of any plans they made.

"We learned about this at school, in Mr. Benson's class." Hailey had drawn level with them. Her eyes were still blank, dreamy, but she seemed a little more focused than before.

"What did you learn?" Tom thought that a mellow discussion about the history of the place might divert her mind from darker thoughts, and even help him to stop thinking about his increasingly uncertain future.

"Well, Emperor Hadrian built the wall. I think it was in AD 122, at least that's when he started. It took – I think it was six years to build."

"Well remembered," said Tom. Lana gripped his hand. "Anything else?"

"It was built as a fortification to keep out trouble from Scotland." She chewed on her lower lip between sentences, as if lost in thought. "But it was also meant as a symbol of Roman power, according to Mr. Benson. He reckons it was like the Romans flexing their muscles. Telling everyone else not under Roman rule to keep back, or they'd get a good kicking."

Tom laughed. "Well, yes, that's a fair point. The Romans certainly knew how to give folk a good kicking."

"Something else, as well: we read this article from a science magazine, and apparently back in the Sixties someone dug up a portion of the wall and found human bones. *Baby* bones. Newborn children were buried alive under the foundations as a sacrifice, to protect the wall."

"Jesus, Hailey... do we really need to talk about that?" Lana shook her head. "What the hell gets into your head, girl? Sometimes, I just don't think I know you at all."

Hailey's voice turned petulant, the tone low and uneven. "It was in the magazine. I didn't make it up."

"Okay, that's actually very interesting." Tom turned to face them, walking backwards across the stony ground and trying to avert the threatened row. "The Romans were a pretty nasty bunch, and they had very demanding gods." Something caught his eye. A small, almost dainty movement far behind them, somewhere back along the route they had taken. It looked like a scrap of white sheet, or perhaps a piece of paper, flapping in the wind. Tom stared back along the trail, but nothing else moved. Even the hikers they'd seen in the car park were absent.

"What is it?" Lana looked in the same direction, and then at Tom. "Are you okay?"

Tom nodded. "Yes, fine. I just thought… I dunno. Something just spooked me."

"Yeah," said Lana. "Probably all this talk of dead babies. So I think that's enough of *that*." She glared at Hailey, who continued walking at a slow pace, watching the ground at her feet.

They followed the relatively straight line of the wall, clambering over small rocky outcroppings and plodding up and down the sudden dips and rises. In places the grass was so worn that it looked bald, as if transparent ice were forming and hardening the ground. The air was chilly – but not cold enough to support the idea of snow – and the slight breeze was stirring, becoming stronger.

Tom kept glancing over his shoulder, trying to catch sight of whatever he had spotted moments before. Each time he turned his head, something twitched at the edge of his vision. But by the time he had focused on the location, there was no longer anything to be seen. It was as if something were teasing him, drawing his attention before ducking back out of sight. The thought unnerved him, and he remembered the weird visions he'd been having lately: the dog with a boy's face, a figure that may or may not be a visual echo of his dead father's abuse.

"How about we stop for a bite to eat?" Lana pressed her body against him. It was warm, firm, and reminded him of reality rather than stupid dreams and visions.

"That would be good. Hailey – what do you think?"

"Whatever." The girl stopped and sat down on a large, damp rock that was sticking out of the ground like a giant's tooth. She picked up a twig and started stripping the bark, rolling it off between her fingers like the rind of some strange fruit.

Lana put the cooler bag on the ground and sat on a nearby cluster of stones. Slowly she began to take items out of the bag: a small checked blanket, bags of sandwiches, a thermos flask filled with what Tom assumed must be coffee. She lined up these things neatly, as if it were important that everything was just right.

"Can I help?" Tom made a move to sit down beside her, but she glanced up and shook her head.

"It's fine," said Lana. "Be done in a minute. The grass is still a bit wet, but it'll be okay if we stay on these rocks."

The sky was now grey as slate, and the dense clouds resembled a layer of dull, dirty plaster across the ceiling of the world. Tom stared upwards, trying to make out the sun behind the billowing mayhem. He saw glints, tiny fragments of brightness, but they were swallowed instantly. "Hope it doesn't piss it down," he said. And when nobody answered, he trudged over the grass towards a low section of the wall.

The stone was old, chipped, and light grey in colour. It poked up above the grass like a giant fossilised spine. He approached the ruin, glancing along it in the direction they'd been heading. Then, as his hand pressed against the cold stone, he looked the other way, trying to pick out the route they had come along.

Something shifted in the grey air, partly obscured by the dimness and the distance. It was a mere flicker, like the sudden twitch of a fish's tail twisting and vanishing into deep, debris-filled waters. The motion filled him with a heavy sense of dread, and he wished that he had not seen it.

Tom kept looking at the same spot, but the movement failed to reoccur, and nothing solid appeared out of the dull, heavy air.

He felt a weight pressing down on him, as if the air above him were turning to stone, like the wall, like the attitudes of the people on that damned estate. His shoulders began to ache from the imaginary burden, and if felt as if he were being pushed down into another world – one that existed either directly beneath or alongside this one. He ran the palm of his hand across his forehead and it came away damp. The sweat was cold, like the perspiration from someone suffering a fever. His vision burred; the churning air far ahead of him shimmered with the promise of more movement.

"Who's there?" he whispered the words, afraid to speak them louder.

Then, fading into existence like a slow-dissolve image on a cinema screen, something took shape a few hundred yards down the track. It hovered in the air, twisting and bucking, filled with an energy that was both frightening and invigorating. It seemed to Tom that he was watching many hands, chopping, punching, and picking at the substance of the air, as if trying to use those small, condensed acts of violence to break through the barriers of reality.

"Who?" Again, it was a whisper. He didn't want Lana to hear.

The hands darted like birds; they opened like wings and then folded shut again, forming solid fists that pummelled the air. Tom heard their impact in his mind, but he knew that the sound was not audible in the real world. Only in that place he had felt shifting beneath and around him, that one that was still trying to open up and pull him in.

He was trapped here, mute and helpless before those rampaging fists – the fists that were now moving closer to him, seeking him out, drawn to his anxiety.

It was like a pocket or envelope of air had closed around those barely visible fists, and they were trying to fight their way out. They were large, bony and monstrous: bigger than life, yet so much less than living. He saw now that there were scores of them, packed in tight like creatures caught up in gossamer netting.

Tom stood his ground. He was too terrified to move, to run. His feet had been swallowed by the earth, becoming part of the footing of the ancient wall at his side. The fists raged; they bristled with energy. If they touched him even once, Tom knew that he would be destroyed. His body would explode on impact.

Then they were gone. The pocket of air seemed to pop like a balloon, and nothing threatening was inside. The sky rose back to its natural position, and his legs were released from the ground's hungry grip.

"Mum said the food's ready." Hailey stood at his side, one hand resting on his forearm. Her face was so pale that he thought he could see through it to the skull beneath. Something twitched inside the confines of her cranium, causing the bone to bulge outward: nothing but a vision that was leftover from his brush with that imaginary realm. He blinked and it was gone.

Tom was under no illusion that her presence had sent the chaotic hallucination on its way, and he could have fallen to his knees in thanks. Instead he followed her back to the cluster of rocks, where Lana sat smiling on the red and black blanket, an array of food set out before her on an improvised table of stone. The sheer banality of the sight helped him to put some distance between this moment and what he had seen – or what he *thought* he had seen.

"This stuff isn't going to eat itself," she said. Then a look of concern crossed her face. "Are you okay? You look... well, you look shocked. Or scared."

Tom knelt down on the blanket, reached for a sandwich. "Sorry. I was just thinking – thinking about my late father."

And then he was frightened all over again, because it was true: he had been thinking about his dead father, but without even realising he was doing so. Those fists – those images of violence – had been all that was left of the man, a representation of his will. His ghost, his phantom, was nothing more than a snatch of unfocused aggression, a flock of fists fighting against something unseen.

After they'd eaten – sandwiches with cheap fillings, freezer-shop-bought *vol-au-vonts*, mini sausage rolls, flattened cheese spheres wrapped in red plastic jackets – Hailey walked across the grass and then started to stroll along the side of the rampart. She bent over to pick up a stone, threw it, and then ran her hand along the weather-worn surface of the wall.

"She was a twin, you know." Lana smiled, but her eyes were flat. "Her brother was stillborn. Thirty-seven seconds after I had Hailey, I delivered a little corpse."

Tom didn't know what to say, so he remained silent. He stared at Lana's face, at the way her hair fell across her cheek and she kept pushing it out of the way; an unconscious gesture, but somehow sad and beautiful.

"I haven't told anyone that," she said, glancing at him, and then down at the ground. "I don't even know why I'm telling you." She shook her head. "Hailey doesn't even know she almost had a brother." She smiled again, and this time it was better, stronger, almost real.

"What's wrong?" Tom waited for her to answer; there was no rush, they had all day. "What's really bothering you?"

"I'm worried about her," said Lana, turning to stare at her daughter's back.

Tom moved round on the blanket so that he was sitting right next to her on the rock. He could feel the heat of her body, even through their fleecy jackets. A flash of sunlight lit the sky above them, and then dimmed but did not vanish. "Why? Is she still having those fainting spells?"

Lana shook her head. She lifted a hand and pushed the hair from out of her eyes. "No, she seems to have stopped those. But there's something else, something wrong."

Tom placed his hand on her knee.

She glanced at him and smiled, but the expression didn't last. "I think she might be pregnant."

"Ah... okay. Has she said anything?" He squeezed her knee, but this time she failed to respond.

"No, it's nothing she's actually said. But sometimes when I look at her, when she's wearing thin clothing, her belly seems swollen. Then, the next time I look, it's flat. I'm not sure what's going on, but it isn't right. It could be a tumour, or something. It might not be natural at all. I think I should take her to see a doctor, but if I tried I know she'd fight me."

The landscape was silent; not even the birds sang. Not a living soul was visible. The sky trembled.

"This all sounds a bit strange," said Tom, unsure of what she wanted him to say. "Her belly – you say it looks like she's pregnant one day, and then the next it looks normal?"

"No," said Lana. "Not normal. On those other days she looks too thin. Skinny. Like she's starving to death. Her skin's all dry, her breath smells, and she's passing blood when she goes to the toilet. She says she's never even been with a boy. I don't know what to do. I couldn't handle it if she was seriously ill."

Tom remained silent. He wanted to help, to offer support, but this was something in which he had little experience. He'd never been a father; his marriage had not produced a child.

"I'm sorry." She hitched closer again, so that her thigh brushed against his leg. "I shouldn't be burdening you with this. All my troubles, my fucking woes." She tried to laugh but it didn't quite work: the sound was shrill, pitched almost at breaking point. "It's just that everything seems to be turning bad, and I have nobody else to talk to."

Tom held her hand. It was warm, despite the chill. "Listen, I'm here for you. I don't know what it is, but we have a connection here. I'm married, you have your own responsibilities, yet we're drawn together. Or am I reading this all the wrong way, and you just need someone to lean on? I can be that, too... if that's all you want."

She shook her head. The movement was vigorous, as if she were trying to convince more than just Tom of her motives. "No, that's not all I want. I need someone to hold me in the night, to make love to me and make me remember that I'm a woman and not just a single mother, a statistic struggling to cope. I need... I *need*. That's all."

Her hand ran along his thigh, moving into his lap to cup him there. She squeezed, softly at first and then harder, and Tom felt like he was about to burst apart at the seams.

"I think I need *you*, Tom." Her eyes were wet, but she did not cry. Her neck blushed red; her cheeks took on a little of that colour.

"We'll work something out. I promise. Because I think I need you, too."

They both looked over at Hailey at the same time, as if she had called out to them.

The girl was standing motionless, turned slightly away from them but with the side of her face still visible, about a hundred metres along the wall. Her hand was outstretched, the palm held flat, and a tiny red and gold bird was perched at its centre. Hailey's lips were moving, as if she were talking to the creature. Then, as they both watched in silence, the brightly-hued bird rose and hovered inches above Hailey's hand before skimming off across the top of the wall, where it disappeared into the shuddering dimness beyond.

CHAPTER FOURTEEN

LATER, AS HE drove away from the Grove, Tom thought about what a strange day this had been. Nothing had seemed to go right on the surface of things – the junkie trying to rip off his own face, the tense mood once the three of them had finally reached Hadrian's Wall, the revelations regarding Hailey's problems, and that odd, insightful moment with what had looked for all the world like a hummingbird – but underneath all this, he felt that it had all been so perfect he wanted to wrap up his memories of the day and lock them away inside a little box.

He had wanted nothing more than to stay for a while at Lana's place, but Hailey's mood had soured once they got out of the car and he thought it best to leave them, to give mother and daughter some time together. It was getting late anyway: they'd remained at the site longer than expected, leaving reluctantly only when the sun began to set. And he had promised Eileen Danby – the neighbour who was keeping an eye on Helen for the day – that he wouldn't be back too late. He had already broken that promise, just like all the others he had broken simply by spending the day with Lana.

He drove slowly through Far Grove, trying to prolong his time away from home, but deep down inside he knew that wherever he went and however long he stayed away, he would always have to return to his wife. It was his duty, his penance. His entire life had been lived in the shadow thrown by an obstacle he could never quite define, and now he was facing the punishment for so many lost years and wasted chances. There wasn't even anyone to blame, not really. Because That Man had not been a monster, just another human being making mistakes like everyone else.

He turned into their street and parked the car on the drive. Then he sat behind the wheel for a while, filled with a dark regret. He stared at his hands on the steering wheel. They looked old, wrinkled. He imagined that in a few years' time liver spots would appear, marking the onslaught of death.

The radio was playing a song by Otis Redding, and despite the hi-tempo beat the tune filled Tom with a sense of regret. Why could he not have met Lana, or someone like her, when he was still young enough and sharp enough and *free* enough to take advantage of the opportunity? Why had it happened now, when he was already resigned to spending the remainder of his years looking after a wife he hated?

Hate. It was such a strong world... but in rare honest moments, like this one, he knew it to be true.

"They call me Mr. Pitiful," he said, smiling, looking for humour in a situation where there was none. His eyes, when he looked at his face in the rear-view mirror, were dull and flat and lifeless, like pennies thrown in a pond to rust, corroded by dreams so heavy that they could not be lifted from the bottom.

He got out of the car and walked slowly along the drive. The lights were on downstairs – Eileen, the neighbour, must still be in there, watching over Helen as she lay sweating in her bed. He paused outside the front door, wishing that he could turn back, run away, and head off into some movie-scene sunset. Then he opened the door and walked inside.

"Tom?" Eileen Danby appeared in the kitchen doorway. She was holding a mug and her face was drawn, tired.

"I'm sorry I'm late," said Tom, taking off his coat. "I hit some bad traffic."

"It's okay." Eileen smiled, and when she did so her tired, heavy face lost at least a decade. He recalled that many years ago, before her husband had left her, she was an attractive woman. "No, it's not that. I don't mind. It's Helen... she's had a bit of a bad time."

Tom glanced towards Helen's room. The door had been left ajar. The handle looked like a weapon, but before he could puzzle over this thought and where it had come from, Eileen was speaking again. "She got a little paranoid." She tightened her grip on the mug, wrapping her fingers around a faded comedy decal of Bugs Bunny dressed as a French Maid. "She seems to think that you've been doing something wrong, or visiting a place you shouldn't."

Tom's stomach seemed to drop into his knees.

"I couldn't really be sure what she meant. Her voice, her words. It was all just gibberish." She smiled sadly.

Tom looked down at the floor, at his walking boots. Dried mud was spattered on the toughened toe caps. "I've been with a client. We went for a walk near where he lives, had lunch in a nice rural pub. There's nothing else." He felt like crying. He always felt like crying.

"I know that, Tom – God knows, you've been loyal to her, caring for her when a lot of men might have walked away. You're a good man, a saint. I know how tough it must be for you."

He felt like grabbing her by the shoulders and screaming into her startled face: *I'm not a good man, I'm a bastard. I've been thinking about nothing else but fucking another woman all day!*

He nodded. "Thank you, Eileen. I really appreciate that."

She took a few steps closer and reached out, one hand still clutching the mug and the other grabbing his hand, groping it before finding purchase. "A *very* good man." Her fingers were hot and clammy.

Tom could not raise his head; he was unable to look up, into her eyes. He knew that Eileen Danby had been attracted to him for years, and that attraction had grown since Helen's injuries. She'd made a blatant pass one New Year's Eve, about seven years ago. Her husband had left her the Christmas before, and she was feeling lonely and neglected. They'd been sitting on the steps at the back of her house, listening to the revellers inside – this was back when Helen was still willing to get around in her wheelchair, so even she was present at the party.

Eileen had placed her hand on his knee, moved it almost casually up his leg. Then, without uttering a word, she'd undone his zip and masturbated him. Right there on the doorstep, smelling of beer and cigarettes and staring away, across the garden, as if the act was separate from her, a part of something else she was thinking of.

And Tom had let her do it, enjoying being complicit in such a blatant act of sexuality.

"I'm not a good man," he whispered. "Never was."

Afterwards, when he was breathing hard and spots of light were scattered across his vision, Eileen had wiped her hand on a paper tissue she'd produced from the breast pocket of her blouse. She kissed him on the cheek, stood up and went back inside the house, all without speaking, without acknowledging in any way what she had done. Tom had sat there for another ten or fifteen minutes, drinking his beer and wondering what the hell had just happened.

They had not spoken of the event since, pretending that it had never happened. Those scant few moments on the back doorstep were like a shared wet dream, something that might vanish if they confronted its memory.

"You know where I am if you ever want to talk." She pulled her hand away, placing it behind her back, as if to hide the evidence of her touch. She always said the same thing, and not once had he taken her up on the offer. But he knew it was there: he still felt the pressure of her grip on his penis, even all these years later, as if she had never really let go.

"I know, Eileen, and it's really appreciated." At last he raised his eyes from the floor, glancing at her. She had stepped back, and her face seemed unable to fix on a single expression. "Thanks."

Eileen smiled, nodded, and then frowned. "She's sleeping now. She slept most of the day, to be honest." She put down her mug on the table near the stairs and grabbed her coat from the hook on the wall. "I'll leave you to it. Tell her I'll pop in on Tuesday, as usual, to see if she wants any shopping."

Tom remained where he was as Eileen let herself out – she'd had a key for years now, and came and went as she pleased whenever Tom asked her to help out while he was away on business. She never overstepped the mark of their unspoken agreement, and had not once given him reason to think that she might have an ulterior motive for doing what she did. Eileen had been a good friend to Helen, despite that one slip at the New Year's Eve party. She had also been invaluable to Tom whenever he needed support. She'd never again strayed beyond these personal boundaries, but the unspoken offer was out there, whether he wanted it or not.

"See you, Eileen." The door slammed shut on his words.

He walked across the hallway and pushed open the door to Helen's room. Every time he did this, stepped into her darkened room, he thought of that film, *The Exorcist*. The one with the possessed girl in an upstairs bedroom, strapped to a bed in the dark. The way the visiting priests' breath misted in the icy air; the oppressive pressure of the silence in the room, apart from the ragged sound of her breathing.

"Helen? You awake, Helen?"

He could hear her breathing, just like the demonic teenager in that film. It was low, heavy, asthmatic, and punctuated by soft little snores.

"I'm home. Sorry it took longer than I thought, but the guy wanted a full report on how I'm planning to save him money on last year's taxes." He hated lying like this, but the demands of his accountancy work were a gilt-edged excuse. Helen knew he had to visit clients, to keep them sweet and reassure them about their money and investments, so she rarely questioned his motives when he left the house for a day, and she always enjoyed Eileen Danby's company.

"No." Her voice was thick; he could tell immediately that she was still asleep.

"It's okay, pet. I'm here. I'm home. There's no need to fret." He approached the bed and sat down on the edge of the mattress. There was a jug of water by the bed, half full, and a crumb-covered plate containing half a slice of buttered toast and a folded chocolate biscuit wrapper. "No need to worry, now."

The television at the foot of the bed was switched on, but there was no picture, just a silent screen filled with surging static.

The top of Helen's head, along with part of her face, was visible above the covers. He could see the sweat glistening on her forehead like crushed ice. Her eyes were closed but her eyelids twitched, holding back a dream. The bedclothes covered her mouth, but he could see by the movement of the muscles in her jaw that she was grinding her teeth and mumbling in her sleep – something she often did when she was uneasy, when she was feeling disturbed or anxious.

He reached out and stroked her forehead. The skin was warm and wet; each furrow or crease was filled with greasy moisture. Tom held back a wave of nausea, feeling guilty for the way he disliked to touch his wife.

"What did you do?" Her voice was louder this time. The covers shifted down a few inches, exposing her open lips. Her teeth were large and discoloured. "What did you do with her?"

"Hush now, it's okay. There's nothing wrong. I'm home…" He was running out of things to say, and knew that she probably couldn't hear him anyway.

"Bastard!"

She did that too, sometimes: swore at him, abused him as she slept. Once he had fallen asleep beside her, curled up on the bed, and woken to find her hands around his neck, tightening, trying to choke him. It had been the last time he'd ever allowed himself to doze in her room. After that he made a point of heading upstairs as soon as he felt tired. Something else she had spoiled; another thing for him to feel guilty about, but on her behalf: a sense of guilt by proxy.

Give me all of it, he thought, bitterly. *A man can never have enough guilt.*

Tom turned and looked again at the television. The static danced before his eyes, threatening to take on forms, to twist into the shapes of dancing figures. He stared at the monochrome blur, narrowing his eyes. Could he see fists in that chaos of interference? Where they swinging, as if throwing punches on the other side of the screen?

Helen moaned: a soft, wordless noise.

A face seemed to loom forward from the screen, breaking away from the mass of dots. Its eyes were closed but its mouth was open, widening as Tom watched. Other, smaller faces poured out of it, dancing around the original features. He was tired, seeing things.

"Tom?" The picture broke apart at the sound of Helen's voice, as though afraid to be witnessed by anyone but him.

"Yes... yes, it's me."

"Where's Eileen?" She blinked into the darkness, the wash of TV light softening her features, making it look as if there were no bones beneath the skin, or like the bones there had melted.

"She went home. It's late."

"What time is it? I... I must've fallen asleep again. I've been very tired today. Exhausted, but I'm not sure why." Her hands fidgeted on top of the bedclothes, exploring like pale stick insects. Her eyes were wide and wet and slightly imbecilic.

"It's almost nine o'clock. I'm really sorry for staying out this long."

Helen shivered. "No. It's fine. You need to work, to bring in the money. I know that." She looked like a plastic doll, rigid and unblinking.

"Just lie back down and go to sleep. I'll clean up and have an early night myself. It's been a long day. Tiring. I need to catch up on a lot of work tomorrow, so will probably be up and about early."

One of her flailing hands settled on top of both of his. Her fat fingers enveloped them, spreading out across his knuckles like a jellyfish. "Okay, Tom. I love you." Her voice was filled with a desperation that he found offensive, even frightening. She said it because she wanted him to say it back – she needed to hear him say the words, to reassure her, to put her mind at rest. He hated it when she got like this, and he despised himself for begrudging her the slight demonstration of affection.

More guilt for him to carry, and it always prompted him to give her what she needed.

"I love you, too," he said, through tight lips. The words sounded like someone else was in the room, speaking for him.

She squeezed his hands and then relaxed her grip. He pulled his hands away, just about resisting the urge to wipe them on his shirt, as if she had left a residue, a taint that he could not bear to feel against his skin.

"I had a strange dream," she said as she nestled her head back against the pillows. Her eyes were open. Even in the darkness he could see the pulse in the side of her neck jerking like a jumping bean.

"Don't worry about that now. Just tell me in the morning, when we're both less tired."

"But I might forget." Her eyelids were flickering shut. The pulse in her neck was slowing, its movement becoming less frantic. "What if I forget it, Tom?"

"Doesn't matter," he said, adjusting his position on the bed so that he could get up without disturbing her. "It's nothing, just a dream. And dreams can't hurt you."

"The TV people told me."

Tom felt his limbs stiffen. His eyes widened in the dark and his shoulders tensed.

"They said that you were with someone – another woman."

He stared at her face, her slack cheeks and her closed eyes. Her small, hard nose. Her slit of a mouth and the multiple chins beneath.

"I don't mind. I know you have needs. You're a man, still a young man, really, and you can't deny your desires."

She was asleep now: he could see that she was. He knew her well enough, and had spent so many years by her side, that he could not fail to recognise when she was no longer awake. Yet her speech was crisp and erudite. She was speaking lucidly, unhurriedly. Her words were as clear as the sound of falling water.

"But they said she's dangerous. The TV people. They told me that she'll hurt you. Something's going to happen, and everyone will suffer. We'll all pay a price, a debt that's owed. We'll all get hurt because of her."

She's sleeping, he thought. *Talking in her sleep. She does this all the time – don't get freaked out. She knows nothing.*

But he *was* freaked out. In fact, he was terrified. How could she know that he had been with a woman, and one whose very presence made him weak and senseless with desire? It wasn't real, couldn't be. This was some kind of fluke, a random circumstance. There was no way on earth that Helen could know, and there certainly were not any people inside the television to divulge the information.

He looked over at the screen, needing to keep an eye on it, to watch it more closely. The static was going crazy. It was like a swarm of monochrome bees trapped in a jar, bouncing off the glass walls, confused and trying to get out, get free, back out into the open.

"She'll break everything. Cause damage. They told me this, the TV people. They had skinned faces and long, bent-back legs. There were tiny birds with bright wings hovering around them and landing on them, sitting in their open palms."

The television screen bulged. Just once, like an air bubble. Then it went dark. Reflected for a moment in that jet black surface, Tom saw something that could not possibly be his father's face, no matter how much it resembled the man's features.

"She'll open doors that should stay closed." Helen's voice was drifting now, growing weaker, quieter. "She's going to let them out, and... she doesn't know... it."

Then she went quiet, apart from her ragged breathing, and the faint sound of her little snores.

Tom prepared to get up and leave the room. The face in the television screen – the one that he refused to acknowledge looked like his dead father – was no longer visible. He shifted his weight on the mattress, causing it to creak and rock slightly beneath him.

I'm seeing things, he thought. *That's all.*

Helen sat bolt upright, her eyes open wide. They were all white: no pupil. Just big white marbles stuck into the pale dough of her face. Her mouth dropped open, her tongue lolling like a fat dead

worm. "Kill me." She said. "You deserve better."
Her eyes were normal now; the pupils were dilated
but at least they'd gone back where they were
meant to be. Her face had regained some of its
firmness, and looked less like the face of a corpse.
"I know you want to, Tom." She slipped back onto
the pillows, her eyes closing. "I know it's what you
want."

Tom stood and backed away from the bed,
terrified that he might disturb her and the whole
performance would start up all over again. He
moved towards the door, keeping one eye on Helen
and the other on the dead television screen.

"Maybe I want it, too."

He could not be certain that she said the words,
but he heard them anyway, inside his head. The
stale air in the room buzzed with energy, like the
air before a storm. Helen's statement – whether
real or imagined – was stuck in his head, refusing
to budge. The words hung there like dead animals
nailed to a wall: a reminder of something bad, the
first bloody act in a chain of events that could not
be prevented from running its course.

He backed out of the room and tried to shut the
door. He could not remove his fingers from the
handle; they were glued there by fear. Perhaps if
he remained where he was, with his hand on the
door, then nothing Helen had predicted would
happen? Perhaps he could stop the world, simply
by standing there, unmoving.

Or perhaps the world would simply keep on
turning without him, unaffected by his ridiculous
protest, and the damage his wife had spoken

of would still destroy them all. One by one, like diseased trees falling in a dying forest, or plastic targets put down by gunshots.

Maybe nothing he did would ever matter, not any more. Not now.

Because what if his life was already over – if in fact it had ended ten years ago, right after the accident – and since then he'd just been playing catch-up?

He shut and then re-opened the door – just an inch or two, the way Helen liked it. When he leaned in close and peeked through the gap he saw a large, grey hairless mass on the bed. Fins twitched above the covers like the legs of a dog dreaming of the run. At last the sea cow was sleeping...

...then it was her again: it was Helen, asleep on the bed, her nightdress in disarray. His wife: the person who depended on him so completely. The woman he was meant to love.

As he moved away from the door, Tom had the terrible feeling that he was leaving behind one kind of darkness only to enter another.

CHAPTER FIFTEEN

HAILEY IS DREAMING again, but this time it's different. She is not naked, for a start, and her surroundings are not at all familiar. She is standing barefoot in a dense wood, wearing sheets of flesh still warm and bloody from whatever animal they have been sliced from. She looks down at her body beneath the pelts, and sees that there are designs painted upon her swollen stomach in blood.

Signs and sigils; numbers and letters in a language she does not recognise.

A spell, a hex: some kind of protective charm?

She rubs at her skin with her fingers, trying to remove the blood, but it has already dried and marked her like indelible ink. She cannot remove the writing; it has made of her a book, a bible: a living chart filled with vague rules and instructions.

"Hello. Is anyone here?" Her voice lifts into the air, hits the canopy of trees, and then falls back towards her. The words fade, become silence.

Silence.

It strikes her all at once that she can hear nothing, not even the sound of her own breathing. Her voice was the only thing able to penetrate that wall of silence, and even her words could not survive for long once they left her mouth.

She feels as if she is standing in the middle of a movie scene with the volume set to mute. Her ears ring with pressure, but she cannot even hear an internal sound. There's just a dull soundless throbbing, a gentle ache that is not entirely unpleasant.

She takes a few tentative steps forward and her feet make no noise on the leaf-coated ground. She feels her bare feet sinking into the mulch, the cold mud seeping up between her toes.

The pelts hang heavy around her, like a royal cloak. Their warm and clammy underside presses against her sin.

The air touches the exposed parts of her flesh, making her tingle where the blood-words have been written.

Her grotesquely distended stomach hangs like a sack of offal. Whatever she carries inside her is still, unmoving. She fears that it might be dead. The bloated flesh sways as she moves, its weight trying to drag her down towards the earth.

As she walks through the woods she begins to make out strange shapes high up in the trees. Weird stick-figures made of twine and twigs, tied and knotted and placed like decorations. They hang suspended from the branches, their tinder-stick limbs twitching in a breeze she is unable to feel: rudimentary bodies twirling, spinning, like children's mobiles.

"Can anybody hear me?" The sound of her voice is shocking, but it makes no impact on this space, just bounces off invisible walls and falls to the ground, defeated. It feels as though there is a sheet of glass between her body and what she sees – and she is trapped, unable to break through and get inside.

The breeze ruffles the grass and fallen leaves but still she cannot feel it against her skin.

Something large and cumbersome moves through the undergrowth directly up ahead, turning a large, shaggy head to glance in her direction. Its haunches are wide and muscled; the flanks have been skinned: pink meat shows where strips of the creature's hide have been cut away. It stops, turns, and looks at her. The face she sees is hairless and vaguely human in aspect. It blinks heavy eyelids, licks its lips with a fattened tongue.

As she watches it opens its mouth to speak, but she cannot hear what is being said. Its teeth are huge, yellow and glistening. These are the jaws of a monster.

The writing on her body begins to liquefy and run, the blood dribbling in narrow streams across her body. The pelts shift as if they are alive, tightening around her shoulders, and she begins to feel even more trapped.

The creature smiles; it is a sad, almost mournful expression. Then the beast walks away on all fours, like a great brown bear. Its humanoid face, in profile, looks fat and unwell, as if labouring beneath the weight of ills and agues.

Where the creature stood only a moment before, a thin, naked body now hangs. Upside down, arms dangling limp and lifeless, the body has been tied with lengths of hemp at the ankles and suspended like slaughtered game from the trees above. The body turns slowly, smoothly, and as she draws near she begins to recognise its shape, the tone of its skin, the colour of its hair.

"Mum?"

Her mother's corpse spins slowly to face her. The torso has been cleaved, the rib cage forced apart like the white-barred doors of a cage. The stomach contents have been removed and the cavity stuffed with dry oak leaves. She is close enough now that she can reach out, take hold of a clump of that makeshift stuffing and pull it out. The leaves are attached, like a rope of handkerchiefs being drawn from the secret depths of a magician's sleeve.

She does not weep. She is calm, existing at a place beyond grief. This is a normal thing, a natural event. Her mother has died and been taken into the bosom of nature, and then reinvented as a part of this enchanted place.

Acorns pour from the savage wound, dislodged by the motion of leaves as she tugs them aside. More acorns than could possibly fit inside her mother fall from her belly, released from where they have been stored in her womb: countless mutant babies waiting to be born into a world of wonder.

She looks at her mother's face and the eyelids flicker open. Her eyes are acorns, too; highly polished, and smoothed down as if by a steady, nimble hand wrapped in emery cloth. Her mother's mouth hinges open and vomits a stream of filth: dead bugs, the gnawed bones of small mammals, and hundreds of tiny wood-dwelling isopods that move in a single wave across her pale face, forming a crisp brown mask.

She drops to her knees and throws her arms around her mother's neck, basking in that fountain of grime. Her mother's skin feels rough as bark, and cold as all the lies she has ever told.

CHAPTER SIXTEEN

FRANCIS BOATER WAS used to waiting. He had been waiting for something good to happen for his entire life, and still the much-anticipated event was yet to arrive. Whatever *it* was – and Boater didn't really know what that thing might be or where it would come from – he was still waiting.

"Is she gonna be long?" He stared at the skinny barman, flexing his massive chest in a way that he knew intimidated people. Boater used his bulk like other people used words: he hid behind it, communicated with the mass of gone-to-seed muscle that had turned to heavy fat. He couldn't remember a time when he had been anything but big – but at least when he was younger, in his early twenties, his physique had been hard and knotted, like a stocking filled with conkers. Now that he was in his forties, he looked like an ageing mountain – or, as he thought on bad days, a stockpile of lard.

"I'll just go and check." The barman – what was his name again? Terry? Trevor? Some soft-shite student-type name, anyway – put down the glass he'd been cleaning and hurried through into the back room, where he vanished up a narrow flight of wooden stairs.

"Fucking bitch," said Boater, necking almost his full pint of lager. He knew about bitches: knew them well, in fact. His mother had been the biggest bitch of all, and she had created what she lovingly referred to as her Own Little Monster when she fucked with his mind during childhood. He remembered coming home often to find her rutting on the sofa with strangers; sometimes she'd even told him to stand and watch, staring at him as her latest beau thrust into her, his eyes closed and his wet mouth pressed against her neck. On these occasions, her smile was like a razor: sharp and dangerous.

Even with intelligence as limited as his, Boater knew that the woman had deliberately twisted him, turning him into what he was today: an enforcer, a man who enjoyed hitting people more than he did simply touching them; a violent sociopath more comfortable in a fight than a lovers' embrace. Yes, even he was aware enough to realise these facts. He'd read enough true-life crime books, and seen too many documentaries on men of violence not to know the limits of his own broken mind.

He glanced around the bar, willing someone to give him a wrong glance, or speak out of turn about him to their drinking partners – a word passed behind a raised palm, a glance held too long or not long enough. But there were no takers; everyone knew who he was, and even if they didn't, his musk was strong enough to scare them. He was a fighter, a warrior, a barely caged tiger. He was Monty Bright's top man, and his reputation went before him like a sword thrust into the darkness.

"She'll be just a couple of minutes."

Boater turned back to the bar, glaring at the stupid little bastard who'd come back with the message. Boater hated the bloke's thin forearms, his pale skin unsullied by prison tattoos, and the keen brightness in his eyes. "Another pint. Now."

The man scurried the length of the bar to use the pump farthest from Boater. This made him smile. Other people's fear always did.

He drank his next pint more slowly, and felt the alcohol dull his rage. No doubt it would flare up later, after a few more beers, some cheap shots, and whatever drugs he could score during the course of the evening. But for now he felt calm and easy. He was out on a promise, and the girl he was waiting for was just about worth the delay.

A few minutes later she came sashaying out from the doorway behind the bar, wearing a skirt so short that it looked more like a belt, a little leather jacket over the top of a low-cut vest top, six-inch heels, and an orange tan from a bottle.

"You look great," he said, leaning towards her and almost swallowing her in his bulk.

"Ta. You look fucking massive, but that's just how I like them." Her smile was plastic, a warped Botox grin, and her eyes were as flat and lifeless as those of a sex doll.

"Let's get the fuck out of here. I hate this shite-hole." He grabbed her tiny hand, swamping it in his warm flesh, and dragged her towards the door.

"Hey, my dad loves running this place. It's his private little hidey hole from the world. Just him and the hardcore drunks." She began to laugh, almost manically, and Boater was confused about the reason why. What was funny about the words she'd said? He just didn't get it, but he rarely got anything these days. Sometimes he felt that the work he did, the life he had led, made him different from everyone else. Another kind of human; one not entirely in step with the others he saw around him. A man apart; a breed not fit for the company of others.

"Where are you taking me, then?"

They emerged from the grotty little pub under the Tyne Bridge. Boater glanced up, at the steel and concrete underside, and for a fleeting moment he realised that the sight represented the prison bars of his life. Then, shaking off such idiocy, he thought about how he was going to shag this bitch until she screamed. Maybe leave her blackened and bruised; her own private tattoo, to remember him by. Where was he taking her? Right up the arse, that's where.

"Well?" her voice was starting to get on his nerves; it sounded small and tinny, like a faulty tape recording.

"I thought we'd have a little dodge along the Quayside for an hour, and then go back to Far Grove for a few beers and a smoke with my mates. I can score some good gear there – something that'll keep us going all night."

She laughed again. The sound grated on his nerve endings. "I like it when you keep going all night, Fran."

It was starting to rain; the charcoal sky looked like someone had slashed it repeatedly with a knife, showing the flat blackness beneath. The clouds were low and heavy, lumbering like pregnant beasts, and the air was turning cold. Boater ducked into a pub doorway, losing his grip on the girl's hand for a moment, and made his way through the hot, sweaty crowd to the bar.

They had two drinks, and during the time it took them to finish he realised that he was already bored of this girl. He didn't even know her name; she was pointless, just another way of wasting time as he waited for that good thing to appear – the event that he knew, deep inside, would never happen, not even if he lived for a million years. Where had he even met her, anyway, this plastic sex toy? He reached inside his memory and plucked out an image: she owed Monty Bright some money, and had taken the option of servicing him once a week to bring down her payments. Growing tired of her, Monty had given Boater permission to take her on, and it had all clicked into place.

It happened all the time, this trading of bodies. Monty got sick of them fast, and he passed them on to his men. This time it was Boater's turn, but each moment he spent in the girl's company was another inch towards the thought of killing her – one more step along the road to oblivion.

He was glad when his mobile phone rang. It pulled him up out of the swamp of his thoughts, made him realise where he was and who he was with – another empty vessel, a cast-off he was about to use as a receptacle for his dead dreams and his dull desire.

He pulled the mobile out of his inside pocket, where it was vibrating against his ribs, and flipped open the lid with his thumb. "Monty. What can I do?" he always answered the same way whenever his boss called; it was a ritual, a habit that he enjoyed. It placed him inside an ordered moment, like a well-oiled hinge in time and space, and made him feel important. 'Doing things' was what he was good at.

"Where are you?" Monty's voice was calm, unhurried – that was good, at least. There could be no trouble if he wasn't on edge.

"In some shitty pub down at Newcastle Quayside." The sound of the revellers inside the building swelled, threatening to steal Monty's response, but he pressed the mobile handset tight against his ear.

"Get your fat arse back here. I've had a phone call. We're going to have some fun."

He could imagine Monty's face and over-gelled hair shining in the low light, and the way he would be leaning back in his chair, perhaps even fondling his crotch as he spoke, anticipating the night's pleasures.

"I can be there in about half an hour. Who is it?" The crowd surged, dragging him sideways. He lost sight of the girl as a host of people spilled between them, moving in a clot towards the back of the narrow space.

"You know – that bitch from the other day. The Fraser woman. The one with the daughter. She's decided to take us up on our offer. She wants to negotiate a deal, payment in kind." His laughter spewed through the phone handset. It was a terrible sound, like the gurgling of a backed-up drain.

"Okay, I'll just dump this slag and be right with you." Her face came into view, over the shoulder of a thin black man in a sparkly shirt that made Boater want to reach out and slap him. She looked afraid, as if she knew what they had in mind for Lana Fraser. "In fact, I'll probably be there even quicker than that." He smiled, but somewhere inside he was aware of something tugging as it threatened to break: a small hand, tightening around his guts. The smile felt wrong, as if it had been manufactured. It didn't quite fit his bloated face. "Just let me deal with this situation, and I'm gone."

Static crawled along the connection, reaching for him. More small hands, but these ones made up of sound. Then, just as quickly, the static cleared. "Okay," said Monty. "Don't be late or we'll get this show on the road without you."

The line went dead but the words hung there, like objects suspended in the darkness of space.

Boater put away his mobile and finished his pint. Then he looked at the girl, wishing for a moment that he knew what to say, how to act like other people. He jerked his head, indicating that she should follow him, and then he set off for the main entrance, barging people out of his path.

"G'night, Boater," said the tall, lean doorman who was lounging against the wall to his right. Boater couldn't remember his name, but he might have sparred with him years ago.

Boater turned around, glared at him. A dull, uninspired rage moved through him, coiling like snakes. "What was that, fella?"

The man's eyes flickered – whatever confrontation was brewing, he had already lost. That was all it took: a faltering glance, a tiny show of weakness. "Nothing... just saying goodnight, like."

Boater squared up to him, straightening his back so that he reared to his full height and with his chest pushed outwards, narrowing the space between them. "No. What did you say, exactly? What were the exact words you just said to me?" He clenched his hands into fists; they were like steel, the joints between fingers sealed shut, welded with sweat.

"I... I just said 'G'night, Boater'." The man took a step back, his spine hitting the wall. That was another show of weakness, his second within the space of a minute; an unforgivable act of defeat that could not go unpunished.

"I'm *Mr*. Boater."

The doorman nodded, looking to his friends for assistance. He raised his hands, but they were open; he held out his palms, surrendering before the fight had even begun.

Boater didn't even need to look over his shoulder to know that the other two doormen would not intervene. He was a known face; his violence was both feared and emulated all across the region. Nobody fucked with Francis Boater, not unless they wanted their face remade into a sculpture of flesh and bone and their family beaten like dogs. He didn't know where to stop; violence was his fuel, his food. He lived to hurt, to cause pain. It had always been his way. That's why Monty Bright had brought him in, trained him up, and trusted him with his life.

"That's *Mr*. Boater, you piece of shit." His hand moved so fast that he barely registered the motion. He was so keyed-up, so attuned to the moment, that he didn't even feel the impact of the blows, just knew in his heart that they had landed true. He saw a splash of red, a blur of pink, and a flurry of spastic movement... then the man went down, hitting the floor like a felled tree.

It was over in seconds. Barely anyone had seen it happen, and those who did failed to understand what they had glimpsed: the raw, brute power of the blows, the finality of the knockout, and the strange compression of time and energy which resulted in Boater walking away the victor. He was always the victor; nobody he had ever met could even come close to besting him.

He left the building, trusting that the girl would follow. They always did. It never failed him, the allure of violence. Not with this type; not with a girl like this one, who always mistook savagery for heroism and confused a beating with a show of passion. He hated her; hated them all. These bitches, these bastards: these fucking empty shells tottering around with nothing on their minds but badly dyed hair.

"Where are we going, Fran?"

He was facing the thick black tongue of the River Tyne, watching people caper like cartoon characters on the other side, waiting in line to enter The Tuxedo Princess, the decommissioned car ferry that now served as a grotty floating nightclub. He refused to turn around, to look at her, but she insisted. Her hand clutched his arm, pulling at him, trying to get his attention.

He focused on the boat and the fact that it was soon to be sent to Greece, where it would probably be scrapped. He'd once worked the door there, pushing around scrawny students and estate kids, flexing his muscles to make the men shake and the women giggle. The end of an era; another local landmark stripped down, floated away, soon to be forgotten. He often felt like his world, his private northeast, was being slowly demolished, bit by bit, memory by memory. Soon there'd be nothing left of the life he'd once known.

Finally, with regret, he allowed himself to be turned.

"Where to now, then?" Her eyes glittered like the stars above them; the skin of her neck was flushed a deep shade of red; her cheeks trembled. She was aroused, she wanted him.

"Fuck off, pet. I have to go somewhere." He breathed deeply, trying to get his rage under control. Even a random act of violence had failed to clear his system, to give him that fix of blood and thunder he seemed to need more and more often these days.

"Take me with you. I'm game. Whatever you want: you, your friends. We can all have a party." She was so eager to be abused, so keen to submit to even a hint of cruelty. What was wrong with these people? What was wrong with *him*?

He imagined breaking her spine with his passion. He thought about cutting off her lips with a pair of scissors. He felt sick; he was dead inside.

That coiling sensation from deep within him had returned, but this time he could not ignore it. There was something going on, a feeling that he couldn't even explain. He felt like crying. That was why he'd given the doorman a slap: because his emotions were running away from him, breaking free, and he needed to at least try to get them back under control. He was not a man who could allow himself to experience normal human emotions. Empathy, understanding, pity, mercy, redemption... these were not for him, not for his kind. He had been flensed of such concerns, a layer of epidermis surgically removed by a blade so keen that its edge was invisible.

The girl seemed to hover before him; her feet were raised several inches off the ground. Her bottle-blonde hair shone like a promise of something better and her eyes glittered again, this time even brighter than the stars. She reached out, reached inside, and Boater felt her small hand grip his ribs, pull them apart, and expose his heart. He heard it beating, beating, and the sound was so close that it was terrifying.

Then, as a crowd of revellers spilled out of another pub and onto the pavement, yelling and screaming and chanting football songs, the moment ended. The cage of his ribs sealed shut and his heart was locked away, where it belonged, deep inside the prison cell of his body. The vision, for what it was worth, had ended.

"Fuck off," he said, turning away and stumbling along the stained footpath like a drunk at night's end. His cheeks were wet; he was crying, but silently and trying to pretend that he wasn't. For a moment, someone else had taken him over – someone real, someone normal – and he hated the feelings that weakling interloper was forcing him to endure. He had been invaded by normality, and it felt... wrong, unnatural.

The Fraser woman – that bitch, just like his mother was a bitch – was really going to get something special tonight. If he had felt sorry for her before, there was no more room for sympathy now. Someone had to pay for the way he felt, and she was going to find herself impaled on the sharp end of his confusion just to settle that debt. He promised himself that it would be an experience she would never forget – even if she walked away with her body intact, her mind would be crippled by the memory.

Boater hailed a cab, flopped down onto the back seat, and told the driver to take him to the Concrete Grove, where the edge of a familiar abyss awaited his arrival.

CHAPTER SEVENTEEN

LANA STOOD IN front of the mirror and stared at her reflection. She was wearing her little black dress, black high-heels and way too much makeup. Bright red lipstick made her lips look swollen; the smoky liner around her eyes gave the impression of light bruising. Ordinarily, she would never go out like this, but she knew what men like Monty Bright admired in a woman: overt sexuality; the image of a whore.

"Whore." Spoken out loud, the word lacked genuine impact. It only hurt when she thought it, when she kept it inside where it could slice her up like a razor.

She turned away from her tarted-up image in the mirror and walked towards Hailey's room. She pushed open the door and stepped inside. The curtains were open; street light leaked through the pane, streaking her daughter's bed covers.

She walked across the room, stepping over Hailey's discarded clothes, and stood at the side of the bed. Staring down, her heart felt heavy and her mind began to clear. What she was about to do, she did for Hailey. She would go to any extreme to put things right, to clear the debt and start all over again. If she had found a way to turn back time, she would have done it without pause for thought, and to hell with any sacrifice time might demand.

She remembered when Hailey was born. The memory still ached inside her. Three in the morning: New Year's Day. She'd just missed out on being one of the first New Year babies, and her sibling had missed out on everything by being born dead. Lana's labour had been long and hard. Her waters had broken fifty-two hours before the delivery, but she had not been dilated enough for the midwife to induce her. The hospital was understaffed and too many pregnant women had been admitted... the whole thing had been horrible, a nightmare.

She recalled a scene a minute or so after midnight, with Timothy standing by the bed, repeatedly lifting and letting drop one of the cheap nylon bed sheets. Worry and lack of sleep had made him fuzzy and weird – he barely even knew where he was or what he was doing. Fireworks were going off outside to welcome in the New Year, but Lana's gaze was drawn to her husband's busy hands, and the sheet as it fell repeatedly onto the bed. Static electricity shimmered in the air; it was their private firework display, a show put on just for them and their as-yet unborn children – the living and the dead.

"For you, honey," she whispered now, in another life.

Hailey stirred in her sleep, one arm coming up out of the creased mass of sheets to cover her face. The bedclothes slipped down to her waist, exposing her midriff. The skin there looked thin, like paper. Lana could almost see her insides through the semi-translucent layer: bunched intestines, and other organs that didn't look quite normal.

When Hailey was born she was floppy and unresponsive, a condition caused by something toxic in Lana's liquors – the fact that her waters had broken so early had led to some kind of infection. The baby's skin was grey; she was barely breathing. They took her away and put her in the Special Care Unit, up on the top floor of the hospital, while Lana continued with her labour. Timothy followed them out of the delivery room; he was clutching one of the tiny woollen hats they'd told him to bring along for the newborn babies. A small, silent Indian doctor drifted in to stitch up Lana after she'd pushed out Hailey's brother, repairing the wounds caused by the delivery of the twins. He worked in silence; he didn't look up from his task once, not even when Lana began to cry. A nurse with short hair and a small tattoo on her neck had carried away a bedpan containing the waste.

"For you…" She leant over her teenage daughter's bed and touched Hailey's stomach. The flesh there was warm, almost moist. She spread out her fingers, forming a fan of the digits. Something fluttered inside Hailey, like a caged bird, and then went still. Her belly remained flat; it did not bulge or distend in the way it had before, when Hailey had lifted her blouse to show Lana the great secret of her anatomy.

I imagined it all, thought Lana. *The stress, the sheer pressure of our situation… It caused me to hallucinate. What I thought I saw… it was impossible.*

Even as she thought this, she was not entirely sure that she truly believed the theory.

Impossible...

Tucking Hailey back into bed, she straightened up and left the room. Everything seemed heavy: her skin, her bones, even the weight of her thoughts. The world was moving slower than it ever had before, as if the nature of gravity had altered.

Her plan was simple, but it was also repellent. She would go to Monty Bright, allow him to do whatever he wanted with her, and then walk away, back to her life. She had been through so much, experienced such horrors because of Timothy and the things he had done, that she believed she could detach herself from the moment and just let it happen.

It might hurt; it would probably haunt her for the rest of her life. But at least the debt would be cleared, and she and Hailey could move forward, make plans to leave this horrible place.

She was willing to do anything to guarantee Hailey's future. Even this: allowing a crude and vicious man – and possibly his friends – to use her body as a plaything. If she thought of it in mechanical ways – she had had a coil fitted a few years ago, so would not become pregnant; she would demand that they all use condoms in case of disease; she would refuse to kiss anyone on the mouth – then she could pretend that it was a job of work. She had grown accustomed to stifling her emotions, and this would simply be one more situation to lock up inside, throwing away the key.

She could think of worse things... like death, or mutilation. Rape – no matter if she went there willingly or not – was better than being maimed or crippled or killed. These men, she knew, were easily capable of all three acts. Penetration she could probably handle and come to terms with, even if it meant losing something of her soul; but losing a *physical* part of herself would be a lot tougher to accept.

But then again, she knew that physical scars healed. Blood stopped flowing; cuts and lacerations sealed themselves shut. Emotional scars, though, never went away: they just faded.

Could she do this? Could she really go through with it?

She glanced over her shoulder, at Hailey's bedroom door. She remembered how that fat bastard, Monty Bright's enforcer, had caressed her daughter's photograph, licking it with his obscene tongue.

Then she asked herself the only other question that mattered under the circumstances: did she really have a choice?

She grabbed her leather jacket and handbag and walked briskly to the door, refusing to look back over her shoulder. She paused at the mirror hanging on the wall by the door, looking again at her doll-like image. She took a packet of baby wipes from her purse and washed off the lipstick, the rouge, the eye make-up.

"No," she whispered. "Not for you." That bastard didn't deserve to see her at her best. She would go to him unadorned, making her sacrifices without the use of war paint.

She kicked off her stripper heels and put on a pair of flat-soled pumps. She would make no concession to eroticism. Let the bastard take her in her most ordinary state, looking like she was on her way to the shops.

Lana opened the door and walked out onto the landing, barged through the fire door, and then stepped briskly down the stairs.

She was on autopilot; her body felt empty, as if she had relinquished all control. She didn't want to do this, but she could see no other way out of her predicament. She did not want those bastards coming anywhere near her daughter. If they touched Hailey, she would kill them all. It was that simple.

The air outside was cold and sharp. Lana tugged her bomber jacket tighter around her body, feeling more vulnerable than ever before in her life. She wished that she'd changed into a pair of jeans. Her bare legs were already feeling the chill. Her body didn't feel as if it belonged to her, and her mind was locked up inside, unable to control what was happening. She knew that she had imprisoned herself in this situation, and the only way out of the jail cell was by doing something terrible... *but sometimes*, she thought, *terrible things can release you.*

But hadn't Timothy thought the same? His actions, when he had been pushed into a corner, were surely the seeds of the terrible thing she was contemplating doing right now. Horror begat horror; bad deeds created even more badness. It was a simple rule of the universe, and one that could never be ignored or forgotten.

Her trapped mind was racing, but it was powerless to intervene. Only the body could perform a meaningful action. The physical Lana was in control now: the flesh-and-blood woman that encased the spiritual being, the shell around the hidden self.

She crossed the road outside the flats, glancing down to inspect the blood stains from that mad junkie, Banjo. The blood had dried to a dark hue; a series of splatter patterns on the roadside and against the kerb. The local news had reported the event earlier, and according to the newsreader Banjo – his real name was Bernard Clarkson – was currently in the LGI, strapped to a bed in an overcrowded ward. They said his mind was wiped. That was the word they'd used: wiped. Like a tape recording or a computer's hard drive. There was nothing left of the person he'd been; the man had vacated his shell, leaving behind nothing but meat.

Lana began to make her way along the long curve of Grove Road. It was the first of the concentric circles that spread out around the Needle. She hated these streets, even more than the outer edges of the estate. They were cold, unwelcoming, and there was always some kind of trouble brewing. Yet here she was taking a roundabout route to her destination – 'going round the houses', as they said in this part of the world. She supposed that she was simply putting off her inevitable arrival at Bright's gym.

She passed a few boarded up houses – security shutters at the doors and windows, graffiti crawling across the brickwork. These abandoned dwellings were flanked by homes in which people still lived. Television light flared behind the windows. Shadows passed by on the other side of grey net curtains and slatted window blinds. Lana felt a deep sense of loss, a strange kind of grief for something that she had not yet given away. She had no idea where this feeling had come from, but it hurt. The pain was like a blade drawn across her chest.

For you, Hailey.

Once again she thought about the tiny baby her daughter had been. It seemed like yesterday. Intense. Immediate. Such a small infant, and she'd been kept in an incubator for two days. When, finally, Hailey was allowed to take her daughter home from the hospital, both she and Timothy had no idea what they were meant to do. They'd stood over her Moses basket, holding hands and crying together, filled with relief that they'd had at least one child to bring back with them. Watching their baby sleep; looking to the future.

Or so they had thought.

Because the future had not turned out so lovely. Instead it had become a bad dream, a series of absurd events that had ended in murder and Timothy's suicide.

Walking now along harsh streets, perhaps even watched by hungry eyes, *hidden* eyes, Lana realised that those events had been the beginning of her downfall. Like a trigger, Timothy's decision not to talk to her about his problems, to get hold of a gun and try to solve them in the most insane way imaginable, had been the moment when her world had started to crumble. Their daughter – their beautiful, bright, lovely girl – had suddenly been cast out into a darkness through which she was still stumbling, looking for an exit.

Lana reached the corner of Grove Street West, where there was a patch of ground upon which a corner shop had once stood, and next to that the Unicorn pub – perhaps the roughest drinking den in the area. She paused for a moment, glancing at the pub lights and its bright yellow windows that spilled illumination onto the cracked pavement. She could hear music, laughter, raised voices. Somebody was singing a football song, while other voices cut in with another crude ditty.

She turned onto Grove Street West, leaving the light behind. Darkness shifted around her, massaging and grasping her like a huge, soft fist. She fought the urge to turn around, run back to the Unicorn, and drink herself free of this debt to darkness. But if she did, her problems would still be there when the hangover cleared. None of this was going away; it was here forever, unless she made a move to rectify the situation.

Bright's Gym was a hundred yards along the street, pushed back from the pavement and with its back to a small gathering of willowy trees which bordered the no-man's-land of Beacon Green. Many years ago, when the area was less poverty stricken, she'd heard that a warehouse depot with its own siding and station had stood on the Green. The old railway line still ran along the eastern edge of Grove Rise, at the bottom of the Embankment, but the old timber sleepers had long since been reclaimed and all that survived were some half-buried metal cleats and a rough trail where people walked their dogs by day but were afraid to visit after dark.

The gym was a small, squat two-storey building that stood alone on this part of the street, opposite a row of derelict houses. Its windows were always covered by metal grilles, with faded, out-of-date posters advertising historical bodybuilding competitions stuck to the glass behind. Nobody could see inside from the street; and nobody inside was able to see out through those windows. The gym wasn't exactly open to the general public, but the regular clientele consisted of local hard men, amateur boxers and paunchy nightclub security staff. These meatheads would go there to pump some serious iron and ingest whatever steroids Bright could supply them with. It was the loan shark's base; he operated every bit of business he dealt with from the shabby premises.

It was his castle, his secure hideaway from the world. The centre of the spider's web.

The police never bothered with Monty Bright. He had the whole area sewn up, and Lana suspected that the local constabulary were of the opinion that they'd rather deal with the shark they knew than the devil they didn't. It all went to prove her beliefs that everyone and everything was either corrupt or in the process of being corrupted. Timothy's actions had formed the basis of this theory, and her experiences here, in the Grove, had merely helped it evolve into a working hypothesis.

She approached the front door and waited, still unsure whether she could go through with her plan. She heard the infant Hailey crying inside her head; her mind was filled with images of Timothy's victims and that of his pale corpse on the mortuary table when she'd been called in to identify his body. A portion of his skull, just above the right eye, was missing. She had glimpsed a blue-grey swell of brain matter through the hole.

"For you," she said, not knowing who she meant: Hailey, Timothy's ghost, or herself.

She lifted her hand, made a fist, and knocked hard on the door. It was opened before she even had time to lower her hand.

"Hello, Lana."

It was the fat man from the other day – the one who'd pinned her against the wall and attempted to invade her with his knee.

She swallowed but her mouth was dry. "I'm here to see Monty... Mr. Bright."

The large man smiled. Oddly, it was a gentle smile, as if beneath the layers of fat and muscle this man might just have a heart after all, hidden within the folds of his cruelty. "I know why you're here, Lana. And, please, call me Francis." His lips were wide and wet. His cheeks were ruddy.

"Okay, Francis. Can I please see Monty? He's expecting me."

The door opened wider, and Francis stepped back into a long, narrow hallway. There were old boxing posters stuck to the walls, promoting fights between combatants whose names Hailey didn't recognise. Dust hung in the air like a light mist; small motes danced before the fat man's retreating form, making him take on a ghostly aspect, as if he were barely there at all.

"This way," he said, turning slowly in the cramped space. His thighs brushed against the wall, unsettling yet more dust, and he moved ponderously, like a whale cruising through the deeps. "He's been waiting for you. We all have."

Following him through the murk, Lana felt the first strands of real fear brushing against her cheek. Like cobwebs, the fear stuck to her skin, drawing her in. They came to a large open space, and to her right Lana could see a dimly lit arena. A boxing ring was positioned at the centre of the room, and along the walls were hung heavy sand-filled punch bags, battered leather speedballs and all kinds of metal bars and brackets meant for performing strength exercises. She'd been in gyms before – in fact, she had once attended exercise classes regularly, back in her old life – but she had never seen such primitive equipment as this. A lot of it looked medieval: crude and cruel and meant for inflicting pain upon the human body, rather than working out the muscles for the sake of physical fitness.

A small man in a white vest and baggy shorts was dancing in the shadows. She had failed to see him at first because of the weak light and the fact that he was positioned in the corner furthest from where she stood. The man's hands were covered in protective wrappings and he was shadow boxing. Each move, every combination, was carried out a lot slower than it would have been in the ring: it was stylised, almost like a silent mummer's play, a weird performance dense with ritual. She watched for a while, entranced, and was only able to move away when the fat man touched her arm and whispered her name.

"We can go up now," he said. "That's Dennis. He comes here every night. Never gets in the ring, just shadow boxes for hours. We leave him in peace. He pays his dues so we let him do his thing."

The man kept moving; he was never still. His feet shuffled across the smooth floor, shushing like the delicate touch of a drum brush against a hi-hat cymbal. His face was stern, almost grim, and his eyes were focused on a single point on the wall. Whatever he was fighting, he would never be able to beat it. The man's private bout would last forever, or at least until the moment when he shadow-boxed into his grave.

"Shall we go now?" Francis increased the pressure on her arm. His fingers were wide, his grip insistent. It was not a question.

"Yes," she said, looking at his face, concentrating on his small, piggy eyes. "Yes, I'm ready now. Let's go and see Monty Bright."

The silent boxer didn't even acknowledge their presence as they passed from his view. She doubted he even realised they'd been there. The thought filled her with a deep sadness that made her flesh tingle.

Her thoughts and feelings were corrosive. She felt like she was on the verge of losing her mind, and she welcomed that madness, wishing that it would hurry up and take her away from all this. Hoping that it would help her to get through whatever happened next.

CHAPTER EIGHTEEN

TOM WAS STANDING on the landing outside his room. He could not remember how he had arrived here, or even when he had woken and climbed out of bed. The last thing he could picture was the bedroom ceiling as he closed his eyes to try and sleep.

He felt like a little boy, dressed in his pyjamas and wandering after midnight through the family home. His fears were those created by a broken childhood; his desperation not to be seen was born of the fact that his father was home and he had been drinking.

He was unable to sleep; his mind was racing with unfocused thoughts that he wished he could suppress. Lana Fraser, Hailey with her strange biology, and a debt that must, at some point, be repaid. He was gripped by a sense of urgent panic, as if he knew that somewhere someone important to him was in trouble, but he couldn't do a thing to help them. Events were racing to some sort of conclusion, but he had no idea how to stop them or even what those events might be.

He padded across the landing to the bathroom and stared at his face in the mirror. His jowls sagged; his eyes were small and narrow, like piss holes in the snow. His skin had taken on a slight yellow hue, as if it were jaundiced. He could not recall ever looking so worn out. He was exhausted yet he could not sleep.

The book he'd been reading earlier was on the shelf by the basin. He must have left it there before going to bed. Dostoevsky: *Crime and Punishment*. He was attempting to wade through the classics he had not looked at since school, when a strict English teacher and his dry methods had rendered them cold and turgid and lifeless.

The title of the book had taken on a resonance that made him feel uncomfortable. Thoughts of Lana and her loan shark floated in his brain, bobbing on the surface while darker, more complex thoughts ran in the deeper currents of his subconscious mind.

He thought about the sea cow downstairs, lost in her paraplegic dreams. Then he thought again of Lana: her dark-sparkling eyes, her hair, her smooth, pale skin.

"I love her," he said to his reflection. The reflection smiled, completely unsurprised, but Tom didn't feel his own face take on the same shape. It was like another person was looking at him, placing him and his emotions under scrutiny.

"I love her," said his reflection, belatedly; but he didn't feel his lips move in harmony with those in the mirror and the voice sounded deeper than normal. He was two people now, or one person split down the middle. His life had been cleaved, as if someone had taken a large axe and brought it down at a point right between his eyes, separating the two opposing sides of his brain.

Was he awake or dreaming? He didn't feel as if he were asleep; the world was solid around him and his senses were alert. No, this was not a dream. He was caught in a space between sleeping and waking, an interstice in which the rules of both of these states battled for supremacy. The imagery of dreams was bleeding into his waking world, and it felt like a drug trip: intense yet hazy, a blend of fact and fiction, a whole new world of contradictory sensations and images. For a moment he smelled wet grass; then the odour became that of rotten meat.

He'd read somewhere that people with brain tumours often experienced phantom smells.

But no, he wasn't ill. Perhaps the explanation was as simple as insanity. Maybe he was losing his mind.

In an attempt to wake himself up, he brushed his teeth. Whenever he looked down, at the sink, he had the impression that his reflection was staring at the top of his head. But when he looked up again to check, his reflection seemed to move with him. He felt twitchy and paranoid; he needed to relax.

He put away his toothbrush and moved over to the bath, where he put in the plug and turned on the hot tap. Soon the room began to fill with steam. He stripped off his T-shirt and pyjama bottoms and sat naked on the edge of the tub, staring at the plumes of water vapour as they rose and gathered in the air. He began to see shapes forming: clenched fists, compressed faces with knotted features. Rudimentary heads shifting in the patterns made by the steam.

He twisted the hot tap off and turned on the cold, adding some bath oil. Testing the water first with his hand, he then turned off the cold tap and climbed into the tub. Despite the addition of cold water, the bathwater was too hot. It burned his skin, turning his legs red, then his belly. He sucked in his breath sharply as he lowered his upper body into the water. This was a small yet pleasurable pain; a brief and biting agony that soon faded as his body became accustomed to the temperature of the water.

As he lay there he pictured Lana, naked. Her soft curves were cupped by shadow, and the visible parts of her skin were almost luminescent. She stroked herself with her fingertips, running a hand across her breasts, down towards her stomach, and then to the dark patch below. A large shadow loomed behind her, stretching like a black sheet around her body...

Tom reached down and began to fondle himself. His hands were clumsy; there was little response to his self-attention. He tried to masturbate but couldn't quite sustain enough focus. That shadow – a vast billowing presence behind the imaginary Lana – was too distracting. He knew what the shadow was, what it meant. It was the shape of her debt, a crude representation of what she owed to that man Monty Bright.

Angry and frustrated, he got out of the bath and stood, dripping wet, before the mirror. His reflection was smiling again, but this time he felt the expression mirrored on his face. The smile was bitter, cynical: there was not a trace of humour evident, just a cruel trace of thwarted desire.

He grabbed a towel and dried himself off, feeling as if he were tending to someone else – a man who was sick and not completely sane. His last ten years spent as a carer – a person whose sole aim in life was to appease the needs of another – had changed him in many ways, and some of them only ever peeked above the surface during times of great stress or anxiety. Sometimes he viewed the world as a place filled with those needs, and he felt as if he'd been cast adrift in a landscape of pain and disability.

He put on his night clothes and went back out on to the landing. The house was quiet; he couldn't even hear the ticking of a clock, or the sound of traffic passing by on the street outside. He glanced at his watch. It was almost 2 AM. Even the night people had quietened down.

He walked to the top of the stairs and peered down into the dimness. It looked like the darkness was a sea. He imagined creatures swimming down there, in the shadows, perhaps even his wife had floated out of her bed to ride the night-time currents, her mouth gaping and her hands grasping.

Tom descended, gripping the handrail tightly. He realised that he was tense, perhaps even afraid. His strange experience in the bathroom had wrong-footed him, making him feel as if he and Helen were not alone in the house. He felt as if a stranger was moving through the rooms below, silently examining their belongings, picking up and inspecting the minutiae of their lives and judging them as worthless.

When he reached the bottom of the stairs he saw the stone wall in the hallway. He knew immediately that it was a portion of Hadrian's Wall – perhaps even the same section where he'd picnicked with Lana and Hailey. It had emerged from the front wall of the house, near the front door, and looped around the door to return through the same wall on the opposite side, forming a barricade to prevent him leaving.

I am dreaming after all. So there's nothing to fear.

But that was a lie. Everything was a source of fear: terror hid in every corner, and was displayed on every shelf and surface.

He stared at the crude segment of the wall. It was a surreal image: the arrival of something ancient in his home, the stone dirty and with patches of fungus spotted along its length. He wasn't afraid of the wall. His feelings towards it were more complex. He experienced a rush of strangeness, a thrill of exhilaration at the sight of the old stone. Then, at a deeper level, he felt honoured that such a vision should present itself to him, a normal man, a struggling husband and potential adulterer. What had he done to deserve this? Why had he been singled out for such a reward?

Then, as he watched, the section of wall slithered, moving like a great, dry serpent. The old folk rhyme returned to him, and he recited it once again in his head:

But the worm got fat an' grewed an' grewed,
An' grewed an aaful size;
He'd greet big teeth, a greet big gob,
An greet big goggly eyes

But there were no eyes on this worm. It did not even possess a face. It was a long, shifting portion of the ruined Roman wall, and its presence here was simply an indication of a deeper mystery.

The wall moved continually now; a moving barrier, blocking his way to the door. He knew it was meant to keep him inside, to hold him hostage. There was a grinding sound, stone upon stone, and he remembered Hailey's comment about baby bones being buried beneath the foundations.

"Dreaming," he said, feeling more awake than he had in days. If this was a dream, then it was a lucid one, and rather than succumb to the logic of the dream he would be required to act, to move freely through the dream and not simply become part of its story.

The door to Helen's room was wide open. Darkness bulged from the doorway, pressing through the frame like oil. He watched it for a while, wondering if he should feel more afraid – his fear was slight now, like a vague notion of how people were supposed to react when confronted with the unknowable.

Without thinking about what he was doing, he began to walk towards Helen's room. It felt right; part of the dream. He was meant to see inside that room.

As he drew closer to the open door he began to make out sounds: a soft, smothered grunting noise, like a pig snuffling at a trough; creaking bed springs; a gentle slap-slapping of flesh on flesh.

It sounded like someone was having sex in there.

That Man, he thought, wildly. *Is it his ghost, returned to finish what he and Helen started? To finally consummate the relationship that was cut short by his death and Helen's paralysis?*

He stood before the door but could not see inside. The darkness was solid. Slowly, he reached out and pressed the tip of his index finger against it. The darkness bulged inward, like a balloon. Yes, that was it: a huge black balloon. But he was stuck inside the balloon and Helen was on the outside, in the real world.

Still he was not afraid enough to turn away, and even if he could, there was nowhere to go. The wall was still blocking his exit. He could either continue on, into the room, or return upstairs to confront his rogue reflection.

He stepped inside the room, his face pressing against the surface of the balloon, stretching the material, forcing it past its elastic limit... and then, with an audible popping sound, he was through and standing on the other side of the darkness.

The sounds were louder now, unfiltered as they were through that cloying blackness. Helen's lamp was on, so there was enough light to see what was happening on the bed.

The bed.

Helen's bed.

The same gathering of fists he'd seen at Hadrian's Wall was inside the room, hovering above and around Helen's bed. The fists were huge – each one the size of Tom's head – and they formed a loose netting around something that was twitching and bucking at their centre. The fingers moved liked birds' wings, flapping slowly; their motion was odd and slightly nauseating. Then, simultaneously, they all tightened once again into hard fists.

It was a flock of hands, all gathered above the thing in the bed. A flock? Was that even the right expression? What was the collective noun for fists, anyway? A pummel? A flight?

No, a flock: that sounded best.

He was using his frantic, panicked thoughts to delay his reaction to the sight on the bed. He could barely understand it, let alone absorb what he was actually looking at.

There was a sea cow on the mattress, a floppy grey manatee. It was huge, flabby, and grotesque. The fact of its existence was bad enough, but the juxtaposition of this fat, struggling mammal lying on its belly on Helen's normal, everyday bed made the image seem even more nightmarish... and Tom knew that he was responsible for this representation of his wife's inability to move, her utter acceptance of defeat. He always thought of her as a sea cow, and here it was, the metaphor made flesh.

But it got worse. Much worse.

Within the enclosure of floating, disembodied fists was a barely formed figure, a large, bulky rendering of a man. The man was naked, and he had his hands on the sea cow's bulk. He was thrusting himself into the manatee, ravaging it from behind. His hands moved away from the thing's plump body, and he began to strike it – slow, hard blows to the sides. Stinging body-shots, just like Tom's father had done to his mother all those years ago, during the dimly remembered episodes of marital rape.

The beast writhed and jerked, but it slowly dawned upon Tom that these movements were not an expression of struggle. The animal was participating in the grim, abusive events: its frantic movements were actually spasms of pleasure. The man and the manatee were making love.

He was witnessing an act of mutual desire, a violent, blasphemous coupling of man and beast.

The ghost-fists shimmered with motion, rising from the bed. The inchoate figure at their core moved with them, carried by their awkward flight. The manatee tried to flip itself over onto its back, but its weight and the fact that it was out of water, stranded in an unnatural element, made the task all the more difficult. Finally, struggling for air, it gave up the fight and just lay there, sprawling and spent on the bed. But during that brief attempt to turn, Tom had seen its face: *Helen's* face, on the body of a slobbering beast.

"Let it come," said a voice that sounded familiar. "You're almost there, but not quite. It's reaching for you." The hands parted, creating a shell-like hollow in the air, and Tom's father stepped out from the fisted enclosure. "It's reaching out for all of you."

His father's image was degraded, like damp tissue paper: his edges were soft and flaking away as he stood there; his pallor was ghastly. His mouth didn't move as he spoke, and as Tom glanced down, taking in the full sight of this shoddy spectre, he saw that the man's form was unfinished. There were no genitals; his sex act with the phantom manatee must have been nothing more than what, as a schoolboy, Tom and his friends had called a 'dry hump'.

He tore his gaze from the ghost and looked over at the bed. Helen was herself again, and she was sleeping. Her skin looked slightly grey in colour. The folds of her bare skin glistened with sweat. The horror he had seen, the sight of the insane coupling, was just another phantom: a ghost of a memory mixed with the detritus of his insomniac mind.

"She used to like it, you know. Your mother."

Tom looked back at his dead father. His face was crumpled, a bloodless mass of deconstructed tissue.

"She enjoyed the pain and humiliation. And then, afterwards, she would go into the bathroom and cut herself." The figure wobbled slightly, threatening to topple forward, and then righted itself. Flecks of it fell away from the central mass; a slow fall of ghastly snowflakes. "She hated herself for what she saw as unhealthy desires. But I just loved all that dirty sex." There was laughter, but it seemed to come from all around the room, emerging from every corner. Parts of the apparition's face slipped away, falling to the ground but vanishing before they reached the carpet.

"Ectoplasm," said Tom's father. "The shit of the spirit world."

Tom backed away; a single step.

His father took an equal step forward. "I'm not here to hurt you."

"Then, why?" Tom was surprised at the sound of his own voice. It was stronger than he had expected. "Why are you here? In my dream."

"It's not a dream. Not really." The figure's shape was becoming less solid. Whatever kind of matter had formed the likeness of his father, that stuff was now losing its adhesive qualities. "This is the space between dreaming and waking. It's where the old place exists – the oak grove and whatever lies beyond. There's a doorway here, and it's starting to open – just a crack, mind. But it *is* opening." The voice had become faint.

"I don't understand."

His father shook his head. More of it came away, his features sliding off like crumbling meringue from a rotting cake. "There *is* nothing to understand. You're there and I'm here. The other place, the one that's reaching out to you and your new friends, is somewhere else. It's simple, really. True Creation is always simple. It's destruction that's the tricky part." Again, the smile; the rumpled, degrading smile.

"Because nothing can ever be fully destroyed. There's always traces, detritus, left behind."

Then, before Tom had the chance to say anything more, the vision was gone. Small flecks of something white remained on the carpet, like crumbs from a midnight feast. Tom walked over, bent down, and tried to pick them up. They dissolved in his hand.

"The shit of the spirit world," he said, quietly. That sounded just about right. It described his father perfectly: the man had only ever been shit, a composite person made of several kinds of human waste. Something better off flushed down the pan.

Tom stood and walked over to the bed. Helen was sleeping soundly. He adjusted the duvet, tucking her in. Part of him wanted to lean down and kiss her, but another part of him wanted to walk away and never come back. Again, he felt like a man split down the middle.

"Sorry," he said, not really knowing what he was apologising for. Then he left the room and closed the door behind him. The snake-like segment of stone wall was no longer there. The darkness had lifted. Everything was normal again, if that word even meant anything now. He suspected that normal was no longer an option; the world had turned, his perception had shifted. That other place, the one he'd been sensing lately, and that his dead father's bespoke phantom had spoken of, had noticed him, and nothing could ever be remotely normal again.

CHAPTER NINETEEN

IT WAS TIME. It was coming. She could feel it.

Her belly was swollen, the skin there pulled so taut that it seemed as thin as tissue paper. When she peered down at those areas of her stomach that were visible between her clutching fingers, she could see rapid movement beneath – a frantic motion in her belly, like scrabbling hands. There was no pain; she was beyond that now. All she felt was a strange hunger, a terrible emptiness despite the thing –

Or things; what if there was more than one? Like twins?

– that was rapidly filling her stomach.

Hailey was lying on her bed, staring up at the bedroom ceiling. Her eyes stung. The back of her neck was burning. But still she felt these sensations as an outsider, an observer. Everything that was happening right now was taking place inside her – the external didn't matter. Her existence had wound tightly around whatever was stirring at her core.

"Come on," she whispered, almost cooing the words. "Come on out and see me." She stroked the mound of her belly, feeling the hot, damp skin shift. "Come out, now."

The hands responded by fluttering again. She knew there were no hands in there – not really – but that was how she had now begun to think of the movements within her body: quick-clutching hands, scrabbling around her internal organs.

The radio was on and voices were debating car crime in Newcastle. It was a late-night phone-in show, one that had won national awards because of its cutting edge approach. The radio was not Hailey's – all of her stuff had been taken by the men who had come to intimidate her mum while she was out at school. She had found the radio in the bottom drawer in the kitchen. It was an old model, like something out of a film: black plastic and with a single tape deck built-in. Hailey only knew what a tape deck was because she'd seen them in magazines, in features on retro fashion and accessories. Like everyone her age, she listened to downloaded or pirated music on her MP3 Player.

At least she had done, before those bastards had taken her stuff.

The pressure on her stomach increased. Whatever was inside was straining to get out.

Hailey knew from physics lessons at school that there were forces constantly being exerted upon the world, the solar system, even the entire universe; pushing and pulling, acting and counteracting: a delicate balance of forces, both cosmic and prosaic. There were forces everywhere, shaping the very nature of reality with their endless activity.

But what if there were also forces that were not generated in this world, forces from somewhere else? A place *beneath* the world she knew. Somewhere with its own physical laws, which acted against our laws rather than alongside them? A place that was always looking for a way in, a breach in the walls between worlds…

And what if the thing (or things) inside her was a part of all that? A spore or a seed from that other place, something she'd picked up somehow, getting it under her skin. What if that seed were growing? And what if she, Hailey, was to be its way into the world?

The thought, however odd, didn't trouble her as much as she expected it to.

She knew that she should be afraid, but she felt as calm as a prayer. Her mind was clear. All she was able to focus on was the movement inside her body, and she was unable to think of it in any terms other than the contents of an egg. A huge egg, its shell pure and white, and with the suggestion of something moving inside.

"I'm an egg," she said, talking to the empty room, the white walls, the cheap-papered ceiling. "I am an egg, and this thing is growing inside me."

She listened to her voice but the words didn't seem like they belonged to her. Not for the first time, she felt like someone else was speaking for her, shaping her lips.

She pressed her hands against her belly once again. This time the movements inside became more frantic, responding to the heat transmitted through her palms.

"It's coming," she said, and this time the voice *was* hers. It could not possibly have belonged to anyone else. She recognised the longing, the desperation that hid behind the words – the same emotions that she detected whenever she said her father's name, late at night, as she stared at herself in the mirror.

She wanted this. She really did. She desired it more than anything – apart from having her dad back, her old life returned to her. But this was the next best thing. It was the best that she could hope for.

New life. Of a sort. Hunger. Need. Maybe even a saviour.

Perhaps what happened here tonight would save her and her mum.

The movement inside her stopped. Silence filled the room. Then she heard a low humming sound. But the room was empty, she was all alone. None of the electrical appliances were on in the other room – the vacuum cleaner had been taken by those men, the washing machine too. Nothing was switched on that would make a noise even remotely like this one.

Even the radio had gone silent. Not even static came from its little mono speaker.

But the humming… it remained, filling her ears. Its volume was constant. Low, regular, and constant.

Hailey sat up on the bed and turned to face the window. The weight of her stomach was a pleasant ache. The curtains were open and the sky outside was dark. She often liked to look at the moon, the stars, and imagine that she was up there, high up in the night sky and flying. Drifting away from all this fuss and bullshit.

There was a large flock of tiny birds hovering outside her window. She could see them outlined against the deep black sky, their wings blurring, sharp beaks glinting in the bleed-off from sodium street lights. Hummingbirds, hundreds of them, perhaps even thousands. The same kind she'd seen in the Needle a few days ago. They hung there, on the other side of the glass, watching her.

Hailey swung her legs off the side of the bed and got shakily to her feet. Her legs ached, but again there was no real pain, just the vague sensation of aching, like muscle memory. She padded across the carpet and went to the window. The birds didn't move. A dense cloud of freeze-frame motion, an unmoving flurry of beating wings. She wondered if anyone else could see them, or if this was some kind of vision meant only for her. Hailey's perception of the world was changing by the minute, and where, before, such a thought would have struck her as crazy, it now seemed perfectly reasonable.

She was carrying a wonder inside her, so why shouldn't there be more wonders on show just outside her window?

"Hello there..." She raised her hand and placed her fingertips against the window. The hummingbirds remained as they were, suspended in the air with their wings blurring, as if locked in place like tiny working machine parts in the mechanism of eternity.

"Yes," she said, struck by the sudden insight. "That's what you are: cogs in the machine. Just like me. Like all of us."

Then understanding slipped away and once again her mind was empty, a container for whatever sights the night might throw at her.

She dragged her fingers soundlessly down the pane of glass, leaving faint marks to chart their progress. The marks faded quickly; the attendant hummingbirds began to float slowly backwards, moving away.

"Come back," she whispered, tears falling down her face. "Don't leave me."

But the birds didn't respond. They drew back, and then shot up into the darkness as one, a blurred arrow ascending to the heavens. Then, in seconds, they were lost to her, gone into the blackness beyond the thin veil of clouds.

Hailey had never felt so alone, even when her dad had died.

She dragged her gaze from the sky and looked across the Grove, feeling abandoned, melancholy.

The top floors of the Needle poked up above the uneven line formed by the rooftops, its peak piercing the thin, low clouds. To Hailey it now resembled the huge fossilised trunk of an ancient tree, its branches grey and withered and its leaves having fallen to earth long ago, before she was even born: a petrified tree, with its topmost branches scraping the sky. A weird organic structure that had its roots buried in that other place.

For the first time in her life she realised how shallow her understanding of things had always been, and that everything has an inner life, an alternative identity. All she had been aware of until now was the surface, but recent events had shown her that the most important things are those which lie beneath.

Her legs felt cold.

She glanced down, at her naked body, and saw that her inner thighs were glistening. A reservoir of cool liquid had burst from inside her, washing her clean, preparing her for the act of passage yet to come.

Hailey knew exactly what was required of her, as if some trace memory, a stored neurological imprint, had suddenly revealed itself. She squatted down on her haunches, knees forced apart with her bent elbows, hands clasped tightly together as if she were deep in prayer. Then she waited to deliver something strange into the world.

...AND THIS TIME, in the dream, she is standing inside a ring of tall oak trees, looking up to watch the sunlight as it filters through the brown-tinged leaves. She squints, momentarily blinded by the light, and then clouds pass overhead and she can open her eyes again.

The creature she saw last time, near the swinging corpse of her mother, has moved on. The corpse has been taken down. She is alone. Her skin is warm, and when she looks down she sees blood smeared on the inside of her naked thighs. Deep red clots cling to the sides of her knees; red patterns decorate her shins and feet.

The sun moves west to east, travelling too-fast across the flat sky, and she is momentarily plunged into shadow. The trees creak, their ancient trunks shifting to accommodate the new position of the light source. Their branches are striving to be touched by the sun's bright fingers.

She feels empty. She is bereft. Something has gone away, leaving her behind. Whatever she was carrying inside her has moved on. She takes a tentative step forward, and then another, gradually moving from the centre of the small grove of oak trees to its outskirts. She reaches out a hand and caresses the old, wrinkled bark as she passes one of the trees, and it moves beneath her hand, twisting like a living body. Her fingertips find a crack in the bark and slip inside, feeling the warm sap beneath. Under the toughened hide of the tree she touches something smooth and unmarred, not unlike newly formed human skin.

She stops and stares at her fingers. They are sunk up to the first joint into the tree trunk. She gently peels away a piece of bark, being careful not to cause too much damage to the delicate structure. The tree moves again, but this time as if it is responding to her touch. There is something almost erotic about the way the trunk slowly spins, turning eagerly to meet her wanton attention.

The underside of the bark is tacky; it sticks to her fingers as she fondles the material. She pulls the chunk of bark away and lets it drop to the ground, where it comes softly to rest on the grass and the fallen leaves next to her bloody feet. Leaning in close, she examines the patch that she has uncovered. It *is* human skin: soft and pink and covered in a red-tinged, viscous liquid, like the wet flesh of a newborn baby.

As she watches, the skin begins to rise and fall. She rests her fingers on the area and can feel a pulse, which beats much slower than her own.

"Alive?" The question is one that barely needs voicing. It is obvious to her now that the tree – or the thing she found beneath the layer of bark, whatever it is – lives. It is breathing; it has a pulse and probably a heartbeat; there is blood, not sap, running through its mysterious system.

She presses against the patch of skin with her fingertips and watches as it pushes inward, making a slight indentation. The tree shifts; a small twitching motion. The leaves above her shudder. The sound they make is like tracing paper being crumpled up in a fist.

"Where is it?" The bark surrounding the area she has uncovered starts to peel away. The trunk begins to strip naked, revealing under its dry covering a vaguely human shape. There is the suggestion of legs, wide thighs, and the smooth curves of hips. Large breasts without nipples. The subtle v-shape of a crudely carved pudendum. It resembles a primitive wooden sculpture, but soft to the touch, and slightly elastic.

There is no head; the body is massive, and visible only to the shoulders. Whatever sits above is covered by the canopy of leaves.

Without thinking, she presses her hand further, deeper into the midriff of the unveiled body. The moist skin yields, and then splits. Her hand enters easily into the hole, that same viscous fluid aiding its passage. She slides both hands inside up to the wrist, gently spreading the edges of the wound, and grasps what she finds waiting within the cavity she has made.

The thing is rigid, motionless. She pulls it out, stepping back to allow it some space.

It is a small, rough puppet: no face, no fingers on the end of its stumpy hands. Just a rough-hewn caricature: a rude representation of a human child. She holds it close, hugging it against her naked chest. Her nipples harden, responding to the puppet's silent hunger.

The puppet does not move. It is nothing more than an empty shell, a half-finished simulacra taken from inside a larger organism, like a splinter of prosthetic bone removed from torn flesh. There is something missing, a vital element. It is hungry but it is unable to feed. She presses its smooth, formless head against her breast, willing for it to partake of her food. Watery milk dribbles from the ends of her nipples, splashing onto this soulless, lifeless hunk of wood.

She doesn't know what else to do.

Nobody has ever prepared her for this.

"Help me." Her voice is tiny, lost in the primeval wood. "Help us. We need you. There's no-one else. I beg you, just help us out of this mess." Tears streak down her face, dripping delicately onto the top of the puppet's inchoate head. Then, in reaction to her fathomless need, the puppet's head slowly begins to move. It turns, pivoting on the broad neck, and the thing looks up at her. The puppet has no eyes but she can feel its gaze.

"Please. Help us. Help me and my mum... we need... we need..."

The trees writhe, their leaves speaking a language she cannot understand. A large flock of small birds flies overhead, darkening the sky and casting a flowing shadow on the ground at her feet.

"We need help."

The puppet begins to shake, its stunted arms and blocky legs wriggling as it struggles in her grasp.

"We need you."

The puppet, she realises, is laughing.

CHAPTER TWENTY

BOATER FELT UNCOMFORTABLE as he led the woman up the stairs to Monty's office. He could sense her close behind him as he climbed the stairs, and hear the sound of her breathing in the enclosed space. She wasn't wearing much perfume, but he could detect the trace of a light floral scent on her skin. She was scared – of course she was; they always were. They knew what they were here for, and what was going to happen to them, but still they were afraid. Monty enjoyed that fear; it was part of the thrill. Boater used to like it, too, but recently things had changed.

He reached the top of the stairs and turned around to face Lana. She was beautiful, even with her face scrubbed clean of make-up. The rage he'd felt towards her down by the Quayside, when he'd been confused and wrong-footed by his own churning emotions, had gone now. It had been replaced with a sense of longing.

"Just wait here for a minute. I'll tell him you're here."

"Thank you," she said, leaning her shoulder against the wall. She had not yet reached the top of the stairs, and stood two steps down from the short landing. The shadows clung to her, roaming over her body like eager hands. Boater thought that she didn't look quite real: an erotic phantom.

"Just a minute... " He spun around in the tight space and knocked on the office door. The light bulb in the ceiling flickered.

"Yeah. Come in." Monty's voice was muffled, but he sounded distracted.

He's probably scribbling in his little book, thought Boater as he pushed open the door and stepped inside.

The table lamps were set low down, near the floor, giving the room a dusky atmosphere. The main lights were off and the window blinds were closed. Monty sat at his desk with his feet tucked up underneath him on the big chair. He was wearing his reading glasses, something that humanised him in a way that Boater found contradictory. Surely monsters didn't wear reading glasses...

"She's here. The Fraser woman. She's here, just like you said."

Monty didn't look up from his book. He held it open on his thighs, studying it like it was a school text. He nodded, distracted and not really listening. "Did you know, Francis, that when the Romans were here in Northumberland they found something strange in the land this estate is built on?"

Boater had no idea what to say or even if a response was expected. Monty had been doing this more and more lately: talking to himself by telling Boater and the rest of the men things, passing on obscure information. It was like he was involved in a lengthy conversation with himself, and all Boater and the others were expected to do was listen.

Monty continued: "Pagan tribes would worship an old grove of oak trees, dancing and fucking and draining their blood into the soil. The Romans murdered this tribe, and then they burned down the oaks and dug up the charred earth, at least that's what the books say, the ones I borrowed from the library. The ones no fucker else bothers to read. Nobody seems to know what kind of power the Romans found, but I like to think that Hadrian built his fucking wall to keep it inside rather than keeping the Jocks out." He laughed, and it was a terrible sound: dull and flat and empty of feeling. "It seems to me that old Hadrian didn't like what they found here. Nobody ever spoke of it again, except to say that the ground was cursed. That it was a Bad Place."

Finally he glanced up from the book, as if realising that he was no longer alone. He closed the cover, running his fingers along the creased spine.

Boater read the book's familiar title: *Extreme Boot Camp Workout* by Alex 'Brawler' Mahler. It was nothing but an exercise manual, a battered old workout book written by some ex-army type. Monty had picked up the book in a second-hand book shop, but he handled the thing like a holy relic – sometimes he even called it his 'Bible'. He was constantly making incomprehensible notes in the margins, or sticking cut-out snippets of newspaper articles to the pages with a little glue-stick. He'd even sketched things in there, filling the margins and the white spaces between blocks of text with doodles that meant nothing to Boater but obviously held some kind of meaning for him.

Nobody else was allowed to touch the book, and Monty even kept it locked in his safe on the rare occasions when he wasn't carrying it with him. But Boater had glimpsed the contents of the open pages on his boss's desk several times, and the things he'd seen there – scrawled, glued and scribbled – were distressing. As far as he could tell, Monty had noted down, among other things, brief snatches of foreign languages, random words and phrases and odd bits of poetry. He had sketched partial maps and diagrams and scribbled monsters on the pages. The book now resembled the decor in the rooms inside a madman's head, and Boater had actually become afraid of it, or more precisely what it might represent.

A book... he was scared of a fucking book. How stupid was that?

"We could learn a lot from the Romans," said Monty, placing the book on his desk and unfolding his short legs so that he could set his feet on the floor. "Sorry to bore you with this, Francis, but it's interesting. Hard bastards, they were, the Romans. Bummers and pederasts to a man, but they were fucking ferocious fighters when they had to be."

Boater shuffled his feet on the carpet. He had no idea what was expected of him, he never did when Monty started acting this way. "Yeah, boss. I'm sure."

Monty spread out his hands on the neat, uncluttered desk and slowly shook his head. He closed his eyes and opened them again. "You're a simple man, aren't you? A few beers with the lads, a bit of frisk in the car park when the pubs chuck out, and a quick shag with whatever slapper you manage to drag back home with you at the end of the night. Simple pleasures." He paused, waited for an answer.

"Maybe." Boater felt his anger rising. He didn't like to be spoken down to like this, not even by Monty, the most powerful man he knew. It sent him crazy, burning him up inside. It made him want to lash out in every direction. He glared at his boss, approaching an imaginary line, one he knew he would be a fool to cross.

"I'm not trying to insult you, Francis. Never that. You're a good man. A top man. You're *my* top man. But sometimes even you must think about the nature of existence. How and why we're here, on this fucked-up planet. There has to be more than fucking and fighting and drinking. Doesn't there? I think about this stuff a lot. Ever since I was a kid I knew this place – the Grove – was special. Things happen here, things that aren't meant to happen. Stuff that doesn't happen anywhere else."

Not unless you've had enough drugs, anyway, thought Boater, trying not to smile. The rage was gone; it had passed quickly, like a brief spell of bad weather.

Boater had heard a lot of this before. It was Monty's pet subject: the theory that the Concrete Grove was a place where forces converged, and ghosts and monsters could be seen. Sometimes he would go on for hours, his monologue deteriorating the longer he talked and becoming more and more like a sort of personal code. It was worse when he was drunk or high; those times he sometimes came across like a religious maniac, thumping the table and shouting and yelling about all kinds of weird shit.

"I know you boys think that this is all just bullshit. But it's not. There's a lot of documented facts available, if you know where to look, who to ask, what holes to dig around in. Recorded UFO sightings and ghostly apparitions. Stories about poltergeists and shape-shifters. It's all around this area, throughout history – the Lambton Worm, the Laidly Worm, the Hexham Heads, the Cauld Lad, the fucking Beast of Benton... so many myths and folktales. Did you ever think that these stories might all be part of a single, greater myth?"

He scratched his cheek, leaving red marks on the orangey, clean-shaven flesh.

"That's what I think. There are others, too, who think the same way. I'm not the only one." He picked up his faded copy of *Extreme Boot Camp Workout* and held it near the side of his face, as if listening to the paper. He gripped the spine, the pressure of his fingers flaring out the edges of the pages. "I bought this in a second-hand book shop in Morpeth. This was way back in, oh, about 1980. I'd been on a dirty weekend with some married tart – she liked to go walking up there, in the countryside. She liked it outdoors."

The ghost of a smile crossed Monty's face, but rather than settling Boater's nerves it made them jangle. He'd seen that exact same smile before, usually when Monty had been reminiscing about violence.

"Yeah... good times." The smile slipped, fell. "I already suspected that this place was special, that there was something weird going on. I'd spoken to a few people, and even seen one or two things myself that I couldn't really explain. Then, it was as if this book was meant to fall into my hands. I picked it up and flicked through the pages, and on page twenty-nine I found a hand-written notation. Do you want to know what it said? I've read that phrase so many times now that I see the words whenever I close my eyes."

Boater didn't want to hear. He really didn't. But he found himself nodding, betraying some inner compulsion for self-torment. Even though he'd heard the phrase repeated a hundred times.

"The note said: 'The Concrete Grove is a doorway to Creation'."

The pause that followed felt vast and dramatic, and filled with so many different meanings that it made Boater's head ache.

"That's *Creation*, with a capital C. It was my first clue, my first pointer. After that it was just a matter of sifting through old books, listening to pensioners tell me their fucking crazy stories, the stories nobody else would ever take seriously. If a scientist wrote a book and made a list of all the ghostly sightings and unusual activity that's gone on here, he'd see that it was well above the national average. It's a melting pot of the supernatural, mate. A fucking *melting pot*." He shook the book, making the pages flutter. "And I've made my own notes, in here, for years now. Lots of notes, and a lot of other weird shit I can't even understand: signs and symbols from history books and parchment papers kept in old church crypts."

Boater smiled. He didn't know what else to do.

"I know, you all just think I'm a madman, using this as an excuse for some of my more extreme behaviour. Maybe you were right, at first. It was an appealing justification. But now, you unbelieving cunts, I know it's all real." He smiled, and his mouth seemed to open too wide, like that of a shark. His teeth were small and pointed. "It's all real."

"Monty…" Boater tried to bring his boss back down to solid reality. It was always the same when he did a lot of drugs, and those new steroids he'd got in from China were messing with him in a way that was particularly intense. "Lana Fraser. She's waiting outside." He really wished that he had not come here tonight. He could have been back at his flat instead, shagging that girl. The one whose name he couldn't even remember. But he didn't need a name to lay down with her; names weren't important, not when all you wanted was a dirty fuck.

He wished he was there instead of here; he wished that he was balls-deep inside that girl, erasing all thoughts of Monty Bright and his twitchy madness, his unnerving talk of ancient powers and festering forces.

"Oh, yeah. Lana Fraser." Monty stood, his crumpled suit looking cheap and vulgar in the dim light. "Bring the whore in here and we'll start the fun." He walked over to the wall and opened the safe, and then placed his beloved book on a shelf. He touched the book's tatty cover once, with the very tips of his fingers, before shutting it away and locking the safe door. He placed the key in his trouser pocket and then turned back to face the room.

He walked right up to Boater, standing mere inches from him. Boater always noted the fact that Monty had a peculiar odour – he smelled of old paper and dust, as if the essence of that book was rubbing off on him.

The top of Monty's head came up level with Boater's chest. He was a small man, and his body was wrecked from years of drug abuse and punishing gym routines. But he was fast, and he was remorseless. Boater had once seen his boss bite off a man's nose and spit it back into the victim's open mouth. He had witnessed Monty laughing as he cut off a woman's hand for refusing to pay a debt, either in cash or in kind. He had seen this man commit so many foul crimes, so much brutality. Rape and murder and mayhem. And in the past, Boater had liked it. He had enjoyed it. Maybe he had even needed it.

But not now. Not today, or for any time afterwards. Something had happened; a window had opened inside him, allowing in the light and a gentle breeze. When he closed his eyes he could see a grove of trees with acres of dense woodland beyond, and his nostrils were filled with the smell of damp foliage...

Something had altered. A transformation had begun. None of this felt right any more. He no longer enjoyed the vileness and vulgarity of his life. He didn't want to hurt people, not ever again. He wanted to see that beauty, to hear the sound of the wind in the trees and lie on the soft earth beneath their branches – perhaps even sinking into the loam, becoming part of it, a part of nature.

"Bring the bitch in," said Monty. "I'm ready for her now."

He was not smiling.

Boater went to the door and opened it. He wanted to scream at the woman on the landing, tell her to run and never stop, to keep on going until she and her daughter were far away from here. "He'll see you now," he said instead. His back was sweating; his legs felt weak. This wasn't right.

Lana Fraser walked into the room, trying to summon from somewhere deep within her an ounce of dignity. Her beauty was enough to make both men take a step back, giving her some space. Her face was her power, but all power, Boater knew, fell down in the presence of greater strength.

"At last you've come to see me." Monty grinned. His orange skin creased around his mouth, forming multiple parentheses. His hair, slicked back with too much hair product, glistened like a beetle's back. "I'm so glad you could... *come*." The emphasis on the last word was not lost on any of them.

Boater wanted to leave, but he knew that he couldn't. He was stuck here, right until the end. There was no turning back, not yet. But perhaps he could try to make amends later, after the fact.

"You mentioned on the phone that I could clear my debt." Her voice was impressively strong. She didn't falter. The words were spoken clearly, and without much inflection. It sounded like she was reading aloud from a written statement.

"Did I, now?" Monty walked across the room

to a door located opposite the one she'd come in. He reached out and opened it, revealing a staircase beyond. "You'd better come down the back stairs, then, and meet my other associate. I'm sure we'll all be fascinated to hear what you have to offer." He stepped to one side, the mockery of a gentleman, and bowed slightly. "We work as a group here. We all like to join in. The last girl left with a face like a plasterer's radio." He was attempting to push her buttons, looking for her breaking point. Boater had seen it all before, and no matter how strong they seemed at the beginning, they all broke down at some point.

Lana Fraser walked purposefully towards the open door. She did not take her eyes from Monty's face. She took in every inch of him – from his off-coloured solarium tan to his whitened teeth and his deceptively weak looking chin. Then she went through the door and stepped down into darkness.

Monty turned towards Boater, smiled, and winked. Then he followed her into the stairwell.

Boater waited for as long as he was able – thirty seconds, perhaps even as long as a minute – and then he, too, went through the doorway and started down into Monty's hidden basement rooms. For a moment he felt that Monty himself was swallowing him whole, and sucking them all deep inside his mad, black heart.

CHAPTER TWENTY-ONE

THIS IS IT, thought Lana as she waited at the bottom of the steep, rickety staircase. *No turning back, now.* She stood in the gloomy little passageway and listened to the sound of footsteps on the wooden treads behind her. Light spilled from a few wall-mounted bulbs, but it wasn't nearly enough to illuminate all the dark corners. Monty Bright and his man Boater were descending after her through the building, entering the belly of the beast... that thought almost made her smile, but then, when she thought about it, the image simply made her more afraid.

The belly of the beast, she thought. *Monty Bright's belly. He's the beast.* Or, if he was not the beast himself, then he was certainly in the service of a beast; a terrible creature ruled by laws of debt and lust and desire: an entity she suddenly and confusingly thought of as Moloch, the false god from the bible.

I will set my face against that man, and against his family, and will cut him off, and all that go astray after him...

Now where the hell had she dredged that quotation up from? She hadn't studied religious texts since high school, in Religious Studies. Her mind was going into overdrive, throwing up insane thoughts and ideas and snippets of things she had learned a long time ago. Words and phrases that were meaningless in the context of what was happening right now.

It's fear. That's what's doing it. Oh, God, I'm so afraid.

Was she really that clichéd, turning to God in her moment of terror? Why not turn to The Beatles? They'd be just as much use in a crisis.

"There's a good girl." Bright had finally reached the bottom of the stairs. He was standing behind her, with his body pressed up against hers. She felt sick; revulsion made her feel as if her skin were trying to turn inside out. She wished that she could peel herself like a piece of fruit and discard the tainted exterior that Bright had already pawed and tainted with his filth. "It's good to see you being so nice and obedient, and waiting for me down here in the dark." He laughed softly, but it sounded more like an expression of hunger than one of mirth.

Bright stroked his trailing hand across her backside as he pushed past her, moving towards a scarred wooden door on the right. It was almost identical to the other doors they'd passed. But this one was different in one major way: this was the one behind which she would find the face of her demon – the slobbering face of Moloch, the great and terrible beast.

She stared at the wall, at the peeling plaster, trying not to look at that closed door. She tried to empty her mind. All the sorrow and regret; the debt and the promises of violence. The only thing she allowed herself to see, in the darkness behind her eyes, was

Hailey's face: her beautiful child for whom she was putting herself through this nightmare.

Noises echoed down the stairwell, strange creaks and moans and popping sounds. The wooden stairs had many dark, dusty old landings, broken and jutting timber balconies that led nowhere, like viewing galleries. But they had only ever been heading to the bottom: right to the very base of Bright's black pyramid. She'd heard the rumours about these basement rooms and corridors, but never had she expected to see them for herself. Nor had she expected those stories to be true – not really; not in a million years.

Standing there, in a shabby underground passageway with a panting man's hand on her arse, she thought about the road that had led her to this point. Timothy's mental breakdown had been the first step, but since then she'd had chances to alter the route she had taken. Surely there had been choices to make along the way – if she believed in anything, it was that. There was always, always a choice, and she had made the wrong ones far too often. Even now, in this squalid place, she was making yet another bad decision. But this time, unlike those other times, she really did have no other option. This was it, the pit, the private hell at the end of the road: a hell that consisted of this dark corridor, two grinning men, and a door to a room where she would have everything taken from her.

"Shall we?" Bright's voice was soft, smooth, as if he were attempting to seduce her.

She set her jaw, tensed her body, and then forced her muscles to relax. "Let's go," she whispered. "Let's get it over with."

Bright nodded once, and then opened the door.

Lana was aware of the big man, Boater, using up all the space behind her, giving her no room to escape, should she even try. She took a step and turned right, into the room.

Inside there was not much to see. A single bulb hung from the ceiling, its paper shade too dirty to make out any kind of design or decoration. The walls were bare stone, with damp stains spread across them like dark, blotchy shadows. There was a double bed pushed up against the side wall, adorned with thin blankets and a solitary shapeless pillow. The floor was stone, like the walls, and there was a crude shower stall in one corner, like something from a book of pictures of a concentration camp she'd once seen. A man stood by the shower. She recognised him from before, when they'd visited her flat to give her Bright's last warning. He'd been wearing dark clothes, then – threatening clothes. This time he was wearing nothing but black trousers and a vest.

More than the man himself, though, she recognised the single black leather glove he wore.

Terry, she thought. *His name's Terry*. It was such a common name for a devil.

He'd been wearing two gloves the last time she'd seen him. This time he only wore the one; his other hand was bare... his *prosthetic* hand. It looked like some kind of out-dated contraption, with thin metal levers visible at the wrist and wide leather straps holding it in place on his forearm. He raised his arm as she stood there, standing just a foot over the threshold, and clenched his plastic fingers.

Then, as she began to lose all sense of reality, he undid the leather straps and removed the false hand to reveal a shiny pink nub of flesh.

"Just wait 'till you see what he can do with that stump," said Bright, standing right beside her. She turned and looked into his shiny face. His eyes seemed to have doubled in size and there was white spittle gathered at the corners of his mouth.

Terry, waving his stump around in the air, began to laugh. It was a quiet sound, almost polite: a gentle chuckle that was completely out of place given the situation.

She looked down, at his bare feet. He was wriggling his toes on the stone floor. For some reason the sight was more sickening than that of the naked stump, and Lana felt a wave of bile rising at the back of her throat.

She took another couple of steps, trying to impose herself in the weird isolated space that was the room, to exert some measure of control. She heard the door shut behind her. Then there was the sound of a key rattling in the lock, and then a series of blunt clicks as the only way in or out of that room was sealed, perhaps locking a part of Lana inside there forever.

"So, Lana Fraser," said Bright, slipping off his jacket. "At last you deign to come and visit us, to offer us some kind of payment on your debt." His body, beneath the jacket, was clad in a tight grey shirt. His arms were huge, the biceps oversized. He could barely even bend his arms to remove the outer garment without having to angle his body to aid its movement. He was deformed; a man made monstrous by the abuse of muscle-building chemicals and heavy weights. Like most small-time criminals, he had an obsession with physical strength, but his had become so acute, so outlandish, that it had altered his exterior to reflect, more or less, how he saw himself in his mind's eye.

"Yes," she said. "I'm here to pay it off. I want to bring this to an end, finalise the deal. Just like you said on the phone."

Terry, still standing by the primitive shower stall, laughed again. He flexed his gloved hand; the leather creaked loudly in the silence that followed his abrupt laughter. He stared at her face, her eyes, and never broke eye contact even as he stripped off his vest. His torso was well-muscled, but not as barrel-like as his boss's broad trunk. Blue-black prison tattoos – at least that's what Lana assumed the crude, thick-lined renderings to be – decorated his upper arms. An odd-looking dragon draped its badly-drawn tail around his shoulder.

"Is that what I said?" Bright walked around and stood directly in front of her, cutting off her view of Terry as he began to loosen his trousers. Bright was pulling his shirttails out of his waistband. Then he began to undo the shirt buttons from the bottom up. "Yes, I suppose I did say that, didn't I?"

"I know the score," said Lana, trying to find strength from somewhere, anywhere. "I know what's expected of me, and I'll do it all. I'll do *you* all, if it keeps you away from me in future, and away from my daughter." She clenched her fists and refused to look away as he slipped off his shirt and folded it neatly before placing it on the floor, near the end of the stark double bed.

Beneath the shirt he was wearing what looked like a wetsuit. It clung to his oddly-shaped form like a second skin, accentuating the ugly, disproportionate muscle build-up around his upper body. Lana was so surprised by Bright's ridiculous get-up that for a moment she forgot to be afraid, and a tiny smile flickered across her lips. She cut the smile short before it got out of control, wishing that she could have prevented it altogether. The last thing she wanted to do was antagonise these men: there was too much aggression in the room already; unless she was careful, there was the risk that they would lose all control and cause her some real physical damage.

They could fuck her, by all means – she was just about prepared for that – but please God, don't let them break her.

"Monty, I have some things to do... I'll just go back upstairs while you sort things out down here."

Sort things out, was that how they thought of it? What they called gang-rape? Lana felt her back stiffen as Boater brushed up lightly against her.

"Don't be silly, Francis. We're all taking part. We're going to have some fun." Bright smiled at her. "Aren't we, Lana?"

She didn't have it in her to reply, but she somehow managed to keep staring at him, pressing her gaze into his soft face. There was something going on here – something below the surface, a situation that was nothing to do with her but in which she seemed to have a pivotal role.

"But, Monty–"

"But *nothing*, Francis!" Bright's eyes swivelled away from her and glared over her shoulder, at his mammoth henchman. "But nothing. We all stay here, and each of us takes our fill. We owe it to this kind lady, who has put herself to a lot of trouble to be here. Never, Francis, *ever* look a gift horse in the mouth." He smiled but it looked all wrong, as if his face were splitting in two. "And don't ever let a free fuck go to waste."

Lana felt her legs start to shake, but she fought to control the movement. She wouldn't give him the satisfaction of witnessing her fear. She was strong; her mind and body were one. This bastard wouldn't break her, not ever. She vowed to remain intact to the very end, even if she ended up dead. This fucker would not see a single tear roll down her face, or hear a scream pass from her lips. She was stone. She was already dead.

"Are we ready?" Bright rubbed his hands together. His wetsuit absorbed the meagre light, glistening like the flesh of some hideous black lizard. "Are we all ready?"

"Fuck, yeah," said Terry, moving forward, away from the shower stall. He was standing in his white wife-beater vest and underpants. She could see clearly that he was ready for action.

"Yeah," said Boater, still standing behind her. There was something about the giant that Lana couldn't fathom. It was obvious that he was having some kind of crisis of faith; she'd picked up on the fact that he was struggling with his own emotions. He'd almost turned against his boss. She felt it in the air: a sense of suppressed rebellion. Why couldn't he have gone all the way and brought the fight out into the open, giving her some slight hope that this might not happen – that these men might not use her as a sex doll in this grimy basement room?

Terry's pink nub of a wrist shone weakly in the dim light. Monty Bright grinned like a lunatic. And behind her, remaining out of sight for now, a silent giant took stock of his situation far too slowly to offer Lana any form of hope.

Bright took something from his trouser pocket: a thin black scarf. "Here." He said. "Put this on." He opened his fingers and let the scarf unfurl, holding one end between his thumb and the palm of his hand. It was not a scarf, it was a blindfold: a black silk blindfold.

Lana reached out and took the blindfold from his hand. His skin felt cold and clammy, but that might just have been her imagination, conjuring little tricks to transform a bad man into a demon.

"Put it on, *now*." The playfulness had gone from his demeanour, leaving behind a blank, empty shell waiting to be filled by whatever he could take from her.

There was a pause. The room seemed to exist out of time for a moment, as if they'd all moved sideways into another state of being.

When Bright slapped her, without warning, it took her a second or two to register the pain. She heard the sound – quick, high and sharp – and had time to wonder what it was before her cheek started to burn. It was too late to even raise her hand and feel the spot where he had hit her. The pause between the violent act and her realisation of it was too great for her to react without feeling stupid. "Oh," she said instead. It was an ineffectual remark; she wished she'd just kept her mouth shut. "Oh," she said again, thinking, *Shut the fuck up!*

Bright nodded. The walls closed in, squeezing her sense of spatial awareness until it lost all meaning. She realised why Bright had slapped her. The bastard had done it to sharpen her senses, to plunge her into the moment like someone jumping into a cold lake. To make sure she was fully aware when things got under way.

He wanted to ensure that she was trapped firmly in the present and not retreating into some inner chamber where she might distance herself from the outrage. The fucker knew exactly what he was doing. He had done this too many times before to make silly mistakes and allow his victim – his debtor – even a scant emotional reprieve. Maybe his men were just along for the ride, but like most serial rapists, Bright was interested in mental rather than physical penetration.

"Let's get this show on the road," said Bright, softly, almost lovingly – as if he were savouring the taste of his catchphrase on his tongue.

Lana covered her eyes and waited for the suffering to start.

AFTERWARDS, WHEN IT was all over and done with, she stood in the shower stall and let the cold water chill her battered body. Hot water would have been too much of a kindness, and men like these were not known for their acts of generosity.

Lana ached everywhere, inside and out. The stink of semen clung to her. She had vomited so much in the shower that her belly felt mercifully empty. She had not taken the blindfold off. She didn't want to see them again until she was clean. She faced the wall and let the sound of the water deafen her, but still she heard the door as it opened and closed, and the footsteps approaching across the hard floor.

"Hurry up. We have things to do."

It was Terry's voice. She would never forget that voice, even if she lived to be an old woman. He had whispered such terrible things in her ear as they'd used her body, entering every orifice. Such terrible, terrible things. He'd spoken of Hailey, and how she looked. He'd talked about her daughter's young body, and what he would like to do with it. The words he'd used had been ones she'd heard before, many times, but in the situation she was in they became something new: another language, and one that expressed only depravity.

These were surely not men; they were animals. Beasts. They had no souls, no morals. They were demonic.

But, no. They were just men: Bad Men.

She fumbled for the taps and turned off the flow of water. Then, wincing as her limbs burned with pain, she took off the blindfold. Then she turned to face the one-handed man who had defiled her. He was fully clothed and his prosthetic was fixed back in place. He was once again wearing both of his black leather gloves.

"Put your fucking clothes on." The contempt in his voice was almost as hurtful as what they'd done to her. Almost, but not quite. Not at all, if she was honest. That was just another lie to tell herself, a flimsy barrier to wedge between her and the memory of what had been done here in this shabby little basement room she would always think of whenever she heard the word 'hell'.

The door opened again just as she was putting on her blouse. She watched Bright walk in as she buttoned it to the neck and smoothed out the collars.

"So, are we done?" Her voice was hoarse. Her throat felt like it had been filled with cement. "Are we square?" She shuffled forward. Each tiny step made her thighs blaze, her crotch burn, her torn anus clench, and set off a series of dull explosions deep inside her lower abdomen.

I'll need to get checked out, she thought. *For STDs. AIDS.*

This grim note of reality, even more than the acts she'd been made to perform and submit to, threatened to tear her apart. The aftermath – the thought of the countless small, intimate and desperately embarrassing tasks she would need to undertake before declaring herself clean and safe – were like daggers in her belly.

"*Well?*" She was amazed that she still possessed enough strength to raise her voice. She certainly wouldn't be able to raise her hands to defend herself if one of the men chose to slap her again. Such physicality was beyond her right now, at least until she started to bruise.

"For now," said Bright.

Terry laughed softly, but when Bright glanced at him he fell silent, and then lowered his head and left the room. He shut the door quietly behind him, as if that one look had caused him to fear even the slightest sound.

The games were over.

Bright was once again wearing his suit, but was not wearing any shoes. He reached into the inside pocket of his jacket and took out a fat cigar – *probably Cuban,* thought Lana, madly, focusing on absurd details rather than the larger canvas of the picture taking shape before her. He lit the cigar and took a long drag. Smoke trailed from his lips; Lana thought it moved too slowly to be real.

"What do you mean?" Her hands dropped to her sides. She felt boneless, as if the men had filleted her on the bed. "You promised." But she knew that any promises made by such a man were subject to the whims of his fancy. She'd been a fool to let herself believe that this would make any difference to her situation, but what else did she have to cling to other than foolish belief?

"I promised you nothing," said Bright, looking at the cigar in his hand. The tip glowed bright red, like a single devilish eye. "Consider this visit a down payment. The way I figure it, you'll have your debt cleared in, say, six to eight months. Even quicker if you bring the girl along next time. Nice and tight and pretty, isn't she? I've seen her through the school gates, playing with her little friends. I think *my* friends would like to play with her very much."

Lana knew that she should rush him, maybe go for the throat, the eyes: attack the soft parts, just like a cornered rat. But it was futile. He was too strong, and had always possessed the upper hand. Right from the start, he'd played her along, upping the odds until she came to him and offered him exactly what he wanted and could have taken at any point, if that had been his choice.

But Monty Bright did not want to take; it was the very act of *offering* that turned him on, made him shine.

Where's your compassion?" she said, failing to penetrate his armour. "Where's your basic human decency?" She hated the desperation she heard in her weakened voice, but it was all she had left to offer, the only thing she could dredge up from inside her poor, defiled wreck of a body.

Bright walked towards her. He was shorter than she remembered; he barely came up to her shoulder now that she'd put her pumps back on. His skin looked soft, malleable, and his eyes protruded like boiled eggs from a face as flat and round as a polished plate. Bright's shoulders were hunched; his posture was awkward, as if the years of self-abuse disguised as exercise had mutated his basic geometry. He slowly raised his hands and began to slip off his shirt. He still wore the wetsuit underneath, as he had done during her ordeal, and she stared in horror as he slid his fingers under the neck of the garment and began to peel the material downwards, as if he were calmly removing a layer of skin. He extracted his arms from the rubbery suit and rolled it down towards his waist.

"For that, dear Lana, I'd have to be human."

The blindfold and the wetsuit had prevented her from seeing anything before, and most of the time her arms had been pinned down or back behind her, but his naked torso was a mass of lumps and abrasions. More and more of this was revealed as he continued to drag the garment down over his belly. The malformations looked like ripe tumours: they dangled in grapelike clumps from beneath his armpits, clustered around his nipples and made a ribbed embossment down the faint seam of his hairless belly.

Even now, after everything she'd gone through, Lana felt sick to the stomach.

There were small mouths in there, amid the globules and curlicues of flesh, and bright little eyes that blinked uncomprehendingly. A nose or a sex gland twitched; snot or semen spilled from its shiny, puckered end. Here was a whole community of beings, perhaps even the physical representation of the souls of people he'd consumed as repayment for debts even greater than her own, loans whose rate of interest was infinite.

"Bring the girl next time," he said, smiling around his cigar. "I'll show her a whole new world of hurt." The cigar's fiery red eye winked: just once, but it was more than enough to ensure she got the message.

PART THREE

FACES

*"The things you do have
begun to repel you."*

– Monty Bright

CHAPTER TWENTY-TWO

"So, FRANCIS, DO you have anything you'd like to tell me?"

They were back in Monty's office. Boater was standing on one side of the desk while his boss poured two glasses of fifteen year-old Glenlivet on the other side, from the comfort of his chair.

"No," said Boater. "Not that I know of, anyway."

Monty raised one eyebrow, finished pouring the whiskies, and then looked directly at Boater. "Well what was all that about, downstairs? Why did you want to leave before the fun started?" He slid Boater's glass across the desk, and then leaned back, raising his own glass to his lips.

Boater wasn't comfortable; he hated confrontation unless it involved extreme and sudden violence. He was not a talker: he was a puncher, a kicker, a head-butter, a stomper-of-heads. Social intercourse was not one of his strengths, but kicking the shit out of people was.

"Well, Francis?" Monty put down his glass and smiled. "Talk to me. Tell me what's on your mind. We're not animals, we're men. And men should be able to reason with each other."

Boater reached for his glass. His hand was shaking. He was twice the size of the other man, and probably weighed three times as much, yet he was afraid. It wasn't that he was scared of Bright physically, not really. What instilled him with this wholly unreasonable fear was the thought of Bright's madness. He knew that now; he could see it at last. His boss, the man he had served without question for almost two decades, was fucking insane.

He took a large swallow of the whisky. It burned his throat, but as the liquid travelled down the intense burning sensation changed to a gentle heat that helped calm him. "I just feel different these days, Monty." He licked his lips, getting a second taste of that hot, sweet mouthful. "It's been happening for a little while. I've started to hate what I do, what I am. The things I'm capable of... they make me feel... fuck, I dunno. I can't use words like you can." He looked down, ashamed of his lack of vocabulary, his inability to express himself as clearly as he would have liked.

"The things you do have begun to repel you." Monty stood and walked around the desk. "Is that it, Francis? Is that what you're trying to say?"

Boater nodded. He raised his head. He felt tired, so very tired.

"Look around you, Francis. Look at my walls."

Boater turned his head and stared at the framed pictures and photographs. He'd seen them all, many times before. He didn't know who any of the people in the portraits were, and the other stuff – sketches and diagrams of weird objects, buildings and places – left him cold. He didn't appreciate art or culture. His idea of a good night out was to drink until he fell over, and the only films he liked featured lots of car chases and gunfights.

"That man over there. See him?" Monty walked over to the portrait in question, which hung next to a strange three-panelled print of demons cavorting in giant teacups and fragments of broken egg shells. The painting showed the face of a man with thinning hair and fleshy features. *A funny-looking bloke*, thought Boater. *I bet he didn't get much fanny*.

"That's Arthur Machen. He wrote stories and novels, a lot of them about another place that exists alongside our own. A place where there are angels and demons. A real place, mind you, not some daft country you can get to through the back of a wardrobe. No, Machen's other place was a realm of spirituality. It was a world where faith and belief were very real, and they had faces... sometimes they were hideous faces, and sometimes they were beautiful."

Boater stood there in silence, unsure of what his boss wanted from him. He looked at Monty, and then he looked back at the framed portrait. He pressed his lips together, and then moved them apart so that he could finish his drink. It was just a picture of an ugly old man. There was nothing more to see.

"What I'm trying to say, Francis, is that a lot of people have strange feelings and ideas. Some are equipped to express those ideas, and others keep them locked up inside. You're changing, that's all. Something is changing you. We're all very close to something that's exerting a kind of energy – a psychic power, I suppose, that's altering the way we look at the world. It's the place I've been trying to find for years, ever since I found that book, my little Bible. And possibly before that, without even knowing." He pointed over to his desk, where his beloved copy of *Extreme Boot Camp Workout* was laying face down amid some scattered papers. "It's all in there – even some of Machen's words on the subject. He wrote a story called 'N', where he said that a fragment of Creation had broken off and landed in London, where it acted as a doorway to allow the mystic to intrude upon the everyday world."

Boater's head was throbbing. He felt like a man standing on a ledge, thinking about whether he should leap or turn around and walk away. Jumping had never felt so appealing. He understood none of this.

"I need you to do something for me, Francis." Monty had changed the subject again. He often did this, swinging his conversation in unexpected directions. "This is a big favour. You're the only one I can trust. Terry and those other clowns, they're okay in a fight outside a nightclub, or to use as muscle when I need to claim a repayment, but you have certain sensibilities – especially now – that make you unique. You're my man, Francis, my fox-in-the-box. You always have been." He smiled, but his lips were stuck to his teeth and it made him look slightly odd, as if he were wearing a mask.

Boater resisted the urge to shudder and returned the smile. But it felt wrong, as if he too were forcing the muscles of his face into an unnatural expression.

"First let me show you something. Grab that bottle and let's go back downstairs. There's something I think you need to see." He waited for Boater to move, and when he did Monty waited some more, watching his man, his fox-in-the-box, with eyes that betrayed a mean, seedy hunger.

Boater kept the whisky bottle in a firm grip. It felt like the glass neck of the bottle might break if he gripped it any tighter. For some reason, he wanted desperately to uncork the bottle and swig the entire contents down in one. He thought that if Monty attacked him he'd use the bottle as a weapon. Then he wondered why he was even thinking such a thing.

"Let's go down, Francis."

Boater glanced one more time at the portrait – what was his name, Arthur Mackem? The subject's watery gaze seemed to take him in and then spit him out again, judging him as unworthy. He looked away, feeling ashamed. Why did he always feel so ashamed these days, as if he were somehow seeing the real Francis Boater for the first time and judging *himself* as worthless?

They went through the door and once again descended the old wooden staircase, with Monty in the lead. The disembodied landings seemed creepy and shadow-filled, as if figures stood just out of sight on the timber boards. When they reached the basement level, Monty turned and walked in a direction that led away from the 'play room' where they'd taken Lana Fraser.

Boater rarely came down here if it could be helped; he wasn't comfortable with all that earth, and then the weight of the building above it, pressing down on his head. He liked to see daylight, a way out of the darkness, and this felt like they were turning their backs on the world above to seek solace in the musty darkness under the ground.

"I've never shown you this room." Monty's voice sounded flat, as if he were covering his mouth with something. "The only other people to have seen this place are dead." It was not a threat. Monty was simply imparting knowledge.

Boater remained silent. The bulbs in the wall lamps guttered like candle flames. He listened to the sound of their footsteps as they made their way along the narrow passage, and ran his hands along the cool stone walls. He didn't know why these underground rooms had been built – perhaps they were originally meant to be storage areas – but Monty loved it down here, in his private maze. There were rooms where beatings had been dished out, quiet corners where women had wept and other small chambers filled with drugs that would be sold on the streets of Newcastle, or handed out to the local dealers in the Grove for distribution closer to home.

Part of the myth of Monty Bright was stored here. The stories people told on the streets, the facts they twisted to become legend, had all started here, as fragments of Monty's self-built reality.

"In here," he said, pulling up short at yet another ordinary door. The paint had peeled. The wooden surface was pocked with small abrasions. "This is where I keep them." His focus had drifted again, like it sometimes did when he spoke about the knowledge he had learned and the things he had written in his worn copy of *Extreme Boot Camp*

Workout. Monty's voice sounded like it was coming from miles away.

Boater was on the verge of turning around and making his way back above ground, where he could breathe some fresh, clean air, or at least the air that passed for clean and fresh in the Grove.

"Let's get this show on the road," said Monty, with a rehearsed air. Indeed, Boater had heard him use the phrase many times, usually in the moments before someone was beaten or cut or raped. Sometimes it even preceded a killing blow.

Monty unlocked the door, pushed it open, and blackness pulsed in the room beyond. Boater followed his boss inside, wishing that he had walked away after all. He didn't like the feeling he got when he crossed over the threshold. It felt like someone had died in there.

"This is what I wanted to show you." Monty reached out a hand and flicked a light switch. Dim light spilled down the walls and crept across the floor, failing to fill the far corners but illuminating the very centre of the space like a spotlight on a shabby stage. "I wanted you to meet my secret council."

Boater looked down at the floor and saw a bunch of old television sets. Most of the screens were cracked; some of them were partially shattered. Each set was of a type that was now rarely sold. There were no flat screens here; no HD-ready plasma models. Just a lot of old, busted television sets like the one his mother used to have in the parlour when he was growing up.

"Monty…" But he didn't know what to say. This was too weird. None of it made any sense.

"This is where I get my information. Can you see them in there? They tell me things: the bad stuff that's going to happen unless I do something to prevent it." Monty was down on his knees in front of the first row of televisions. He was reaching out a hand and brushing the screen with his fingertips, as if he were cleaning the surface of dust. "They help me. They advise me what to do."

The screens were all dark. These television sets had not worked in years, maybe decades. Even Boater could see that. There was no doubt in his mind that nobody had watched anything on these things since the days when there were only three terrestrial channels available through a roof-mounted aerial or antenna.

"These are the lords of all I survey. They see everything. Their eyes are all around the Grove. They travel to different places, to people's homes, through the airwaves and they spy on my debtors. Then they bring back snippets of news, like little carrier pigeons." There was an element of awe in Monty's voice, but also one of love.

"I see," said Boater. "That's... good. It's handy, isn't it?" He backed up slowly, making sure that he was close to the door. Just in case Monty flipped. He gripped the neck of the bottle tighter.

Monty turned his head. He was still down on his knees in the dirt, as if praying before the host of broken television sets. "You don't, do you? You don't see them." He smiled, and for a moment Boater thought that he saw cold, flat TV light play across his features.

"No," said Boater, shaking his head. "I'm sorry, but I don't see a fucking thing. There's nobody there, on those screens. The TV sets can't talk to you." He held out his hands, a placatory gesture. "They aren't even plugged in."

"Not on the screens, Francis. *In* the screens. They're inside there, like baby birds waiting inside their eggs. They hatch out sometimes, but only to feed. They take back the sights that television has given us, and when it happens they leave behind a blank slate. People are nothing without their borrowed visuals, their hand-me-down ideas. When they're removed from the great glass tit they become empty very fucking quickly..." He turned back to the televisions, as if they'd all come on together to show him the different channels they could receive.

Boater was locked in place. He couldn't move. So he just stood there, and he watched.

"That's what happened to that stupid druggie thief, Banjo. They stripped him clean, taking back the visions and washing his brain as clean and smooth as a baby's arse."

Boater remembered the guy, that junkie. They'd brought him down here and beaten him, and then Monty had told them to leave him alone with the fucker. That was the last Boater knew of him until he saw a report on the local news, stating that the junkie had been found walking the streets trying to rip his own face off. If he remembered correctly, Lana Fraser and some bloke had seen it happen.

"That rotten little bastard got what he deserved. He got wiped clean, retuned to an empty channel."

The longer Boater stared at the TV screens the more he thought that he could see something behind them, coiling in the darkness. It looked like snakes made of smoke, or limbs of mist. A writhing mass comprised of long, twisting shapes was packed in behind the broken glass, and they were slowly becoming clearer, gaining resolution. Then, as though a visor had been lifted from before his eyes, he caught sight of huge, twitching, insect-like legs, folded over and stuffed tightly into the spaces behind the screens. "I think I see something," he said, taking a few steps forward, into the room. "They're in there, aren't they? They're really in there."

"Yes, they are." Monty stood and walked to Boater's side. He laid a hand on his forearm. "They told me to take the girl."

Boater glanced at him. "What girl?" But he knew; of course he did. He'd been keeping an eye on her for almost a fortnight now, since Monty had asked him to swing by her school a couple of times a week, and perhaps follow her home every now and then. If she had ever seen him, all she would have noticed was a fat man in a car parked by the Arcade, or some burly bastard standing outside the Dropped Penny pub waiting for someone.

"First they told me to watch her, and I put you on the job. Now they've said that I need to take her. That Fraser woman, she's going to try to kill me. She'll come back here very soon, and perhaps she won't be alone. I need an insurance policy, a little leverage, some collateral on the remainder of her loan." He gripped Boater's arm. His fingers felt like steel rods. "Get the girl for me, Francis. Get that cunt's daughter and put her somewhere safe." His eyes were manic, filled with an energy whose intensity was terrifying.

Boater's head felt like it was expanding, and a strange droning noise filled his ears. He watched Monty's lips move but he could barely hear what was being said.

"Get her and hide her until I tell you it's safe to bring her back out into the open."

Even though his hearing was impaired by the keening sound inside his head, Boater understood completely what he was being ordered to do. The only problem was he didn't know if he could go through with it.

"But first," said Monty, smiling again. "You can help me carry these fucking televisions upstairs."

LATER, AS HE sat in his car outside the gym, Boater stared at his tired reflection in the rear-view mirror. He looked different; his features had altered subtly, as if he were trying to physically become someone else. But then the light from passing headlights briefly illuminated the interior of the car and he was once again the same old Francis Boater, with his bloated face and his small eyes. But for a moment there, in the shadows, he had almost been able to convince himself that he was a different person entirely.

He thought about the girl, and what Monty had told him to do. He pictured all the times he'd seen her recently, walking along on her own, heading either to or from her school. She was always alone; she never walked with friends. Like Boater, she seemed to travel through her life alone.

Right then, sitting motionless in his car on a darkened street, he decided that this time he was going to make his own decisions. This time, whatever he did he would do for the right reasons.

CHAPTER TWENTY-THREE

TOM HAD NOT slept; he had merely dozed in the armchair, grabbing eagerly at the promise of rest yet gaining only scraps. So when he opened his eyes he knew immediately that he wasn't dreaming. Not this time, anyway.

The first thing he saw was a scruffy dog walking slowly across the doorway, left to right. The dog was huge, more like a wolf, and as it turned to look at him he saw by the lamplight that it had the face of a boy. It was a familiar face: it was *his* face, but when he was much younger. The dog, and its stolen features, had once stalked him through the rooms of his father's house, warning him off, shepherding him away from sights that he should not be allowed to see, and now it had returned to resume its role as guard dog to Tom's psyche.

Tiredness allowed him at last to see this truth. Exhaustion had opened his eyes and shown him the reality that was hiding behind the illusion.

All this time he had thought the dream-dog meant him harm, but it had actually been trying to save him. The realisation made him simultaneously sad and afraid.

"I'm sorry. I never understood. I always thought you were a monster. I didn't realise that you were just a part of *me*."

But the dog was gone. The doorway was empty. Not even its shadow remained.

He got up and walked out into the hall. The darkness there had form and substance, like a cluster of earthbound clouds. He felt like he was dreaming awake – it was a sensation he now recognised as being a signal that he was partly in that other state, the one he had sensed so keenly during the day trip with Lana and Hailey. When he turned to face the front door, he half expected to see another animated section of Hadrian's Wall slithering in and out like a serpent through gaps in the building. But this time he was awake, and the vivid dream imagery was nothing but a memory.

Something moved on the stairs behind him. It was a slow, heavy sound, like someone dragging themselves on their belly across the floor.

He glanced at the door to Helen's room. It was open. He crossed the hallway and peered inside. The television was on, tuned once again to the static between channels. It bathed the room in an eerie light, and showed him that the bed was unmade and empty. But Helen had not been out of bed in years.

So where the hell was she now?

Tom turned to the bottom of the stairs. In the dimness he could make out a trail of moisture leading upwards. The carpet was wet; each step glistened, as if a giant slug had made its way up to the first floor.

He began to climb the stairs, keeping to the edge nearest the wall and clinging to the handrail. The light receded, staying down on the ground floor, but there was enough illumination bleeding in through the upstairs windows for him to see by. When he reached the top of the stairs the sound was much louder: a slow, moist slithering. He turned on to the landing and saw it there, hauling itself towards the bathroom at a slow, monotonous pace. A patch of light from the window at the end of the landing seeped towards it, like a yellow puddle. Its heavy grey body moved slowly; the large, clumsy fins pressed weakly against the floor and failed to get much traction as the animal inched along the floor.

The sea cow's journey was agonisingly slow, but it at least had intent and purpose.

Tom walked along in its wake, watching the oversized mammal as it made its way towards the open bathroom door. The taps were running, filling the bath with hot water. One of the small lights above the mirror was on. Tom had no idea who had started to run the bath – certainly it couldn't have been the manatee: that was impossible. Maybe he had done it, in his drowsy state. He could believe anything right now. He could even believe that a sea cow was hauling its massive bulk along his upstairs landing towards a bath-full of water.

"Helen." His voice sounded tiny, so he said her name again. "Helen."

At first the sea cow didn't register his presence. Then, abruptly, its fins ceased their awkward movement on the carpet. The beast started to hitch its body around, pivoting on its belly and swivelling through 180 degrees to face him. It seemed to take ages for the thing to turn, and when finally it did the beast stared at him with tiny black, baleful eyes from a square, grey face that looked somehow familiar. It opened its black-slit mouth and made a strange hollow clicking sound. Its tongue was long and thick. The teeth in its upper and lower jaws were huge and jagged, like fragments of rock stuck into its gums.

Are they meant to have teeth like that?

The clicking sound came again. He'd heard it before; the other night on the telephone when no-one had spoken. On that first occasion, Tom had put it down to a wrong number or a crossed line, but that damn clicking sound had blocked his thoughts... just as it was doing now.

Clickety-clickety-click...

"Is that you, Helen?" Tom felt ridiculous, but at the same time he knew that the animal was indeed his wife – somehow, once again, Helen had become in reality exactly as he thought of her in his mind, taking the physical form of his imagined insult. But this time it wasn't a dream; this time it was part of the waking world. The two elements had clashed, and this creeping horror was the result.

A fracture had appeared between the states of waking and sleeping, living and dreaming, and what crawled through that rift was the stuff of fantasy. The mental power utilised during the usual dream-state was finding another outlet, and Tom knew, without having to question the thought, that something was using that energy as fuel. Some *thing* was trying to break through, to open a doorway and move from one realm to the other.

He remembered his father's warning and the phantom flying fists. The way the old man's ghost had abused his bed-ridden wife, as she had taken the form of the manatee. It all meant something, but he was unable to solve the equation. This otherworldly form of mathematics was beyond him. He didn't have the skills; the numbers would not add up.

The sea cow lurched in his direction, moving faster this time but still slow enough that he could easily outmanoeuvre it as the beast rocked towards him across the landing, clickety-clickety-clicking like a broken spindle. Only when he stumbled on the top step and fell badly, momentarily trapping his left leg in the gap between two stair rails, did he begin to fear what the sea cow might do if it caught up with him.

CHAPTER TWENTY-FOUR

How the fuck did that happen?

Lana was sure she'd walked along a narrow ginnel that should have brought her out somewhere near The Dropped Penny pub, but somehow she found herself standing on top of the Embankment and facing in the wrong direction entirely. She stared down the slope and into the shadows at the bottom of the old railway cutting, picking out the broken timber railway sleepers in the sodium-tinted darkness.

The route she'd taken should have delivered her outside the pub. She knew that; it was a fact, non-negotiable. So what the hell was she doing here, at the opposite end of the Grove, and facing the wrong fucking way?

Her stomach ached, her legs hurt. Her insides felt battered.

"Keep calm." She spoke out loud in an attempt to dispel the fear that was creeping up on her from behind, wrapping its arms around her shoulders like an old lover. Time was slowing down. She felt like she'd been out here for hours when in reality she'd only just left Bright's grotty little gym.

She turned around and stared at the domineering shape of the Needle. This was the closest she'd been to the building in ages. She didn't like how it looked; the phallic tower made her nervous in a way she could not easily define. It was worse now, at night, and standing so close to its graffiti-covered walls. Out here, in the cold darkness that was bruised by yellow street lights, she could imagine that the place had a consciousness – that it was sentient, and that it was watching her just as closely as she had watched the impassive tower block from her window, night after night, hating it for what it represented, her new life at the bottom of the pile.

"Bastard," she said, directing the curse at both the building before her and the rotten excuse for a man she'd just left.

She knew what had to be done now. There was no other way. She had offered herself to Monty Bright and he'd taken his fill. Then the fucker had reneged on his end of a bargain he claimed had never been struck. Bright had proven himself to be a liar, a rapist, and a welcher. And in some ways this last was the worst of all.

He had never intended to cancel her debt, nor had he meant to leave her alone once she had given him what he wanted. This debt, she now realised, would never be paid. It was forever. He had his fingers in her life right up to the knuckle joints, and there was nothing that she could do to break his grip.

She started walking again, past the silent frontages of darkened houses and towards other buildings that had been boarded up and abandoned. Trying to ignore the pain, she kept her eyes on her surroundings. She didn't like it here, at the centre of the Grove. The air felt different from that on the outskirts. It was as if the callousness that dwelled here had its source on, or under, the very streets she now walked.

Another narrow alley opened up like a mouth in the darkness, a street light picking out its redbrick sides and showing her the way. She headed for the opening, glancing back over her shoulder, and then ducked inside. The alleyway was long, the walls on either side of her were smooth and covered in the same kind of graffiti she saw everywhere around here: badly drawn sex organs, phone numbers and promises of gratification, declarations stating how big someone's cock was and how deep someone else's vagina. These primitive designs and renderings all seemed to focus on the subject of sex, as if that were the only language the artists knew how to use. There was nothing erotic about this paintwork, as there might be in true art: there was only crudity and banality, a strange, dull obsession with body parts and their basic functions.

When she emerged from the opposite end of the alley she found herself this time at the south end of the Embankment. She'd been heading east, yet somehow she had ended up facing south. This was wrong; it couldn't be possible. She felt like she was becoming lost in familiar streets, and each time she tried another route the arrangement of the maze reconfigured itself to strengthen the delusion.

Down on the disused railway line, far enough away that he probably couldn't even see Lana on her raised vantage point, a man was walking what at first she assumed to be a large, shaggy dog. As the moonlight and the wash of pale illumination from the streetlamps highlighted these figures, Lana saw that the animal was not a dog at all. It was something unusual, an animal she was unable to identify. Its furry body was close to the ground and it possessed far more short, thin legs than was necessary – like a nightmarish cross between a bear and a centipede. Then, as she strained her eyes to make the image clearer, the man and his companion slipped into a patch of shadow and failed to come back into view. She tried to tell herself that the man had not been so thin that he resembled a fluttering paper cut-out. Nor had his arms been so long that his hands reached down past his knees.

Fighting panic, she walked south, along the lip of the Embankment, and then crossed the empty road to walk the fence line of the old factory units. Grove Drive lay on the other side of the blackened factories, and if she walked to the end, then doubled back on herself, she could approach the block of flats where she lived from a different angle entirely. Maybe that way she could solve the puzzle and find her way home.

But when she turned the corner onto what should have been Grove Drive, she found herself back on Grove Road, one of the central rings of the main circle of streets at the heart of the Grove.

It was impossible. She should not – *could* not – be here. But here she was.

Lana's hands were shaking. She stuffed them into her coat pockets to try and still them, but as soon as she did so her legs began to tremble. The fear she had managed to repress earlier that evening, when she'd given herself to those men, was now finding a way out into the open. This surreal journey through insanely shifting streets had somehow uncorked the feelings she had forced down into the deepest part of herself.

It was almost a kind of relief.

"I'm going to kill you." The words, when they came, sounded like they were being spoken by someone else. "I *will* kill you, Monty Bright." She hadn't even known she was going to say these things until she opened her mouth, and even that felt like it was beyond her control, an impulsive act rather than one she had thought about beforehand.

"Kill you." She didn't feel ashamed by the threat, or even frightened by the depth of her conviction. She felt strong now that she'd made the decision and confirmed it out loud. The night seemed to steal her words, taking them and stashing them away in some secret nook or cranny made of pure darkness. Those words would remain there, resting on a shelf of night, until the act was done; and only then would they be returned to her, like a promise or prophecy sent home to roost.

As if borne by her newfound sense of righteousness, Lana made her way out of the circle at the centre of the estate, cutting along Grove Lane until she saw the mini roundabout adjacent to The Dropped Penny. She crossed the quiet road, glancing at her watch as she made it to the kerb on the other side. It was 2:30 AM. She felt like it should be close to daybreak, but it was still deep in the early hours of morning, and a long time before most of the denizens of this place would even stir in their beds or even think about waking. The dreams here lay as thick as clouds above the houses; when she glanced up, at the sky, she could almost see their formless gyrations above the rooftops. The Needle stood behind her. She felt as if it were bending forward to mock her while she had her back turned, but nothing could have forced her to turn around and take a look.

She made her way to the Grove Court flats, fumbling with her key as she walked along the path to the main door. Once inside she stood with her back against the door, glad that she had some kind of barrier between her and the labyrinth through which she'd been stumbling like a lost child. She paused there for a while, trying to control her breathing. Finally the shakes had come, and the asthmatic reaction of delayed fright.

"I'll kill you," she said again, between rushed breaths. "Kill. You."

Once she felt calmer she climbed the stairs and entered the flat. The lamp was on in the living room; there was a small black and white television playing on mute. Hailey must have borrowed it from one of her few friends. She couldn't imagine any of her neighbours dropping it over for them to use. This wasn't the kind of place where you helped each other out. People kept to themselves, and hid behind their doors at any hint of trouble.

She watched a giant white cat as it tried to climb the Post Office Tower on the tiny screen, and realised that it was a late-night repeat of an old comedy programme from the 1970s: *The Goodies*. She'd loved the show when she was a young girl, and had never missed an episode. The sight of that stupid cat – a bad special effect from a dated TV show – brought her close to tears for the first time that day.

She exhaled and turned away from the television, heading into the kitchen. She poured herself a large whisky in a tall glass, added a couple of ice cubes from the freezer (there were two left, looking sad and fluffy in the plastic mould), and stood leaning against the workbench as she drank. It was pointless going back into the other room to watch the rest of the show. There were no chairs to sit on, and her lower regions ached too badly to sit on the hard floor.

Tears poured down her cheeks as she finished her drink, but she refused to acknowledge them. If she ignored them, they didn't exist. She poured another tall drink and drank it without ice – there was none left anyway, and she didn't feel like scraping it off the inside of the freezer. She was desperate but she still had standards.

She laughed out loud, wiped her face with the back of one hand and used the other to tilt the glass against her open lips and tip the remaining whisky down her throat.

"Mum?"

Hailey's voice pulled her out of the state of hysteria she'd been dangerously close to embracing. She put down the glass on the bench and pushed herself into the middle of the kitchen. "Hey, baby. Yes, it's me. I've been out for a late drink with Tom." She smiled but knew it was fooling nobody – not Hailey, and certainly not herself. "What are you doing awake at this time?"

"Mum, something's happened. Something weird…" The girl was standing at the end of the short hallway, partially inside the living room. She was wearing a white terrycloth robe that was hanging open, the belt undone. Her belly was loose and wrinkled, like a fleshy bag, and it hung down over her waist. There was blood on her thighs. It looked dark in the lamplight, like deep red ink.

"Hailey. What's wrong? What happened?" She moved quickly, grabbing a couple of tea towels from the top drawer beside the sink and kneeling down in front of her daughter. "What the fuck's happened, Hay?"

"They've come," said Hailey, her pale face turned slightly upward. "I asked for help, and help's arrived."

"Talk to me, Hailey. Tell me what you've done." Frantically, she checked her daughter's arms for signs of self-harm or needle marks. Then, finding nothing but smooth white flesh traced with delicate blue veins, she turned her attention to Hailey's lower anatomy.

She'd given birth, that much was obvious. Her belly was hanging in such a way that it was clear something had recently vacated it. She pushed the loose flesh aside, inspecting the area beneath. There was blood on Hailey's pubes, and stringy matter pasted to the inner surfaces of her legs. The blood was congealing; it was not running fresh. Whatever had occurred, it was over. The damage was done.

"You've had a baby?" She could not believe that she was saying the words.

Hailey laughed. It was an awful sound: empty and uncomprehending. "No, Mum. Not a baby. I've delivered something, but it certainly wasn't a baby." Hailey's voice sounded strange, like she was a grown woman and not a little girl. She spoke like an old crone, battered and beaten by life's traumas but not yet ready to lie down and quit.

Lana decided to change the course of the conversation, to give Hailey some room in which to find her focus. "Where did the TV come from, honey?" She rubbed her daughter's forearms, as if she were trying to warm them up, to help circulate the blood in her veins.

"Tessa's mother brought it over. Late on, after you'd gone out."

Lana had no idea who Tessa was.

"That was nice of her." She kept rubbing Hailey's arms. She couldn't stop. "I'm sorry, honey. Mummy couldn't make it better." Tears ran down her cheeks and she stroked Hailey's cold wrists. "I tried, I really did, but I couldn't manage it. I'm sorry for your illness, I'm sorry for the things we've seen and done. I'm sorry your daddy isn't around to see how beautiful you are."

Hailey's eyelids flickered, and then her eyes slowly closed and opened again. They were completely white, without a trace of pupil or iris. She opened her mouth and a trail of saliva ran down her chin. She was having some kind of fit. Another one.

Lana grabbed her daughter by the shoulders. "Hailey?"

Hailey's body began to shake. Lana was almost used to this by now, but combined with everything else she was going through it seemed much worse this time.

"Oh, Hailey. Oh, honey." Lana cradled her child in her arms and reached out to something she didn't believe in. If there was a God, or some kind of greater power that watched over the fallen, then why would it not answer her pleas? The doctors were useless; they didn't know what was wrong. None of them could make a proper diagnosis. Maybe all she had left to rely on was whatever might be listening to her prayers.

The shuddering motion stopped. Hailey pushed herself out of her mother's embrace. Her eyes were normal again. White flecks of spit speckled her chin.

"The Slitten," said Hailey, her voice low and cold and even. "They'll help us. Just ask. *Ask*."

After everything she'd seen lately – and all the horror she'd experienced in Monty Bright's basement room – Lana was ready to believe in anything. Any slim hope offered to her looked appealing, even the private fantasy belonging to a damaged teenager. She let go of Hailey and shuffled backwards on her knees, clasping her hands in a clumsy prayer. She lowered her head and gathered whatever energy still inhabited her battered body.

"*Just ask*." Hailey's voice was a whisper, an echo.

Lana stared at her hands, clasped before her in an idiot's plea. Suddenly this seemed like an absurd children's game. She pulled her hands apart and wiped them on the front of her dress, as if they were covered in dirt. "No. This is stupid," she shook her head. "Like I said before, it's just fucking stupid." She stood and walked over to Hailey, manhandling her in a more aggressive way than she first intended. "Let's get you cleaned up. I always seem to be doing that lately."

Hailey said nothing. She just allowed herself to be led to the bathroom.

Lana ran the hot water until it was steaming, and added just a little cold so that the water was tolerable to sit in. Then she helped Hailey undress and guided her into the bath. The room was filled with steam. The window glass was opaque. The surface of the mirror was like a cataract-blinded eye. She felt close to a place where all of this made some kind of sense, an alternative world in which pain was simply a method of gaining entry, where trauma was just the price of admittance.

She put Hailey to bed and then took a shower to relax – the faulty shower head decided to work on the third attempt, the water spluttering at first but then flowing with renewed force. But no matter how many times she bathed herself, Lana knew that she would never be rid of the stain of this evening. She was polluted; her body had been changed by what she'd allowed those men to do to her. And the sight of Monty Bright as he shed his wetsuit had imprinted itself on her mind, altering the geometry of her brain forever.

After her shower, she dressed in clean clothes and returned to Hailey's room. The girl was sleeping, lying in exactly the same position as when Lana had left her before midnight. The girl's eyes moved rapidly beneath waxy lids; she was seeing something other than the depressing sights around her. Maybe even something wonderful. Lana reached out and stroked Hailey's forehead, fighting back tears.

Hailey's eyes opened.

"*Just ask.*"

Lana took away her hand. She stared at her daughter's pale face, at her dull, hard eyes. Then she relented. If it made Hailey happy, she could at least do this for the girl, feed her crazy little fantasy.

But somewhere deep inside her, where her hopes and dreams lay dry and withered, like dead flowers, hope stirred.

Lana closed her eyes, once more pretending to pray.

"Help me. Please help." Lana's voice sounded different. Her words felt strange as they left her throat. They were like solid objects regurgitated into the room. The words had shape and form: they were alive; and once released, they went out in search of something incredible.

When Lana opened her eyes, Hailey was sitting up in bed, wide awake now. The expression on her daughter's face was one of bliss, like a child on Christmas morning. She held her hands together in front of her chest, and then slowly, and with great intent, she began to unbutton her nightdress.

Lana leaned back. "What are you doing, honey?" That faint fluttering of hope was gone; the fragment of belief was spent. There was nothing here in this room but a girl who had lost touch with reality and a mother who had failed to protect her.

"I'm *summoning* them." Hailey's breasts looked bigger than when Lana had bathed her earlier; they spilled out of the open neck of the garment, full and firm and lactating. Watery milk striated with pale crimson streaks leaked from the rigid nipples, drawing wet lines down Hailey's bloodless, paper-thin chest.

Lana stared at her daughter's body. It had changed. Something beyond understanding had happened.

The sound of rain clawing at the windows. But it wasn't raining; hadn't rained for days. Spindly, twig-like shadows crept across the walls and ceiling, pasting darkness upon the walls; the bricks and floorboards creaked as if in preparation for the arrival of something glorious. The air turned dusty and grey light seeped from invisible cracks to baptise the room.

Gossamer filaments drifted down from the ceiling, like the webbing of a spider, but longer, firmer, thicker. At the top of each frosted strand there was a small bundle, like an oversized, blackened fist, which slowly began to unfurl and reveal a lighter underside. Dusty petals opening. Striving for the light.

Lana stared at the ceiling, and at the things making their way down towards her.

"What are they?"

"The Slitten." Hailey bared her chest to the room, throwing back her head and closing her eyes in an expression of near ecstasy. The Slitten responded *en masse*. Scores of them dropped like desiccated spiders from the ceiling, rolling across the floor towards the bed. They were shadow and half-light, lines and slashes, more thought than substance. Their features were vague, like stolen shards of daylight trapped in sealed rooms, and their limbs were many and sharp-clawed. When Lana stared straight at them they became blurred, lacking focus. But when she looked off to the side, they solidified and took on form in her peripheral vision. Their desiccated reptilian mouths gaped. The ragged holes in their crisped bodies showed only hollowness within. They were like living fossils, the calcified shells of reanimated prehistoric beasts.

Hailey's behaviour – along with the baggy clothes, the moodiness, the increasing secrecy – all made sense now, at last, in terms of this virgin birth. She had not been impregnated by some boy on the estate, but she had been filled with wonder. And now those wonders had been delivered into their care.

Her daughter, she now realised, was a being of contrasts: guardian and wet nurse; victim and criminal; strength and fragility; darkness and light.

The Slitten crawled up onto the bed, swarming over their birth-mother and obscuring her lower torso. One by one, they reached up and began to suckle, taking it in turns to slake a thirst born in darkness. Lana watched in awe. Her beautiful daughter was now a mother to monsters and for some reason the thought did not fill her with terror or repulsion. Instead, she felt a strong sense of purpose, and the potential solution to their problems began to take on a kind of clarity that she had not even dared to dream of.

Soon the Slitten were satisfied. They rolled off Hailey, slid from the bed, and gathered around

Lana, their movements slow and heavy. They had taken their fill. Their hunger was sated, at least for now.

"Ask them," said a tired voice from the bed, its owner lost in the growing shadows – shadows that had not been there even seconds before. "Ask them again. It's why they're here, to help us. Tell them what you want them to do."

Lana looked at the resting entities, but only out of the corner of her eye. Then she reached out her hands and began to speak.

CHAPTER TWENTY-FIVE

WHEN HAILEY GOT out of bed her whole body felt drained and empty, as if something vital had been siphoned from her during the night. She had a vague memory of her mother coming home in the early hours, and of them having some kind of heated conversation. But the details were fuzzy. Whenever she tried to think about what had been said, she drew a blank. It was as if the majority of her immediate memories had been scraped painlessly out of her brain.

She brushed her teeth, washed her face, and put on her school uniform. Her stomach ached, and the emptiness seemed to grow. She wasn't hungry, but she felt the need to fill a gap inside her body that had not been there when she went to bed last night.

She remembered a dream. Something about a wood or a forest, and a creature (or creatures) that were important to her in some way. That was all; nothing else came when she tried to pinpoint the memory.

"How are you feeling?"

She turned around and saw her mother standing in the doorway, her face pale and drawn. She looked like she'd aged a decade overnight.

"A bit weird."

"I'm not surprised."

Hailey paused in tying her shoelaces. "What do you mean?"

Her mother shrugged her shoulders and pulled her dressing gown tighter. "Don't you remember last night? When I came home?" She leaned against the doorframe.

Hailey shook her head. "The last thing I remember was Tessa's mum coming round drunk and waking me up to give me that telly. She wouldn't take no for an answer because she was so pissed. I think she was trying to make herself feel good by giving us some charity."

Her mother smiled. "Who on earth is this Tessa? Have I met her?"

"She's a friend from school – one of my only close ones. You remember, the girl with the big feet who keeps knocking stuff over."

Mum smiled, but still she looked vaguely ill. "Ah, yes. The clumsy girl. She came round for dinner that time. Broke my bloody vase."

Hailey laughed, which seemed to break the mood. "That's her. She still feels bad about it."

"You look tired, honey. Are you sure you want to go to school? You've had a… well, a rough time."

Hailey stood up and approached the mirror above her dressing table. She combed her hair and tied it up in a loose ponytail. "What's wrong with me? What happened last night? I'm so hungry I could eat a scabby horse, but if I did try to eat anything I know I'd be sick."

"You really should have some breakfast. I've made toast. Just try and eat a slice. If you really insist on going to school, we'll talk properly when you get home." Her mother folded her arms across her chest. "There are still things we need to talk about." She scanned the room, as if looking for something specific. "Have you been having strange dreams?"

Hailey watched her mother in the mirror. Nodded.

"Me too, baby. Scary ones. But I think they're more than just dreams. Last night... things happened last night, when I left you here. Stuff we need to discuss."

Hailey kept her eyes on her mother's reflection in the mirror. "I'm ill, aren't I? There's something seriously wrong with me." Did she have a brain tumour, was that it?

"I think there was something wrong," said Mum. "But now I think you might be getting better." The ghost of a smile crossed her face and then she turned away, heading back to the kitchen. "Come and have some toast."

Hailey finished getting ready. She packed her school bag and made sure that she had all of her books and her pencil case. Giving herself one final glance in the mirror – she didn't look too bad now that she'd made a bit of an effort – she left her room and went to the kitchen.

"Would you like some fruit juice? I could pop out and get some from the shop. Or maybe a cup of tea?"

Hailey sat down opposite her mum. "No. I'm fine. I'll just try a bit of that toast." She reached out and picked a slice off the serving plate. The butter had melted and the toast wilted. When she bit into the toast it was cold. The texture of the limp bread almost made her gag.

"Just a few bites," said her mother, trying to smile and almost making it.

"Where were you last night?" said Hailey, once she'd swallowed the mouthful of bread. "I remember waking up. It was late. Or early. Was that when you got home?"

Her mother looked away. Her eyes roamed over the kitchen surfaces. "Yes, that was me. We had a little chat and I put you back to bed."

"So. Where did you go?"

"I had to go out and see a friend. Nothing you need to know about, not really. Just an errand I had to run."

Hailey chewed the toast. The more she had the more she got used to it. Her stomach still felt empty but it no longer ached. "You're not getting involved in anything crazy, are you?" Her eyes began to sting. The kitchen lights were too bright and they made her head throb.

"No," said her mother. "It's nothing like you think. But this is one of those things we need to talk about. I made a big mistake and it's going to affect us both."

Hailey's ears were ringing. The sound was distant yet incessant, like an alarm. "Okay, we'll sit down and talk tonight, when I get home from school."

Her mother shuffled in her chair. "I might have to go out again later, so it'll probably be late. Will you be okay on your own again, just until I get back?" She paused, not really waiting for an answer. "I promise not to be too long. We can talk then."

"That's fine." Hailey put down the remains of the toast: the soggy piece of crust, with melted butter smeared along its length. "I can watch the TV now, can't I?"

"Yeah, I suppose you can."

Hailey saw the tears sparkling in her mother's eyes, and for a moment she felt like going over there and throwing her arms around her, telling her that she loved her more than anything in the world. But something held her back. She heard a faint skittering noise from the other end of the flat, coming from the direction of her bedroom. Her mind was filled with images of tattered, flyblown shapes falling in tandem from the ceiling. She felt her nipples stiffen and fluid leaked from their tips.

The Slitten.

The thought came to her from nowhere, and rather than summon memories it conjured a feeling, a sensation: then she felt an overpowering urge to protect. She had no idea what was happening – or what had happened last night – but she did know that this was not the time to talk about the situation. But they must discuss things soon, and try to fathom a way of solving their problems. Hailey had the idea that a possible way out had already presented itself, and if she could only remember what it was then she could bring up the subject with her mother.

But not now, she thought. *Not yet. She has to come to the same conclusions on her own first.*

Again, she felt like her thoughts were not her own, that somebody else was putting them inside her head. There was some kind of barrier between them, and she needed to wait until it came down before digging into this subject.

"I have to go, Mum. I'll see you later."

Her mother didn't answer; she was staring into space, her eyes large and moist.

Hailey grabbed her things and left the flat, followed by the nagging suspicion that she was turning her back on something forever. This was not a rational thought, but somehow she felt that once she had walked out the door she would be unable to turn back. The world had altered too much; the fabric of their lives had been picked apart at the seams. Everything was too broken to be repaired, and the only way to change things was through further acts of destruction.

Out on the street there were very few pedestrians, apart from groups of kids on their way to school or to bunk off elsewhere, far enough away from the estate that they wouldn't be seen. Hailey kept her head down. She didn't want to make eye contact with anyone, even her few friends or the few other kids who gave her the time of day and didn't tease or bully her. She wanted to be left alone. Her thoughts required sorting, sifting, putting in order.

Instead of heading along Grove End, in the direction of the school, she turned right and crossed the mini roundabout onto Grove Road. Then she cut through Grove Side and headed towards the centre of the estate.

She knew the man was following her. She had spotted him in his car immediately, waiting at the kerb opposite the old Grove End Primary School. The fat man behind the wheel had watched her intently as she left the block of flats. She had seen him before, many times; she suspected that he had been watching her for a couple of weeks now, always keeping his distance and never hanging around for too long. Today, though, he got out of the car and followed her conspicuously. He stayed a few yards behind, never straying too close, but it was obvious what he was up to. Even Hailey could see that he was purposefully trailing her through the estate.

She turned left onto Grove Crescent, and then used the nameless ginnel to access the Roundpath – the narrow dirt track which ran around the perimeter of the patch of land upon which stood the intimidating structure of the Needle. When she looked up at the tower she saw several phantom images reflected against the windows – those which had not been broken – on the upper floors: a dark, busy mass, a flurry of wings, distant trees that were not really there. Hailey closed her eyes. When she opened them again the few unbroken windows reflected only the blue-grey sky and the pale, slow-moving clouds.

The emptiness inside her reached out towards the Needle. For the first time she had an inkling of the reason why she was drawn here. She yearned for whatever was inside that old building, the secrets it kept within the fabric of its structure. Another world lay between the mortar joints and the connecting members of timber and steelwork, and all Hailey had to do now was find a way to get through to the other side.

She waited at the end of the ginnel, pressing her body flat against an old timber hoarding with a faded motif. When the big man appeared, holding a mobile phone to his ear, he looked surprised for a moment, shocked to find her there. But then he smiled. It was a tired smile, as if he were pulling it up from somewhere dark and painful. He lowered the hand that was holding the phone and put the handset in his jacket pocket.

"What do you want?" She clutched her empty belly. The remnants of whatever she had carried there gave her strength. She could remember now – she had birthed something in the night, a brood that had come to help her and her mother. "Why have you been following me?" The Needle seemed to bend forward behind her, enclosing her within the protective dimness of its shadow.

"Am I really seeing this?" The big man stared up, his eyes huge and wet and unbelieving. "The building… it moved. It actually leaned towards us."

Hailey smiled. "Things are different here, in the middle. Tell me why you're following me and I'll show you." She heard the creaking and groaning of the building behind her. The earth vibrated softly, as if a minor tremor were following a fault line located directly beneath her feet. "I'll show you something amazing."

"I was told to keep an eye on you, and then to come and get you. My boss is a bad man. I was a bad man. But now I don't want to be bad. Not anymore." Tears gleamed on his smooth, round cheeks. "I'm sick and tired of being bad… I want to be someone else now."

The air filled with the sound of the Needle shifting on its foundations. Hailey didn't turn to see, she just listened to the music of its movement:

the high, sharp keening of twisting steel beams and stanchions, the crisp cracking of concrete, the gunshot-popping of old timber frames.

The big man raised his arms above his head. Hailey wasn't sure if he was fending off the sight or trying to embrace it. "I can see trees in there." His voice was quiet, awed. "There's a forest behind the windows. A fuckin' forest…"

Hailey stepped forward, out of the shadow of the Needle. Her feet felt quick and light; her body moved through the air as if carried on invisible wafts and currents. "Come on, Mr. Bad Man. Let's go inside."

"My name's Francis," he said, softly, his gaze still locked onto the Needle.

Francis reached out to her and she took his hand. It was huge, like a slab of meat. She gripped his fingers tightly. She was trying to reassure him, to transmit to him by touch alone that there was nothing to be afraid of, not unless whatever had possessed the building was afraid of you. It was a simple equation, one that even she could work out: Fear plus Fear equals Death. The opposite – because every force must have its equal and opposing reaction – was that Peace plus Acceptance equals Survival. This wasn't something she had ever learned at school: it was knowledge gained from a tantalising glimpse of another world.

And if the price of admittance to that world was suffering, then once the toll was handed over her remaining currency had to be left behind at the door. No change would be given; exact payments only.

Hailey led her giant companion to confront whatever waited for them inside, within, and behind the walls of the estate.

PART FOUR

THE KILLING OF A NORTH-EAST LOAN SHARK

"I won't let anyone hurt you."

– Francis Boater

CHAPTER TWENTY-SIX

THE BLACK-PAINTED steel frame of the bridge formed a shadowy grillage around her as Lana strode along the walkway. Sunlight danced through the gaps, stuttering in bright little flashes to blind her momentarily as she made her way towards the waiting figure she assumed was Tom. The dazzling light behind him didn't allow her to make out any details: he was just a tall, dark silhouette standing with his hands in the pockets of his overcoat.

When she'd called him on the telephone earlier, desperate to hear his voice once Hailey had left her alone in the flat, he had seemed distant and elusive. When he had asked her to meet him here, at a point suspended above the River Tyne, she had at first been filled with trepidation, but then her desire to see him had overcome any doubts prompted by his odd request. Of course she would come, she'd agreed. Of course she would meet him on the bridge.

What else was she supposed to do?

The riverside air was cold. The water below her looked as thick and black as crude oil. People stared at the water from the riverbank on either side – Gateshead and Newcastle – and watched as a small working boat moved slowly under the bridge, following the flow of the river towards its mouth, and then possibly out to the open sea.

Tom didn't turn to greet her when she approached. He just stayed in the same position, staring eastward along the Tyne, perhaps looking for a way to follow that little boat out to sea.

"So what's with all this *Man from Uncle* shit?" She tried to glimpse what it was he was looking at, but all she could see were the things right in front of her: the low-set red and white Swing Bridge with its stumpy blue watchtower, the green-webbed assemblage of the Tyne Bridge, and the broad curve of the river as it swung around to the right beyond these manmade structures. "I mean, why are we meeting here like spies, at the middle of the bridge?"

"I... I'm not sure." He kept staring along the river. Then his gaze drifted down and off to the right, towards the tacky nightclub-boat that was always docked at the south side, beside a grubby concrete access road. His hands remained inside his pockets. "It's just, this has always been my favourite place. Ever since I was a kid, when I used to come down here with my parents, I loved it, the sense of being cut off and standing above everything. And I didn't want to meet you in that awful place – the Grove."

"Why not?" She looked at him. The side of his face was slightly swollen, the skin shiny and red. She'd not noticed before, but there were fresh bruises smudged along the edge of his jaw. "I don't understand."

Finally he turned to look at her, and as he lowered his face towards her the sun blazed behind his head, creating a glaring nova. "Neither do I. There's been some stuff happening that I just don't get. It's like I'm living inside a dream."

"Or like a dream that was living inside you has finally broken free?"

"You, too?"

She nodded. "It isn't just you. I can't explain anything that's been happening, but the only part of it that feels real – feels *right* – is us. You and me. What we seem to have between us." She lifted her hand and opened the fingers, like a pale pink flower. Sunlight bulged through the gaps.

Tom removed one hand from his coat pocket and grasped her wrist. "What's going on? What have we started?" He licked his lips. The nova around his head dimmed as he shifted position, turning fully to face her. He held both of her hands with his own, squeezing them firmly but not so tight that it hurt.

"I don't think it has anything to do with us. Not really. A lot of different things are combining to create something that's bigger than us all. Hailey's condition, that loan shark Monty Bright, his hired hands... and it all starts with the Concrete Grove. I think what's coming through the cracks we've created has always been there, and that it's using our desperation as a doorway." She tried to laugh but all she managed was a sort of croaking sound. "I know how stupid and melodramatic this all sounds, but I've been doing a lot of thinking. I've seen things, stuff that I could never have thought of as real before now."

"I've seen things, too." Tom smiled but it seemed to pain him. He raised a hand and touched the side of his face.

"Those bruises," said Lana. "What happened?"

"Last night. I fell down the stairs. I'd been drinking, and thinking about us."

She could see that he was lying. He couldn't even maintain eye contact; his gaze drifted back to the river, the route to the sea at Tynemouth.

"Don't start lying to me, not now. I think all we have is the truth. If we lose that, then everything will just turn into a series of fictions, all linked by whatever's in the Grove. Like a giant spider in a web." She didn't quite understand her own analogy, but something about the words made sense. It was the image of a giant spider, sitting at the centre of a web made of human life lines and spinning its own stories. Somehow that seemed right: it was an apt image. She could feel it, right down in the marrow of her bones. "Just be honest with me."

Tom stared down at the ground. A soft wind ruffled his hair. He looked back up again, and there were tears in his eyes. "My wife. Helen. You know about her, of course, that she's a paraplegic. She lost the use of her lower body, from the waist down, when the car her lover was driving crashed."

"Yes. You told me all about it." She moved closer to him. A group of teenagers ran by on the other side of the bridge, laughing and throwing coins into the river. Several cars and a bus drove towards the Newcastle side of the river, thumping over the steel joints in the tarmac decking.

"She did this to me." He turned his face so that she could see clearly the bruising. "Last night, she... changed. She became something monstrous and she attacked me. She hasn't been out of that fucking bed in years, but last night she managed to get out and drag herself after me through the house. I fell. She grabbed me and tried to smother me..." he turned away again, ashamed.

The sunlight flashed, making Lana close her eyes for a second. Then she couldn't stop blinking. When he had mentioned monsters, she couldn't fail to think of Hailey: and of the things she'd been carrying inside her. The monsters – if that's what they truly were – she had delivered. Along with these thoughts came ones about Monty Bright. The deformities on his body; the screaming faces trapped in his flesh.

"We can help each other, you and me. If we stick together and use the strength we seem to have when we're side by side." She took a step back. More cars passed them on the roadside. A young couple strolled by, hand in hand; the man stared at Tom, as if he could see something strange about him. Then he looked away. "Last night I went to see Monty Bright. He and his men... they did things to me. Raped me."

Tom made a sound deep in his throat: half sob, half moan.

"I thought I was doing the right thing. I thought they'd leave us alone if I went there, and did what they wanted. But it didn't work out that way." She kept her eyes on his battered face, refusing to look away in shame. Even though she'd kept quiet about what had happened with Hailey last night, she felt that she was being as honest with Tom as she ever had with anyone. She realised now that she'd placed her heart in his hands. All he need do was to squeeze it tight, or open his fingers and let it fall. Either way, it would hurt; but one way would cause far less pain than the other.

"I don't know what you want me to say." His mouth was a slit in his face. His eyes were now hard and empty.

"I want you to tell me that it doesn't make any difference. That you still want me, and still want me to want you. I want you to say that you'll help me. We'll help each other."

Another bus chugged by. Raised voices were carried to them from the riverbank. To Lana, the moment felt as if it might shatter like glass at any minute. "Of course I still want you. I mean, you're the only person I know who's as fucked up as I am."

It was a feeble joke – desperate, really – but in that moment she loved him for even trying to lift the mood.

They walked along the side of the bridge, holding hands and looking up through the steelwork at the wedges of bright sky visible between the girders. Traffic grew heavier and as they approached the south side they began to see people making their way across the arching eye of the Millennium footbridge towards the old Baltic Flour Mill. There must be some kind of exhibition in the new gallery; the redevelopment of the building had raised the profile of the area and brought with it a fresh interest in the local art scene.

"I know a little place where we can have coffee. It's nothing flash, just a greasy spoon café where the taxi drivers go." Tom led her sharp right off the end of the bridge, heading down Bottle Bank, where there was a row of old shop fronts, most of them boarded over. "It's just down here."

A few taxis were parked at the kerb on the narrow cobbled street that led back down to the river's edge. Set amid the timber-boarded frontages were two premises that had not succumbed to financial ruin. One of them was a taxi rank and the other was a tiny café with no name and badly whitewashed windows.

They went inside and sat down at a low table. The place was gloomy; not much light could get in around the patches of white on the window glass. If she twisted her head and leaned across the table, Lana could catch a glimpse of the street outside. "Nice place," she said. "How many Michelin stars does it have?"

Tom laughed. "I used to do a lot of business round here, when these were all going concerns. I have a few clients on Gateshead High Street, too. Whenever I'm in the area I come in here for a morning coffee and a read of the papers. Nobody bothers you here. They all want to be left alone."

There were three other customers in the café. A skinny middle-aged man with a facial twitch sat near the toilet door reading a battered paperback novel, and two other men sat in silence drinking milky tea from large mugs.

"They're all taxi drivers," said Tom. "Nobody else even knows this place exists."

"Except you." She reached across the table and stroked the back of his hand.

"Yeah, except me." He stood and went to the counter, where he ordered two black coffees from a shapeless woman in a long grey sweater and grubby jeans who appeared from a door to one side. She went back through the door and emerged less than a minute later with two mugs filled with what looked like tar.

"You expect me to drink that?" She took the cup Tom offered her as he sat back down, peering into the contents and pretending to be disgusted.

"Just think yourself lucky I didn't ask for it with milk. At least black it's drinkable. Just about." Tom added sugar to his mug from a chipped bowl on the table. The end of the teaspoon was frosted with an off-white crust and the discoloured clusters in the bowl looked like singed crystal meth.

Someone turned on a radio – probably the saggy woman who'd served them coffee – and a droning traffic report filled the empty spaces in the room.

"I have to ask you something." Lana curled her fingers around the mug. The coffee was hot, but she liked the way it made her skin hurt. "Something important."

Tom took a sip of his drink and put down his mug. "I'm listening." His swollen face looked better in the dim light. Not so damaged.

"I plan to-," she licked her lips. "I plan to kill Monty Bright. It's the only way out of this I can see now. I have to kill him." Just saying the words in daylight, even at such a low volume, forced Lana to fully consider their true meaning. It didn't sound so bad, she thought. Not in terms of the chaos invading her life. What was a little murder to add to the mix, especially when the proposed victim was no longer even human? "I need to know if you're willing to help me do that."

Tom stared at her. His face went pale beneath the fresh contusions. He swallowed. The radio droned on. "If you'd said this to me a few days ago I would've run a mile. But now – after everything that's happened – I'm still here. I'm still listening."

Lana paused for breath, took a drink of the scalding coffee, just to drive the moment home, and then continued. "He isn't a man. I think he used to be, a long time ago, but he isn't now. Not anymore. Prolonged exposure to whatever's festering in the Grove has changed him into something else." She examined Tom's face for signs of doubt, or possibly a hint that he might stand up and leave.

"Okay. Go on."

"He showed me something that I still can't quite get my head around. He has these tumours all over him – on his chest, mainly. But they aren't tumours. They're not cancers. I think they're the remains – or maybe even the souls – of the people he's bled dry with his debt. He doesn't stop at money. What he wants from them – and what he wants from *me* – is everything. Everything his victims have to give. He wants it all. He starts with the money, and then the possessions, and then moves on to the flesh. Finally, all that's left is the spirit, and he wants that, too."

Tom leaned back in his chair. The legs scraped loudly across the floor, drowning out the radio newsreader's voice. A fragment of the report caught Lana's attention: "...the prisoner, known locally as Banjo, last night escaped police custody. He is not considered dangerous, but if anyone knows of his whereabouts they are requested to..."

Lana knew the man they were talking about – it was the drug addict they'd seen trying to rip his own face off in the street. *God*, she thought. *Right now, that seems like it happened a lifetime ago.*

She returned her attention to Tom.

He was looking up at the dirty ceiling, as if inspecting it for cracks. Without moving, he began to speak. "Last night my wife physically turned into something else. I meant it literally when I told you that." He lowered his head and looked at his hands, which he laid out flat on the table. He looked like one of those old-time circus sideshow performers, just before they start to slam a knife into the table top through the gaps between their fingers. "She turned into a creature and attacked me. If it wasn't so scary it would be funny," he dipped his head, exposing a tiny bald spot at the centre of his scalp that she'd not noticed before. She wanted to reach out and touch it, to penetrate his armour.

"I think we've both moved way beyond the normal now," she said. "The decisions we make here, the way we act, will define how this all ends. If we ignore the obvious – that there's something, well, *supernatural*, happening, then we're fucked." Talking about these things made her feel that she was actually doing something to fight against the situation. In all the books she'd ever read and all the horror films she'd seen, the main characters only ever admitted far too late that the supernatural had invaded their lives. That was the thing that usually got them killed: a refusal to accept the obvious, no matter how insane it might seem.

Lana was not willing to make the same mistake.

"There's some sort of power in the Concrete Grove and, for whatever reason, it's noticed us. Killing Monty Bright won't send it away, but it will get rid of an immediate threat and give us a chance to think about what we do next."

Tom rubbed a hand through his hair. He winced as he did this, causing his injuries to flare up in fresh pain. "After what happened to me last night, I'm willing to believe that anything is possible."

The radio broadcast changed to a music chart show. The woman behind the counter turned up the volume and began to hum along to the tune. Her feet shuffled dryly across the dusty, crumb-littered floor.

Accompanied by the soundtrack of the latest number one record, playing from a tinny little radio on a shelf in a cheap riverside café, the deal was sealed, the pact was made. Such were the circumstances under which two ordinary people became murderers.

CHAPTER TWENTY-SEVEN

TOM'S CAR WAS parked on the Gateshead side of the river. They left the cafe and headed up the hill, away from the water, to the small parking area behind a row of terraced houses that had been converted into shops and offices: a solicitors, a print shop, a DVD rental outlet.

They sat in the car and stared through the windscreen, across the short cobbled lane at the tall wall guarding the yards at the rear of the buildings. The wall was topped with razor wire and there were No Parking notices painted across the garage doors.

"I'll drop you back at your place," said Tom.

Lana gripped his hand on the steering wheel. "Thank you."

He nodded. Started the car.

They drove back across the bridge and along the bypass, heading towards the Cramlington exit. The traffic was heavy but it moved freely.

"How about driving past your street on the way? I want to see where you live."

Tom glanced at her, and then returned his gaze to the road. "Why? It's just a normal house on a boring street outside boring old Far Grove."

"Because it's a part of your life I know nothing about. I've only seen one side of you – the side that comes to visit me and takes us on day trips."

"And agrees to help you kill people." He said it without a trace of sarcasm. He wasn't making a joke.

"Yes. That part, too. The part of you that wants to help me, no matter what the cost."

They both fell silent for a while, and only when they saw the first road sign for Far Grove did Tom break that silence: "Okay. We'll swing by my place first, just so you can see how dull and tragic my life really is." This time he smiled, but it seemed slightly forced, as if he was trying just a little bit too hard to act normal.

Lana watched the streets go by. The houses were mostly suburban new-builds, residential boxes made by development companies to house people who didn't care about period detail and a sense of history. Red bricks, plastic window frames, double glazing. A small plot of garden, a garage and a concrete drive. It was all so strained that Lana felt as if the image might crack, like something painted onto a sheet of glass.

"This is mine. Ours." Tom drove slowly along his own street, not even looking at the houses. "Number Sixteen."

"I didn't really have you down as a new-build man. I thought you might live somewhere a little more... well, interesting."

"It was Helen. Her dream. She always wanted to live in a nice middle class area, with a new kitchen and a driveway. Flowers in all the borders and a fucking rotary washing line on the back lawn." His voice was filled with bitterness. Lana could hear it, like a whining sound behind the words. "Her cosy little fantasy."

"I'm sorry. I shouldn't have asked you to bring me here."

"No." Tom stopped the car and then turned it around in the road to face the way they'd come, performing a neat three-point turn. "It's good that you see all the sides of me." He still hadn't looked at his house. The curtains were closed. None of the windows were open even a crack. "There are things in that house that I never want to go back to, but I know I will. I can never leave for good."

She knew that he meant the memories, and the elements of the life he and his wife had stored there behind the closed doors and windows, but somehow she got the feeling that there was another layer to what he was telling her, a subtext that she couldn't quite grasp. It was puzzling, and slightly disturbing. He seemed to have changed from the last time she'd seen him. Nothing major, just subtle details about his character that she couldn't even attempt to isolate without feeling that she was simply reading too much into his reactions.

But *something* about him was different. She could feel rather than see those changes, but nonetheless they were there.

"I'll take you home," he said, as the car approached the end of the road. "We can talk more there, away from this mess that I've made."

From one mess to another, thought Lana. *But at least this one's of your own making.*

She felt guilty for pulling Tom into her problems, yet at the same time she was grateful that there was at least someone she could turn to for help. Other than Tom, she had no one. Her life had emptied of real friends as soon as Timothy had taken it upon himself to use murder and suicide as a solution to his problems.

But wasn't that now what she was about to do? Wasn't it exactly the same as Timothy had done?

No, she thought. *It's different.* But in what *way* it was different she couldn't tell. Was she more justified in murdering a rapist loan-shark than he had been in killing people-trafficking gangsters? Could you even define crimes in this way, deciding which was worse and calculating what would represent a right and just punishment? Wasn't it all just vigilante justice, like some absurd *Death Wish* film? If that were the case, then she suspected she made a shitty Charles Bronson substitute.

"What's so funny?" Tom's voice pulled her out of her thoughts.

"I'm sorry. I didn't realise I was smiling."

"You laughed. I was wondering what the joke was. I could use a joke right now."

"I think we both could." They were entering the Grove now. A group of teenagers dressed in gaudy tracksuits and hooded sweatshirts were standing on the corner of Far Grove Way, staring down the passing traffic. Tom glanced at them. He smiled.

"Jesus, there's always kids hanging about." Lana turned away.

"Little shits," said Tom. Something hit the side of the car – a stone, a bottle – and Tom slammed on the brakes. The kids ran off in the direction of the skateboard park, laughing and pushing each other as they moved as a pack along the middle of the street.

"*Cunts*." The amount of venom in his voice shocked her. This was the first time Lana had heard him use such extreme language.

"Forget it," she said. "It isn't even worth getting upset about."

Tom put the car into gear and it moved forward, but at a slower pace than before. He kept glancing into the rear-view mirror, looking for someone upon which to take out his frustration. This was another change: the anger, the barely repressed aggression. It frightened her more than she could say.

Tom parked the car outside the flats but made no move to get out.

"Are you coming in?" Lana took off her seatbelt and waited for him to respond.

"Sorry," he said. His voice sounded rough and hoarse. "My head's all over the place right now. I'm finding it difficult to stay focused. Everything that's happening… it's just confusing me."

"Everything with us?" She placed her hand on his knee and squeezed lightly. Just a small gesture; it was all that she dared.

"No, not just that. Things are spinning out of control. It feels like being at the centre of a whirlwind and watching the edges come apart." He turned and looked directly at her for the first time since they'd got in the car. "Know what I mean?"

Lana took her hand off his knee. "Yes. Yes, I do. I know exactly what you mean. It's happening to me, too – there are things I haven't told you yet but really should. Other stuff that's happened to me and Hailey." She took a deep breath. "Come up to the flat and we'll talk."

Tom opened the door and got out of the car. He still looked slightly dazed, as if he hadn't slept for days, but he was a lot calmer than before. He went round to the passenger side and opened the door for her, stepping back onto the kerb. "Madam," he said, and this time his smile looked natural.

"Thanks," said Lana, stepping out of the car. She took her keys from her purse and walked towards the flat, certain that he would follow.

Once they were inside, with the door locked, Lana began to relax.

"New TV?" Tom was standing beside the set Hailey had been given, reaching out to touch the screen.

"No. The mother of one of Hailey's friends brought it round. A drunken act of charity." She put down her bag and headed for the kitchen, craving a drink. "Wine okay?"

"I'm driving, but why the hell not? I mean, after all the shit that's been raining down on us lately I doubt a drink's going to kill me." Again he smiled, and again it was a normal expression, completely unforced, if a little stiff and weary. "So you weren't here when this woman brought the TV?"

"I was out. At Monty Bright's gym." She took the stopper from a half-finished bottle of cheap white Zinfandel and poured the wine into two glasses. Her movements were forceful and exaggerated; she felt angry that he kept talking about the stupid television.

"Sorry." Tom walked over to where she was standing. He stopped on the other side of the partition shelves and reached for one of the glasses. "I'm babbling. I feel like I'm already drunk."

"Well," said Lana, "maybe a couple of glasses of this crap will sober you up." She raised her glass and tilted it. "Chin-chin."

They both drank in silence, not lowering their glasses until they were almost empty.

"I think we needed that," said Tom. "Okay. I'm assuming you have a plan." He didn't say the word, but it stood between them like a third presence in the room: *Murder*.

"Yes, I have a plan. There's something you need to know – to see, actually. I can't explain it to you without showing you, and even then you need to look sidelong." She went to the fridge and took out a fresh bottle of wine. Her hands shook as she opened it.

"I'm struggling to keep up with you here." Tom took the bottle from her and finished the job, then poured the wine into their glasses. He kept drifting away from her: one minute he was there, in the moment, and the next his eyes seemed to fog over and he was elsewhere.

"I need you with me, Tom." She moved closer to him, placing a hand on his elbow. "You have to be right here beside me, not thinking about anything else."

Tom smiled, and she didn't like the look of his face: sickly, feverish. For a moment he looked like a crazy man, standing there in her kitchen with a big shit-eating grin on his face and a bottle in one hand. Right then, he looked like a killer. Lana was torn between feelings of gratitude and fear.

"Are you here? Are you with me, or are you off somewhere else?"

The smile vanished. His eyes regained their focus. "Yes. Sorry. I keep doing that... drifting off inside myself. My mind's wandering. There's too much... too much going on."

She walked into the lounge area, clutching her glass. Her steps felt light, as if she were floating an inch above the carpet. This whole conversation felt like one she'd dreamed before, or maybe it was a premonition of a dream she'd not yet had. Even these thoughts were dreamlike; as vague and elusive as handfuls of dust.

She walked to the hallway, stopping and turning around to face Tom. "Listen, this is really fucked up. Okay? What I'm about to show you – you've never seen anything like this before." She put down her glass on the floor, standing it next to the skirting board.

"Do you ever get that feeling?" said Tom, his shoulders slumping. "You know the one, where everything feels like its slipping out of your control. Like that dream, where you're running on sand, moving your legs as fast as you can, but you're getting nowhere. You're just running on the spot while the world flows by, quick as a flash." He looked like he might faint; his face was pale and his pupils were tiny black pinpoints at the centre of his eyes.

"Come on. Stay with me. I need you." Lana was beginning to doubt that he was capable of what she had in mind – something had happened; he had changed too much. Was it something he'd experienced last night, back at his cosy little semi in suburbia? "What's gone on? Why are you being like

327 Gary McMahon 327

this? It's like you're on drugs or something." Was that it? Had he turned to chemicals to try and tune out the madness around them?

His head snapped forward and he looked directly at her, his pupils returning to their natural size. "She's not the person she used to be. Helen... she's become someone else. Some*thing* else." There was such a look of imploring in his face that it made her feel sick.

"Stop feeling so guilty about betraying your wife. We didn't set out to hurt her."

Tom shook his head. "No, that's not what I mean."

"I *know* what you mean. We all change. Every one of us, and sometimes we have to leave people behind. You and me, we've changed, too. We've come together, changing from individuals to become a team." She believed approximately half of this – the rest was said just to put him at ease, to make him less self-pitying. "Everybody changes. People get hurt. That's just how life is for the likes of us."

Tom leaned against her. She could feel his erection pressing against her thigh.

"We're all victims. Every one of us. None of us gets out of this unscathed." She kissed him, and he responded with force, pushing her backwards so that she slammed into the wall. She lifted one leg, wrapping it around his thighs, and pulled at his hair with her right hand while the left hand rubbed at his back, his arse. "*We're all hurting*," she whispered, between kisses. "*We all get hurt.*"

She fumbled with his trousers, tugging them loose and pulling them down as far as she could. She slid one arm down between their bodies and grabbed his cock, pulling that, too, so that he moaned in a mixture of pain and anticipation.

"Are you sure?" His voice was shaky.

Lana nodded. "It won't hurt, not if we're careful."

He bit at her throat, licking under her chin, and slammed his body against her. His hands grabbed at her clothing, ripping her T-shirt and rolling her leggings down past her waist.

When the telephone rang she didn't even hear it, not until he stepped back, blinking, looking like a man who had just been rudely awakened from a dream. Lana's hand was damp. He had peaked before they'd even begun...

"What?" then she heard the sound of the telephone. "Just ignore it." She kicked off her shoes and leggings and stood there in her torn T-shirt and knickers. Her legs were shaking; adrenalin coursed through her body, putting her on edge and ridding her body of the aches and pains. This was a fight-or-fuck moment, and her flesh knew exactly which of the two acts it had chosen.

"No," he said, tucking in his shirt and buttoning up his trousers. His cheeks were flushing a bright shade of red. "You should get that." He looked ashamed, as if he'd been caught in the act of something terrible.

She walked across the room, her bare legs growing cold now that the heat of the moment was gone. She was still wearing her black socks. She felt vaguely ridiculous. Her hand was sticky, so she wiped it on her T-shirt.

Lana picked up the phone and tried to ignore Tom, who was shuffling about near the hallway. "What." The coldness in her voice made her feel better.

"What kind of welcome is that for an old friend?" Bright's voice was even colder than her own.

Lana felt as if her guts had just dropped into her uterus. Everything between her legs tightened like a fist at the sound of his voice. Memories of the night before came flooding back: the rubbery feel of his wetsuit against her skin, the groping hands, the hard dicks, the brutal invasion of her private self that she could never put right, the emotional damage she could not ever repair. If Tom was different today, then so was she – and this person, this *monster*, was the reason why.

"What do you want?" Her voice was an octave higher than she would have liked, and she hated herself for showing fear in that way. Fear was exactly what he wanted, what he thrived upon.

"Oh, Lana... Lana, Lana, Lana: you always want to get right down to business, don't you? No small talk, no chit-chat. A man could quite easily get offended, you know." His laughter was horrible. There was no other word for it. The sound provoked such a sense of horror within her that for a moment she felt like weeping.

"Tell me what you want or I'll hang up the phone." Her voice wavered again.

The laughter stopped abruptly. "I have her."

Lana had no idea what he meant. "Listen, Bright, I don't have time for your bullshit."

"Time... ah, yes. Do you realise what time it is?"

Angry, afraid, baffled, she glanced at her wristwatch. It was 4:30 PM.

I have her.

Hailey should be home by now. Her High School was only a short walk away, in Far Grove.

I have her.

Even if she'd dawdled back from school, walking slowly and daydreaming in that way of hers... even then, she should be home by this time.

"Where is she... where?" Her hand gripped the receiver. Tom walked up beside her and raised his eyebrows: *What is it?*

"She's safe," said Bright. All trace of humour had left his voice. It was his turn to be 'all business'. "Don't worry about that. She hasn't been harmed. Not yet."

Lana's stomach clenched; knots tightened inside her body.

"She isn't here, with me, but she's safe. One of my associates has her. He called me earlier to say that he had everything in hand. You remember Francis, don't you? The big lad?"

The giant. Boater. Francis Boater. He was the one who'd spoken out – albeit briefly and ineffectually – when they'd all been down there in Bright's basement room. It was a slim hope, but at least it was something: he'd shown signs of regret, remorse and doubt. Maybe he was keeping her safe, and hadn't laid a hand on her young body. Perhaps this giant was in fact her best chance for safety?

"So what do you want?" This time her voice was steady. Quiet, but resolute.

Tom grabbed her wrist but she shook him off. She couldn't deal with him now.

"I want you to come and see me, Lana. I know that's what you had planned anyway, there's not much I don't know right now. I'm in a special position, with access to all kinds of information." He chuckled softly. It felt like his breath was right in her ear. "I have friends in low places, you see. *Very* low places."

"When?"

"Tonight. Midnight. The witching hour. It's so appropriate, isn't it? I'll be here alone... well, apart from Terry and some friends that can't really be classed as *being here*, not really. I suppose you could say they're partway here, and partway somewhere else."

"What will you do when I get there?" It couldn't be sex, not this time. There was no reason for such extreme methods. Last time, she had gone too willingly. The friends he mentioned were not the ones from before. She suspected that he was talking about another kind of friend entirely.

"I think you and me need to have a proper chat. A wee talk about things. It's about time we put our heads together and discovered all our common concerns." He was almost whispering now.

"Common concerns?"

"Well, your daughter for one. She seems to have gained access to somewhere I'd like to go – a place I've been trying to find for a long time. I don't know how she's done it, or what she's used as a key, but a door has opened to let her in. And I want her to do the same for me: to open it up and escort me inside so I don't get hurt or killed or changed into a fucking werewolf."

"I have no fucking idea what you're talking about." She closed her eyes. The dream that had become her life was taking another violent twist, leading her down a road she wasn't keen to follow.

"Oh, you will. Once we have our talk, Lana, you'll understand everything." He cleared his throat: a small cough, dry and delicate. "Until midnight, then. Then we can get this show on the road."

Lana was about to speak again, but the line went dead.

"What did he want?" Tom stood there with his hands crossed over his belly, unsure whether to touch her or keep his distance.

"I don't know what he wants, but I do know what he's going to get."

Tom backed away. Just a single step, but it was enough to tell her everything she needed to know about the balance of power in this relationship. Tom's help was limited now; his strength was finite, and he had almost reached the end of his reserves. He was merely a helper, an assistant.

It was up to Lana now. She had to take charge.

"Come on, Tom. There's something I need to show you."

"Is it the thing you were going to show me earlier, before?" He looked away, embarrassed by his premature reaction before the phone had interrupted them.

Lana didn't care. Not now. All that was over; there was something else to be done. "Yes, that's right. I'm going to show you how we'll kill that bastard and get my daughter back."

CHAPTER TWENTY-EIGHT

"I WON'T LET anyone hurt you." Boater stared at the girl, wondering if she'd ever wake again. "I promise…" She wasn't moving. She hadn't moved for what seemed like hours. He was pretty sure it was late – it certainly felt as if they'd been there all night, maybe even a lot longer than that. But the windows were covered with curtains of foliage and very little light was able to get through the dense green drapery.

When he'd followed her into the Needle everything he'd been feeling for the past few days had come into sharp focus. The vague yearning, the newly developed sense of shame, the fact that he no longer felt the urge towards violence… it all coalesced into a big ball of hurt inside him, at his core, and he had realised that he never wanted to hurt anyone again.

Somewhere deep inside the spirit of Francis Boater, a trigger had been pulled. Now all that remained was a delayed detonation: the single gunshot that would signal the completion of his redemption.

He'd had a long time to think about things, here in the seething darkness. He remembered his countless childhood agonies: his mother, the whore, who had made him watch while she entertained her clients;

the constant struggle with his weight, and the fights he'd been in because of hurtful schoolmates. Then, after leaving school, there was the amateur boxing and the weight training that made him feel so alive and full of self-worth; the many emotionally-damaged women who'd been drawn to him because of his physical bulk and his capacity for violence, and then been repelled and ran from him for exactly those same reasons. And finally there was his time with Monty Bright, when he'd become a hired hand, a lump of muscle-for-sale: a Bad Man.

His entire life had been a tapestry of pain, an intricate pattern composed of interlinked traumas. Only now could he stand back and take in the full scarred picture. The girl had enabled him to see what had been so fucking obvious all along.

When he'd walked into the building she had slowed down until he was level with her, and then she'd taken his hand, encouraging him. They'd walked deeper inside, hand in hand, and Boater had felt a connection deeper than any other he'd experienced in his life. This girl, this small, vulnerable victim he had been sent to abduct, was his saviour.

They'd come into this room, and she had lain down on the floor, curling up her legs into a position that made her resemble a resting infant. Then, just as the shadows began to crawl across the walls and the sound of unseen trees creaking and leaves whispering in a wind he couldn't feel started up all around them, she'd spoken to him:

"Keep me safe," she said, her small eyes watching him in the darkness. "Watch over me and make sure I'm not harmed."

"Of course I will," he replied, his body growing cold but his spirit starting to rise. "I promise."

"I'm tired." Then the girl had closed her eyes. And she had not opened them again since.

"I promise," he said now, hours later. The room had changed around him, becoming outside rather than in, taking on a quality of the external.

Thick fingers of creeping vines had sprouted from the walls, covering them like some kind of blight. The concrete floor had erupted in places, and thick roots had burst through, snaking in loops to return underground. The ceiling was now a dense canopy of leaves. When he looked up, Boater could see distant starlight through the heavy matting. The moon was full, even though outside, in the old world he had left behind, the moon had been a mere crescent.

Boater wasn't afraid. None of this felt threatening. The real threat came from out there, back in the urban wasteland he'd turned his back on. The feral kids, the clamouring debtors, and Monty Bright's lust for whatever power lay at the heart of the estate. But in here, sitting under the whispering canopy and held tight within an enclave of ancient trees, there was nothing to fear but the badness inside him – and that was something he was now abandoning, like so much unwanted rubbish.

"I was lost before, Hailey." He knew that she wouldn't respond, but had faith that she could at least hear him. "I was stumbling around out there, not even knowing who I was or what I could be if I really tried. But now that you've found me, I can see the potential I've always had. I can sense another man locked up inside my skin, and he's fighting to get out." Tears poured down his cheeks but he didn't wipe them away. They were good and clean and pure; a baptism in this new world he'd found. Or had the place in fact found him? "He isn't a Bad Man. Oh, no. He's a good 'un, this one. He's the good Francis Boater." He was smiling. It felt strange, as if he'd never been able to smile before. He supposed that he hadn't, not really. Not like this.

He got up and walked towards the door. It was closed, but it no longer resembled a normal door set within a fabricated frame. This door was a solid slab of living wood: a natural barrier. There was no handle, no keyhole. He reached out and pushed it open. The door swung on hinges of fibrous vines, helped on its way by the weight of Boater's body as he leaned against it.

Beyond the door there was a crumbling section of concrete wall. Where before there had been a long grey corridor filled with dumped trash, there was now a shadowy landscape of trees and bushes and uneven ground that bled into a thick, syrupy blackness. The broken concrete wall looked like ancient ruins against this dark backdrop. Rotten teeth of brickwork poked up through the ground here and there, like reminders of another forgotten time in history.

A series of oak trees stood proud and massive and implacable, forming a tight circle around him. Darkness bulged in the gaps between their trunks. It looked as if the trees were protecting the small, ruined room in which Hailey Fraser now slept...

"The Grove," whispered Boater.

He turned around and saw that the door was shut. The concrete wall was covered in a layer of plants; leaves and stalks criss-crossed to form a natural skin over the man-made shelter.

The landscape was gradually smothering the unnatural structure.

There were sounds of movement in the undergrowth. Nocturnal creatures hunted for food, made their way between entrance holes to their sets and burrows and led their young on secretive night-time journeys, exploring the limits of their world. Boater looked around, at the strange florae which hid so many scurrying scavengers. Huge hand-like leaves twitched beneath his gaze, exotic flowers closed their petals over bulging stigmas and stamens, and the tall stems of large plants shuddered like eager lovers in the night.

Boater fell to his knees, raising his hands in a mockery of prayer. The trees creaked; their language was splintered, unknowable. A chorus of plant life created a kind of song with nothing but their excited, jittery motion.

The vast, eternal woodland stretched away into a primeval forest of forever outside the circular grove of ancient oaks. The borders swelled fractionally, increasing in size as the landscape fed from the dreams of a broken man with nowhere left to go. He could almost feel the place breathing.

Somewhere out there, at the edge of his imagination, Boater knew that there was a better place, an alternative to the world he had always known. But he couldn't enter that place – he didn't have permission to stray past its invisible boundaries.

Yet still, he felt that he was being allowed to know a little of its history.

Whatever power he had stumbled across here was neutral and existed in a realm where human terms like good or bad meant nothing. Tattered and flyblown, the energy stored here responded only to human emotion – until then, it lay dormant, a battery awaiting a charge. But the Concrete Grove estate was a receptacle for negativity: only failure and regret could be produced in such a misbegotten location.

So the power here had mutated, becoming a reflection of the stew of fear and desire upon which it fed. Boater sensed that over time things had altered here, and once-ambivalent creatures had evolved into ravenous beasts, taking on grotesque faces. New shapes had formed amid the dregs of muddy magic, and they brought with them brand new hungers.

This place – Monty Bright's so-called 'splinter of Creation' – had eventually been polluted by the world inside which it was hidden. And toxins had leaked back out through rips and fissures, slowly returning to the world outside the Grove, but in other forms entirely.

This realisation hit Boater like a blow to the stomach. He felt unmoored from his life for a moment, as if his entire body had been shaken off the planet by a violent force.

"If this is a dream, or if I'm lying dead somewhere and I've come here on my way to someplace else, please let it never end. Let me stay here forever." He clenched his fists and held them high, making a promise that he could never put into words. This vow came from deep inside, beyond blood and tissue and bone: this was the promise of the man who was imprisoned in the hidden chambers of his own heart, the fabled Good Man that he had never been allowed to become.

"I promise," he said, not even knowing what he meant by those words. But the Good Man knew. He understood everything, even the things which lay beyond words, behind the mask of language.

The Good Man knew it all.

"I promise."

And the Grove responded as it always did: with infinite patience.

After a while Boater felt calmed. His tension slipped away, lifted from him by the tranquillity which had returned to the Grove. The undergrowth was still and silent. The night felt empty and airless. The stars flickered in the vast black sky, providing just enough light so that he could see.

He stood and returned to the room, going back through the hewn timber door and closing it firmly behind him. When he looked, it was a normal door once more. Cheap plywood panels, a plastic handle, steel hinges.

He turned to face the gloomy interior of the room. The rate of growth across walls and floor had intensified, making the mulch beneath his feet seem thicker and the covering on the walls even denser than before.

Hailey's sleeping body was obscured by what he at first thought was a dark cloud, or a mass of shadows. But as he moved further into the room, drawing closer to the girl, he saw that she was being shielded by scores of tiny, coloured birds. There was no sound; they didn't move. The entire tableau was like a painting, a still-life image.

Then, just as the birds noticed him, movement returned to the scene: their wings beat faster than his eyes could discern, creating a Technicolor blur; the sound of humming filled the air.

"Don't hurt her..." But he knew that the birds were not here to cause the girl harm. The birds, like Boater himself, were intent on protecting Hailey. They would see that she was safe.

"Safe and sound," he said, sitting down on the floor nearby. He was too afraid to move any closer, in case the birds mistook him for a potential enemy, yet he wanted to remain at her side until the birds took her from him and set her free in this world. So he sat there on the soft forest ground – no concrete now; just damp earth and rotting vegetation – and stared at the hummingbirds in wonder.

Whatever happened next, he knew that he had a role to play. For once in his life, Francis Boater felt like he might just make a difference.

CHAPTER TWENTY-NINE

TOM HAD TAKEN drugs in the past, when he was a student. It was something he'd done only occasionally, whenever he'd been hanging out with a certain group of friends who were into the scene. Just a few joints, one or two tabs of LSD, and, once, a line of cocaine snorted from the top of a toilet cistern in a Newcastle nightclub. He'd never enjoyed the loss of control, so his drugs phase had lasted all of five weeks. After that he had never felt the urge to try them again, and he drifted away from those friends anyway, moving on to a group whose drug of choice was alcohol.

Now, walking alongside Lana through the streets of the Concrete Grove, he felt as though he had once again ingested a mild hallucinogen. In truth, he'd felt this way for days. His mind was lost in a soft fug, enveloped in a mist that kept shifting and altering the way he felt and how he viewed the world around him.

Last night, when he had been stalked and then attacked, was the culmination of these feelings. He knew that it hadn't happened – nothing so absurd could possibly be real – but at the same time he also knew that there was in fact the corpse of a sea cow at the bottom of his stairs.

"Hold my hand." Lana grabbed his and clutched it tightly. "The last time I made this journey I got lost."

His mind raced for an instant, and then slowed right down, as if that fog was getting thicker. "Lost? How do you mean, lost? It's only five minutes away."

She squeezed his hand again, as if she were seeking reassurance. But Tom felt incapable of giving her what she wanted. His strength was gone; he was a shell, a husk, an empty shape walking what felt like a predetermined path towards damnation.

"I know. But I kept going along streets and ginnels and coming out where I shouldn't. And it was never the same place twice. I felt like somebody was rearranging the streets as I walked along them, trying to make sure that I didn't know where I was going. It took me ages... ages..."

The sky was vast and clear. Stars shone brightly, like tiny light bulbs strung across the blackness. The moon was a slender curve of silver.

Tom tried to remember what they'd done since Monty Bright's call, but he had only a vague memory of drinking bland white wine and listening to Lana talk about her daughter. There was little sense in doing anything else. They didn't know where Bright's man had taken Hailey. It could be anywhere, even somewhere off the estate. All they could do was try to kill some time before meeting the loan shark on his own terms. Lana was desperate. She had even got out photographs at one point, and made Tom look at snapshots of them both in happier, more prosperous times. There had been tears, and then there had been rage. Finally, like an afterthought, there had been another failed attempt at lovemaking.

It was all a blur. Nothing was fixed in his mind. If he tried to grab hold of a specific recollection, Tom felt that it might slip from his grasp like a wet, thrashing fish.

"Nearly there," he said, just to hear the sound of his own voice. When he looked up at the tops of the streetlamps, he saw strange writhing motion at the centre of the fluorescent glow: foetal light; unborn illumination. His ideas were just as crazy and confused as his emotions.

When they reached the top end of Grove Lane, near the junction with Grove Street West, it was apparent that the door to Bright's gym was unguarded. There were no burly men waiting outside, and the shutters were down across the windows. Tom could hear music from the Unicorn, the pub around the corner. He'd been told stories about that place, and none of them had happy endings. It was an old-school Northern boozer, with dusty wooden floors to absorb the blood from fights, and the landlord kept a baseball bat behind the bar just in case things got out of hand.

"It's open, just like he promised." Lana pushed open the main door of the gym – a heavy wooden barrier with a steel kickboard along the bottom and wire mesh over the small safety-glass window pane at the top.

Darkness seemed to bleed out through the doorway, but Tom knew that it was simply an illusion, another rogue vision.

"Come on. Let's go up." Lana led the way, letting go of his hand as she crossed the threshold. He knew that he could run away now that her attention was focused elsewhere, but somehow he managed to convince himself to stay.

Get it over with, he thought. *Then you can go home and see what's what.*

Somewhere at the back of his mind, where he was struggling to keep it pinned down, a voice said: *you don't really want to go home. Not ever again. You know exactly what's what.*

Tom followed her inside, every inch of him screaming to turn around and leave. They had come here to commit premeditated murder, and they wouldn't get away with it. People like them never managed to commit a crime without being caught. Only the real criminals went free, boasting about their dirty deeds as they planned the next one.

Monty Bright had killed people. Everybody knew this; it was a fact, as much as local gossip was capable of producing such a thing. But the police had never managed to link him to any of the victims he was supposed to have either murdered himself or had dispatched by others. He was always somewhere else, with someone who would sign a statement or swear in court that they'd been with him all night.

No, only one-off murderers got caught. They always did. This was another fact of the streets.

They walked past an open doorway on their right, and Tom paused to look inside. There was a boxing ring in the centre of the room, and various heavy bags and speedballs set up along the walls. He thought he saw someone shadow boxing, but when he looked again it was simply a shadow.

It moved like a pro, bobbing and weaving and ducking, fighting itself back and forth across the length of grubby wall.

More tricks of the mind; another absurd mental hiccup.

If he wasn't careful, he'd see a sea cow lurching towards him across the floor, dragging its bulk over the exercise mats and around the piles of free weights and medicine balls...

"This way. I remember... from last time."

He followed her up the steep flight of stairs, gripping the handrail as he climbed. The walls leaned towards him, creating a vertical wedge into which they moved. The sound of the stairs creaking seemed to happen a second or two behind each footfall, as if there was some kind of aural delay. He kept his eyes fixed straight ahead, watching Lana's narrow back and her slim backside, as she gained the upper landing.

They paused there, outside another door.

"He's in here," Lana whispered. "This is his office." She pressed an ear against the door and closed her eyes. "I can hear movement."

"You'd better come in." The voice came from the other side of the door. Bright knew they were there; he'd been waiting for them. Of course he had. He'd probably watched them every step of the way after they'd entered the building, sitting behind his desk with his eyes on a CCTV monitor.

"The door's unlocked."

Lana turned to him and nodded. Her eyes were wide and questioning, seeking confirmation that he was still willing to back her up.

"I'm ready," he said, and steeled himself for the unexpected.

Lana turned the handle and opened the door. Light spilled out onto the dim landing. Tom followed her inside. Lamps gave off low-level light, which spilled across the carpet. The walls were covered in framed pictures and portraits. Some of them were nightmarish, others bland and unremarkable. Images of monsters hung next to stiff-backed men in Victorian suits, their eyes narrow and their faces stern and unflinching.

"Come on in," said Monty Bright. "Let's get this show on the road." He sat in his office chair, with his feet resting on the desk and his hands clasped behind his head. His hair was slicked back, tight against his head, and shone in the oddly lambent light. His face looked like one of those paintings: unmoving, placid, hiding real feelings behind an immobile mask.

Another man stood against the wall at the side of the desk. He was broad, dressed in a dark suit, and was wearing leather gloves on his clenched hands. Six or seven old television sets stood on the floor, their screens cracked, their casings dusty and showing signs of handling, clean patches where large swathes of the dust had been cleared as they were carried into the room.

"You remember Terry, of course. And his stump." Monty Bright grinned. For a second his teeth looked false, as if too many of them had been crammed into his mouth. "And you are?" He inclined his head, indicating that he was speaking to Tom.

The other man – Terry – took a single step away from the wall.

"I'm nobody. Nobody important." Tom closed the door behind him.

"Oh, but we're all important here." Bright stood up. He wasn't very tall. "We all have a role to play. This is something I've learned. Even the most humble of us has a part in all this." He picked up a book from his desk – some kind of workout manual. It looked old; the cover was worn and faded. One of the desk lamps – the one situated nearest Bright – flickered twice.

Tom suddenly found the man's name amusing, like an irony that was only now becoming apparent. He wasn't bright at all – he was dark; as dark as they come. Even the light shuddered in his presence.

"Where's my daughter, you prick?" Lana stood with her fists clenched. She looked ready for a fight, perhaps even to the death. She had put on an ankle-length black coat just before they'd left her flat, and she kept it buttoned up to the throat as she confronted the loan shark. Part of Tom wanted her to keep it fastened, but the vengeful side of him couldn't wait to see her open that coat and get things started.

"She's safe, just like I said on the phone." Bright came around to the front of the desk. His chunky shoes, with their inch-high heels, clumped softly on the carpet. Everything to Tom seemed hyper-real, as if the world had taken on extra levels of vividness.

"Where."

Lana stared right at him.

"Is."

She opened her hands, slowly flexing the fingers. "She."

She was utterly in control of the moment.

"My, my..." said Bright, trying for amused nonchalance but failing, and betraying the fact that he was shaken by her apparent lack of fear. "My, but how you've changed, and in such a short time, too. The last time I saw you, you were washing spunk off your skin." He folded his arms across his wide chest. The suit jacket strained at his upper arms and shoulders, as if the seams were about to burst.

"Tell me now, before it's too late."

Terry remained where he was, silent and threatening. Tom felt like he and the other man were simply an audience for this confrontation. The meeting playing out before them was like high drama: the finale to a play whose first two acts had been performed in private.

He watched copies of the scene repeated in miniature on the reflective surfaces of the television screens.

"Remember my associate, Francis? The large man. He has her. I don't know where, he didn't tell me, and I can't get a signal on his mobile. Unless, of course, he has it turned off. I think he imagines he's hunting down some kind of redemption, and your daughter is the means to him finding it."

Lana's posture relaxed. Her shoulders slumped.

"I've had Francis following your pretty little girl for a few weeks now, but lately he's turned against me. I wanted him to bring her straight here, so I could put her downstairs, to keep her safe. But he had other ideas. Or maybe she did."

"What is it you think she can do for you, Bright? A monster like you, trying to put your hands on a young girl. If you think I'll let it happen, you're even crazier than I thought." Her voice was hard and clear. She was unafraid. Tom saw the steel within her, and it was almost enough to make him fearless, too.

"I've been looking for a way into somewhere that's been hidden for a long time. It started for real with this book." He held up the fitness manual. "It gave me the pointers, and I've kept looking for more ever since. It's all in here: the evidence." He leaned back against the desk, too short to actually sit on its top. Instead he just rested his backside against the edge. "It's all in here; all the information I've managed to find. There isn't much, but news about the place isn't exactly in the public domain. Your daughter found an open door, and she's been welcomed inside. She reached out and touched the power at the heart of the Grove, and it liked what it saw. She has a strange combination of innocence and yearning, and it seems that was all she needed to get over there, to the place I've been kept out of for so long."

"What the fuck are you talking about? And what the hell is going on with all these TVs?"

"More evidence."

Right then, as if they'd been waiting for a cue, the televisions sets flickered into life. The damaged screens flared, giving off a dull glow, and there was a series of clicking noises as the old cathode ray tubes sparked into life.

(*Clickety-clickety-click...*)

"What is this?"

Bright smiled. "Oh, just a little light viewing, to demonstrate what I'm talking about." He looked at the screens, his face pale and washed-out, like a degraded image of itself.

Tom glanced at them, too.

On each of the screens there appeared the same scratchy, flickering image: a grove of massive trees, and at its centre what looked like a group of men in Halloween costumes. But the costumes were too sophisticated to be anything other than real – these were monsters, plain and simple. And Tom had already been introduced to their human counterparts.

Their legs were long and muscular, bent back like the limbs of giant crickets or grasshoppers. Their faces looked burnt; they possessed the shiny quality of scar tissue. It was difficult to make them out clearly, because the image was so grainy and incomplete, but there seemed to be five or six of them gathered at the centre of the grove of trees – the same as the number of television sets in the room. They jumped and hopped around the clearing, twitchy and excited.

"These," said Bright, "are my friends. They came to me one night, as I was watching an old porno movie on a TV in some junkie's squalid little bedsit. I can only see them on old television sets, for some reason. They don't show up on digital technology. These monsters are old-school."

Terry took a step forward, staring at the screens. "There's nothing there, Monty. They aren't even switched on."

"Can you see them, Lana?" Bright waited for her response.

Lana simply nodded.

"And what about you – is it Tom?"

"Yes. I can see them." He didn't look at Bright. His gaze was fixed on the screens. Amid the crowd of jittering bodies he was sure that he could make out a familiar shape. If he peered hard enough, and concentrated, he could see what looked like a large sea cow writhing on the ground between their massive, concertinaed legs. "I can see."

"I've seen a lot of things here, in the Grove." Monty's face seemed to slacken; he was turning inward, lost in his own thoughts and memories. "I remember one night, when I was about seven years old, my mother sent me to the Dropped Penny to get my father. He was a drunkard, good for nothing but pissing his life away…"

Nobody moved; the man's anecdote, the sheer force of his memories, acted like a binding agent, bringing them together inside the room.

"When I got there, he was regaling his cronies with stories of his youth – utter bullshit, like always, but they were a captive audience. When I interrupted him, he slapped me hard across the face. Instead of letting him see me cry, I ran away. I headed towards the Embankment. I remember the moon was huge… the stars stared down at me like bright little eyes, and when I saw it lying there in the gutter, breathing white mist into the cold air, I thought I was dreaming. It was a unicorn, like in the books I'd read. Something from a fairytale. But its horn had been sawn off about an inch away from its head, and its face was battered and bleeding. So I knelt down and I started to stroke it, crying and still ashamed – still hurting because that bastard had shown me up in front of the whole pub. The beast died in my arms, with me looking it straight in the eye. And do you know what my only thought was, the thing that kept going round and round in my head? Well, I'll tell you. All I could think of was this: I want to meet whatever did this. I want to see what's fucking crazy enough to kill a unicorn."

The silence snapped, like a rubber band stretched past breaking point. Tom could have sworn that he heard it break.

"Monty, I don't like this." Terry was losing his grip. It was obvious. He was no longer a threat; his fear was nullifying him. He wanted only to be out of the room.

"Fuck this," said Lana. "Fuck you and your sad little nostalgia trip. Where does your man have my daughter?"

Bright turned to her, his face ashen in the television light. "I have no idea. Really, I don't. All I know is that he was following her through the Grove, and he caught up with her. That was the last time I was able to speak to him. That's why I asked you here, to help me find her. To bring her in so we can find out what she knows about that place – the other grove, and the infinite garden beyond."

"Do you really think I'd help you find my own daughter? The person I love most in this shitty world?"

"Of course," said Bright, taking a step towards her. "If the price is right, you'll do anything.

You've already proven that. So let's get this show on the road."

Tom felt ill. The television screens were flickering. Their plastic shells looked soft and malleable. He thought about the famous painting by Salvador Dali, the one with the melting clocks.

"Yeah," said Lana, slowly unbuttoning her coat. Her expression was flat and lifeless, like a death mask. Her voice was low. "Let's get this show on the road."

The creatures Tom had seen a few seconds ago were crammed to the front of each television set, pressing against the grubby, cracked glass and clamouring to be let out. Their faces were squashed, their limbs folded, their squat bodies pulsed and flexed, forcing the screens outward.

He glanced back at Lana just as she let her overcoat drop to the floor. It formed a black puddle around her feet, like spilled tar.

Lana was naked from the waist up. She had on a pair of tight leggings and some grubby running shoes, but her upper body was bare. The Slitten hung like bats from her breasts and beneath her armpits, but he could only see them when he looked to the side, watching them from the peripheral. She'd taught him that first, when she'd shown them to him that afternoon, nesting quietly in Hailey's bedroom.

These, then, were the ultimate response to Bright's media-monsters. The yin to his yang. Everything must have an opposite, and if Monty Bright's hideous soul had helped create the things inside the televisions, then Hailey must have generated the Slitten to oppose them. *Sometimes*, he thought, *desperation can be a positive force.*

Everything that came next happened so fast: much too fast for Tom to fully comprehend the order of events. It was all he could do to keep up with the action, and ensure that he played his part to his best ability.

CHAPTER THIRTY

BOATER WAS SO tired that he could barely move. He'd been stuck in the same position for what felt like hours, ever since he'd gone outside the room to look at the scene which lay beyond the borders of everything he had mistakenly believed to be real.

After that, he had been gradually overtaken by a great lassitude, a strange sense of creeping lethargy that began at his extremities and moved inward. Finally he was unable to move from his spot on the ground at the centre of the oaks. Or even to think about moving. It was nice here, comfortable. The concrete walls had been stripped away, dissolved by the natural growth as he had watched in wonder. Small grey protrusions – perhaps the edges of unearthed foundations – could still be seen amid the thick tangles of low-level greenery, but they were too few and too scattered to matter.

The hummingbirds were still gathered around the girl, but now they had lifted her off the ground. It had taken a long time, and much effort had been expended, but somehow they'd managed to raise her a few inches above the soft, damp earth and they held her there, in a delicate envelope of blurred wings and muted primary colours.

Boater glanced down, at his body. Even this small movement took a long time. His muscles were stiff, unhelpful. Large thorns had burst through his flesh, erupting out of his chest. Branches had punctured his back, to twist inside him and exit through his stomach wall. He was being consumed by nature; this place, this ancient woodland, was absorbing him. First it had taken the building, and now it was going to work on him, transforming his flesh and sinew into a strange new entity – something partly human and partly plant. Soon the human parts would be gone, and all that remained would be an exotic new growth on the ground inside the grove, beneath the wonderful canopy of shading leaves and trembling branches.

Soon Francis Boater would be home. His journey could go no further, but even this far was enough. It was, he thought, a fitting end.

It was strange to consider this place as home, but it felt more homely than anywhere else he had been. His surviving family were scum, his friends were criminals, and the man he worked for was a monster. So why not just stay here, where he was truly accepted? Why not become as one with the loam and the natural fertilizer where he had so easily made his bed?

Another clutch of twigs slid out between his ribs, forcing them apart and weakening the bone. He heard the bones snap dryly, like desiccated wood, but there was no pain to accompany the sound. Herbaceous plant life did not know pain: it simply grew and withered, lived and died, as part of an endless biological cycle. His internal organs had fallen into his lower abdomen, becoming deciduous, like ripened fruit slipping from the bough.

Sunlight cut through the grove's canopy, knifing the air and creating prison bars of light around him. Morning had arrived in this place without him even knowing that the night had ended. Boater sighed; the sound was weak, barely even there at all.

"I'll watch over you," he said, his voice breaking off, fading away. "I..." There was nothing more. He could no longer form the words in his spongy, fungal mouth.

The girl was still hovering above the ground, borne on hummingbird wings in a facsimile of flight. Like a broken angel she hung there, her school uniform hanging in tatters, one shoe on and the other cast away, where it sat beside an eruption of vine leaves. She swayed in the air, unsteady yet in no danger of falling back to earth. Her guardians – the birds that had taken over from Boater as her protectors – would not allow such a thing to happen.

Beyond the grove of oaks, in the denser, sun-dappled growth, large forms moved. Trees creaked and moaned; animals scattered through the undergrowth. Something was approaching, and its intentions were as unclear as everything else here – friend or foe, good or evil, the thing could be anything and everything combined.

Boater had realised as he sat there, sinking into the reality of the grove, that whatever forces converged here, they were ambivalent. Neither good nor evil, they simply existed, waiting for a time when they could be harnessed. Everything here was protected, and hidden within the fabric of the housing estate which had been raised upon the site of the original magical grove. He could see all of this playing out before him, like a projection on a screen. He was now a small part of the history of the place.

If only Monty Bright knew the truth. Perhaps then he would stop looking for something that didn't exist, other than inside the mutated husk of his heart.

CHAPTER THIRTY-ONE

LANA STOOD BEFORE Monty Bright as if she were some kind of Old Testament avenging angel. She held her arms out and thrust her hips forward. The Slitten gripped her nipples with their jaws, pinched loose parts of her flesh with their teeth and claws, clinging limpet-like to her body. She could barely even feel them – there was very little sensation, as if the whole of her skin had been anaesthetised.

"I called and they came." It was true: these things had answered her plea, rallying to her side from the dark places, the spaces between love and hate, fact and fiction… and they were the only weapon she had.

In a moment, they leapt from her body and moved like zephyrs across the floor. Monty Bright barely had time to react before they were upon him, snapping at his legs, his balls, his belly, and tearing at his flesh. She watched with her head turned slightly, so that she could have a clear and unimpeded view of the carnage – she was owed at least that. If she looked straight on, all she saw were dusty shadows converging on a man whose clothing and the skin beneath seemed to shred for no apparent reason.

"Monty!" Terry moved away from the wall. "What the fuck?" To him, this was clearly madness. Lana knew that he could see nothing of his boss's attackers. All he witnessed was the rending of flesh from bone.

Tom acted quickly, which surprised her. He was so far gone by now that she'd expected him to just stand there, like a lost little boy waiting for his mummy to come and save him. But he moved quickly, heading off Terry's assault. The two men came together, colliding at a point to the right of Bright's desk.

They went down fighting. Lana watched as Tom rolled on top, grabbing at his opponent. Terry put one arm – the prosthetic – up to ward off the blows, but Tom's movements were so savage, so compelling, that the arm started to come loose from his stump. The straps gave way; the plastic limb slid down his jacket sleeve, and Tom was left holding it. He stared at the glove-clad hand, the thin metal pistons and the plastic casing, like a child shocked by the complexity of a new toy.

Then, reacting quicker than Terry, who was still wedged beneath him, Tom began to beat the other man about the head and shoulders with his own artificial limb. Under different circumstances, it would have been a comical sight: one man straddling another, and hitting him with a plastic arm. But here, now, sharing a room with monsters, both human and otherwise, Lana felt anything but the urge to laugh.

She turned away when Terry started screaming. Blood washed across his face, into his eyes, his mouth, and rendered his features meaningless.

The Slitten had not taken their time on Monty Bright. Their actions were quick and decisive. He was down on his knees, clawing at the shapes that were crawling across his ravaged body. His suit was torn to shreds, and the wetsuit he wore underneath his outfit and been peeled away in several areas, putting on show his distorted physique.

The faces on his chest squirmed, opening their mouths in silent screams. Arms and legs, hands and feet, knees and elbows, popped in and out of the slashes and gouges in his body. There was no blood beneath the upper layers of muscle: whatever fluids had once kept Bright alive were long gone, and his veins had shrivelled and frayed like liquorice root. His muscle-mass fell away beneath the onslaught of so many small claws, sharp teeth, and Lana saw flashes of dull white bone.

As he fell forward, pitching face-down onto the carpet, the television screens exploded, sending shards of glass in a brittle shower across the room. Burnt, toughened flesh, like scorched leather, sprayed in chunks from the cavities left behind. Whatever monsters Monty Bright had allied himself with were now dead to this world. Perhaps they'd gone back to that other place, the one he spoke of so fondly. Or maybe they had never existed in the first place, and all Lana was seeing were the remnants of Bright's bad dreams as they turned to filth on the office floor.

Calmly, she picked up her coat and put it on, and then walked past Bright's twitching form to pick up his book from the desk. The volume had clearly meant a lot to him, so she thought it might contain some useful information.

Bright made a few noises – like high-pitched farts – but then fell silent. The Slitten were receding now, going back to the dust and the darkness. Their job here was done, and she no longer needed them, so the fuel of her desire was spent.

"Thank you," she said, gripping the book in her hands, pressing it against her chest. She had no idea what kind of power Hailey had invoked, or what kind of monsters their need and desperation had summoned, but at least the beings had not meant them harm. She had the feeling that the energies at work in the Grove were wild, untamed, and only certain individuals could harness them. Hailey had done so inadvertently, but what if Bright had eventually learned a way to purposefully control these forces? For that reason alone, never mind all the rest, he was better off dead.

Flames billowed from the televisions. Each one was like an open kiln, giving off an enormous amount of heat.

"What do we do now?" Tom was standing over Terry. The man wasn't moving, but she didn't think he was dead. Not yet.

"Let it burn," she said, feeling nothing. She walked over to Bright's liquor cabinet and opened several bottles of fine whisky, rum and brandy.

Then she started to pour the fluid over anything that was flammable, even Terry's supine form. "Let it all fucking burn."

The flames spread quickly, and as she and Tom left the room Lana heard the sound of someone stumbling to their feet. She let Tom walk out first and then turned around. Terry was down on one

knee, holding on to the edge of Bright's desk. His
bloody face was pointed at her, his wide white eyes
imploring, asking for mercy.

Lana stepped back into the room and picked up
one of the discarded whisky bottles. She held it by
the neck and approached the kneeling figure. Then,
entirely without guilt or remorse, she pulled back
her arm and clubbed him with the bottle across the
side of his head, sending him crashing back to the
floor. Flames caught at his trouser legs; he tried to
kick them away, but it was too late, the fire was
climbing towards his midriff. He opened his mouth
to scream, but all that emerged was a dry, rough
rasping sound, animalistic in its intensity. His eyes
were empty – there was barely anything left of him
to burn.

Lana turned around and left the heat of the
room, closing the door behind her to hold back the
fire for a little longer, just until they could make it
down the stairs.

Tom was waiting for her at the door. He was
standing with his head bowed, his forehead resting
against the doorjamb. His eyes were closed. "What
have we done?" he asked, as if he were talking in
his sleep. "What have we done here?"

"We've taken care of business." She went to step
past him, entering the cold night. The air felt good
against her skin; it tightened the flesh on her face,
drawing it around her skull, and made her feel like
a different person.

She was just about to walk away when a hand
gripped her shoulder. Spinning around, with both
arms raised, she saw a figure lurching towards her

out of the smoky darkness inside the gym. Eyes that were all big, black pupil loomed into her field of vision, a bleached white face hung in the greying air.

"Get off me!" She pulled away, back-pedalling in the doorway and falling out into the street. Tom was already outside; he had moved aside as she had come stumbling out backwards.

The man stood in the doorway, hands grasping the frame. He was bobbing from side to side like a drunkard.

Lana suddenly realised who he was.

It was the junkie, Banjo. His face wasn't ghostly white at all; it was the bandages, the dressings pulled taut across his ruined features. She recalled the news report about his escape from the hospital and reasoned that he must have made his way back here, back home, and come to the last place he could ever remember being before he lost his mind. His hair stuck out of the bandages in random tufts. His eyes rolled. Those huge dark pupils looked like marbles pressed into the front of his head.

"Go on, now," she said, coaxing him as if he were a child. "Go back inside, out of the cold."

He swayed there, uncertain, trying to focus on the sound of her voice. He was empty: a gap in the shape of a man. Whatever had been done to him it had hollowed out his mind, leaving his head as empty and draughty as an abandoned room.

"Go back in there." She pointed over his shoulder, and finally he seemed to glean some kind of understanding. Lumbering like an injured beast, he turned clumsily on his heels and staggered back inside, closing the door behind him. Smoke billowed out around the edges of the door, and Lana felt no guilt for sending him away to burn.

It's for the best, she thought. *What the hell kind of life could he ever have? He's ruined; this place has ruined him, just like it ruins everyone.*

They walked quickly back to Tom's car with the sound of sirens slicing the air, cleaving it like blades as the emergency services raced towards the estate. Someone – a rare concerned neighbour – must have noticed the smoke or the flames and called the authorities. The sirens drew closer as they reached the vehicle, and when they closed the doors they could still hear them clearly, as if the windows were rolled down.

"What do we do now?" Tom started the engine.

"We get away from here. I need to look at this book, see if it gives me any clues to where that fat bastard might've taken my daughter. It's all I have to go on. He won't hurt her, I know that now. From what Bright said, the fool seems to think that she's his only shot at salvation. Funnily enough, she's probably safer with him, wherever they are, than she is with me right now." She smiled, but there was no humour there. It felt more like a scowl.

They drove away from the Grove, heading out towards Far Grove.

"Where are we going?" Lana stared through the windscreen. She could see firelight reflected in the glass.

"My place is less than five minutes away. You can look at the book there, and it's my turn to show *you* something." He was gripping the wheel so tightly that his knuckles had turned white.

Lana turned over the book in her hands, inspecting it: *Extreme Boot Camp Workout* by Alex 'Brawler' Mahler. It sounded ridiculous, like something you'd buy on a satellite TV shopping channel. The binding was frayed and dirty and the edges of the pages were worn thin by Bright's fingers. She opened a page at random, and saw an extract from an A-Z pasted across the middle pages of the book, obscuring the text and several printed diagrams of a man performing exercises.

The glued page was a map of the Concrete Grove, and someone – probably Bright – had handwritten words over certain areas. 'Skeights' was one word, this one scrawled over the section representing Beacon Green. 'Croatoan' was another. These words looked simultaneously familiar and utterly alien – like historical artefacts found under the soil in a backyard. She'd seen the second word before, but couldn't recall where.

A thick arrow, marked in blue ink, pointed off the page in the direction of the council refuse tip close to the old Near Grove train station. There were other words, other phrases, some of them in what looked like a foreign language. Lana couldn't make out what any of this meant, but she knew it all added up to something important.

'Twins' (this one gave her a twinge), 'Channels', 'Captain Clickety', 'Hummers'... all words that must have added to and expanded upon Bright's private mythology of the Grove: keywords and buzzwords signifying events and knowledge that had died along with him.

Located at the centre of the page, directly over

the centre-fold of the workout manual, was the Needle. Someone had drawn crude shapes that were meant to be trees. They'd even coloured in the leaves a dark shade of Crayola green. A big red cross had been inked there, and gone over so many times and so heavily that the pen had torn through the paper. 'Locus?' said the word – which was also a question – written next to the cross.

Suddenly she knew where the fat man had taken Hailey.

"Stop the car," she said, turning to face Tom. It all seemed so obvious. She couldn't believe it had taken her so long to make the connection.

"I am. We're already here."

She glanced up through the windscreen. The house was in darkness. "Why aren't there any lights on?" Tom had pulled up in the middle of the road.

"I told you," said Tom, taking the keys from the ignition and opening the car door. He stepped out and crossed to the kerb. "I need to show you something." His voice was strange: low and husky, as if his throat had tightened.

Lana got out of the car and followed him across the road to the front of the house. She left the book in the car but didn't even notice its absence. The book had given her all the information she required. "Tom, she's in the Needle. He has her in that fucking tower. Come with me, help me get her out."

He walked along the drive and stopped outside the front door. Then, without saying anything, he took out his key and opened the door. He turned to her, smiling, and motioned for her to follow him inside. Then he stepped into the house, leaving the door wide open.

Lana knew that she needed to go back to the Grove, to get to the tower block while everyone else in the area was distracted by the fire. The sirens were still wailing, but they had stopped moving. The fire brigade and police must have reached Bright's gym and begun the process of extinguishing the flames. But still, she walked along the drive and stood at the open door, with one foot resting on the doorstep as she peered inside.

"Tom?" She called into the house, but there was no reply. It was dark in there, but she could make out a figure in the entrance hall, standing at the bottom of the stairs.

Lana took a step inside. "Come on, Tom. Let's get Hailey, and then we can get away from here. We can hide out up in the Highlands, or somewhere. Find a place where they'll never catch up with us." She knew she was lying: there was no way out of this, not now. The best she could hope for was to save her daughter. Little else mattered.

Tom was standing over the body of a very large woman. She was motionless, and lay face-down at the bottom of the stairs, her nightdress hitched up to show her massive, creased legs and her saggy, crumpled buttocks. Her head was twisted brutally to one side, forced around at an unnatural angle.

"It attacked me," said Tom, staring down at the woman's corpse. She was clearly dead: her face was as white and crumpled as old linen sheets. "I fought with it, and we fell down the stairs. Powerful beasts, these things. So, so strong… like a fucking ox, or something."

"Tom... what are you talking about, Tom?"

His head spun around to face her. His eyes were huge, eating up the residual light in the room. "This," he said. "The fucking sea cow." He kicked the corpse but it barely moved. It was too heavy. "Clickety-clickety-click."

She ignored that last part, unable to even grasp at its meaning. "This... this is your wife?"

He shook his head. "Don't be stupid. I don't know where Helen is. This is the sea cow. It took her place, and it attacked me. Up there." He raised a hand and pointed up the stairs.

How the hell had she managed to get up there? She was paralysed from the waist down. Had he dragged her out of bed and up the stairs only to throw her down? "Tom, I think you need to take a look at her and try to focus. *Really* look at her. Look at your wife."

He was crying now. "I wish I knew where she was. I need to find her, to make sure she's okay, and then we can leave. You, me and Hailey. We can leave all this shit behind us and start a new life."

"Tom." She was losing patience now. The old Lana might have taken the time to talk him down, to make him realise his mistake, but the new Lana, the warrior woman, couldn't spare the time or the effort. "I'm going now, Tom. I'm going to get my daughter. You've killed your wife, do you hear me? You killed her. I can't help you, not with this. There isn't the time."

He sunk down to the floor, onto his knees. Slowly, with great care, he reached out and began to stroke the dead woman's fleshy cheek. Her eyes were open. White foam was dried around her mouth, like a crust of salt. "Where's Helen? Such gentle creatures when you see them on telly, but *you're* not gentle, are you? You stole my wife."

Lana turned away and made her way slowly to the door. When she stepped outside, emerging into the cool night air, she reached behind her and shut the door firmly, making sure that it was tight to the frame. She could at least do this for Tom: give him some peace and some time to figure out what he had done.

In the distance, over the estate, the sky was bright with reflected flames. She could see the Needle beyond the capering yellow light, sticking up like a thick, grey finger pointing towards the stars.

"I'm coming, Hailey," she whispered as she started to run. "Mummy's coming."

CHAPTER THIRTY-TWO

It DIDN'T TAKE Lana long to reach the outskirts of the Concrete Grove. People were milling in the streets, trying to get a good look at the fiery display. Two fire engines were parked on Grove Lane, with groups of firemen working to put out the blaze. It looked like they'd managed to catch the fire in time to stop it spreading, and they were in the process of limiting the damage. The gym was already ruined, a blackened shell, but the nearby properties were undamaged apart from soot-stains on their frontages. Most of them were empty, anyway, and the rest were rented properties. Nobody in authority would care about the fire: even the landlords could claim on their insurance, and the evening's destruction would be considered nothing more than an inconvenience.

Not a living soul would mourn the dead. Men like Monty Bright, and his enforcer Terry, were never really loved. They were only ever feared, and when they died the communities they lived off like parasites let out a collective sigh of relief.

Maybe later, when all this was over and if she survived the night, Lana would return here to lay flowers for the poor junkie, Banjo. It was the least she could do, even if by sending him to his death she had shown him little mercy.

The air was hot as she jogged along Grove Side, towards the centre of the estate. She moved away from the blaze, and by the time she had entered the mouth of Grove Street, along which she could join the Roundpath, she was once again growing cold. She pulled the overcoat tighter across her chest, all-too aware that she was still half-naked beneath its thin covering. She checked the buttons, making sure that they were secure, and continued along the street to the end, where she slowed her pace once her feet crunched on the loose material of the circular pathway which ran around the perimeter of the Needle.

Pausing for a moment, she glanced up and looked at the tip of the building. A dark mass had gathered around its pyramidal glass peak: not smoke, not clouds, but hundreds of tiny birds. The air was filled with a distant humming; now that the crackling of the fire was behind her, she could hear the sound of the birds' wings as they beat gracefully against the air.

Hummingbirds, she thought. *More fucking hummingbirds.*

Were these things guardians, or harbingers of some kind? She recalled one of the words she'd seen written across the map of the estate in Bright's workout book. Psychopomp.

A soul conductor; a creature whose job it was to guide the souls of the recently deceased to the afterlife, the other side, the place that she had never believed in. Was that the role of the hummingbirds?

Did they accompany people as they crossed over, journeying from this place to that other – from the Concrete Grove to the grove beyond?

Her mind was racing. This was all mad conjecture, but it made as much sense as the ravings of that crazy man Monty Bright – him and his alternative world, his parallel universe that existed within the estate. His rambling speech and the book – what little of its contents she'd had the chance to skim – both seemed to suggest that Bright had been searching for a fragment of Creation, a sliver of the Garden of Eden. But what if he was only partly correct and the garden he had been seeking for so long was actually a wood, a forest, a dark tree-filled land that acted as a depository for lost dreams and nightmares? And what if the doorway to that place was a grove of ancient oak trees, over which had been constructed a concrete tower block?

Hailey had found a key to unlock that door. Bright had called it a mixture of innocence and yearning, but whatever unique qualities her daughter possessed, they were currency here. Lana had always told Hailey that she was special, but had never really known it for sure, until now.

Something deep within her responded strongly to the theory: she felt that the place towards which she was now heading, the realm Monty Bright had died trying to find, was like a failing battery, powered by the dreams and desires of the people who gathered around it. And in a place like the one she'd left behind, a blasted, godforsaken pit like the Concrete Grove, the only charge this battery could receive was negative.

So the forces here had mutated, becoming toxic. They had changed, and sprayed out their waste like a buried nuclear core going into a slow, decades-long meltdown.

She ran towards the old construction hoardings that formed a barrier around the tower, looking for a way inside. There had to be one – a gap in the fence, a slight depression in the ground under one of the boards, or perhaps a couple of damaged sheets of timber panel through which she could force entry. Soon she saw a loose board, and not caring who heard or even saw her, she set to work on pulling it free. This took several minutes and she tore one of her fingernails, but finally she managed to tug the board far enough away from the makeshift barricade that she could squeeze through the gap.

She tore the sleeve of her coat, and one of her running shoes came off, but she didn't stop to pick up the shoe. Instead she took off the other one and proceeded barefoot, stepping on splintered timber and old nails, tearing the soles of her feet but barely even feeling the pain.

More sirens sounded a long way behind her. She didn't turn around to see if the fire was out; she kept on going, heading towards the main entrance of the Needle.

This time she didn't need to struggle to find a way inside.

Because the doors were open.

Something had been waiting for her to arrive.

Above her, the humming sound continued. Around the base of the tower block, thick roots squirmed and writhed, tunnelling into the earth and then emerging again, displacing the turned soil and the building debris. The earth was alive with motion; something was straining at the boundaries of her perception, trying to be seen.

"I'm coming, Hailey." She walked into the Needle, and entered another world, passing from night to day in a heartbeat.

The floor was not concrete; it was soft earth covered in a layer of mulch. She felt it soak the soles of her feet and ooze between her toes, cold and invigorating, placing her in the moment. The sounds of the forest filled her ears; its rich, loamy smell invaded her nostrils. She was not inside a precast concrete frame building, she had instead entered some kind of woodland glade… no, not a glade: a *grove*.

Stood in a circle around her were several ancient oaks. Their rugged trunks were thick and imposing. The branches reached up, entwining, grasping, meshing, to form a dense canopy. Hairy conical nests hung from those branches, and hummingbirds darted in and out of the tiny entrance holes. The sky above the canopy seemed miles away, as if it had receded to a point where it was barely visible to the eye. All she could make out was a vast emptiness; a canvas upon which was painted thin, wispy clouds, behind which there burned a high, hazy sun. Lana turned her attention to the very centre of the grove of oak trees, and there, amid a small cairn of grey stones that might have once been part of a concrete structure, she saw a huge man-shaped mound of mossy ferns and leaves. The mound twitched as she approached, and when she stood before it she realised who it resembled: Francis Boater, Monty Bright's redemptive hard-man.

"Where is she?" She stared at the huge mound, not expecting it to be capable of speech. She knew that she should be afraid – indeed, the person she used to be would have been terrified – but all she felt now was a deep sense of pity. This man – this torturer and rapist – had been exploited by the forces here and then left to be absorbed into the fabric of the place. It was a correct end, she supposed, yet still there was something rather sad about his prolonged demise.

A sound came from the mass. Like a breathy whisper.

Lana went down on her knees and leaned in close, pressing the side of her head to the damp, mossy lump.

"*I protectsssssssssssssssssssssssssss…*"

"Thank you," she said, and got back to her feet. "Thank you for watching over her, you piece of shit. Thanks for that, if nothing else." She backed away, repulsed by the thing that had once been a man, or had at least called itself a man.

Daggers of sunlight pierced the foliage, slipping between the leaves and branches of the big, old trees. At the outskirts of the grove, something moved, slowly stalking her. It padded in a wide circle, biding its time, waiting for the right moment to reveal itself to her.

"Hailey? Is that you, baby? I'm here. I've come to get you."

The air inside the grove began to darken, as if a dense black cloud had crossed the sun. Shadows crept into the open, sliding through the gaps between the trunks and out from beneath low-lying foliage.

The thing outside the grove started to move inward, making its way through the trees. It was huge, bulky and covered in thick, dark fur. Like a bear, it moved first on all fours and then reared up on its hind legs to clear felled trees and other random obstacles.

"Oh, no…" Lana looked around, but there was nowhere to go, nowhere to hide. The beast had seen her; it knew exactly where she stood and how vulnerable she was.

The thing dropped and loped on all fours into the clearing, with its large, shaggy head turned to one side. The creature's flanks were huge and glossy and blood-flecked. Its heavy paws were large and threatening. Sharp claws curved like sickles from the ends of its rudimentary fingers; they scraped across the bases of the trees, cutting out swathes of bark.

"Please. Don't." Lana was powerless. Finally, she was afraid. She saw now the stupidity of coming here, of trying to bring back her daughter from a place that did not want to let her go. In fact, how did she even know that Hailey wanted to leave? What if she had been coming here for months, seeking solace and some kind of communion with the dormant forces that were now beginning to awake? Perhaps she had found her true home here, among the lost and ruined artefacts of other people's dreams.

At last the beast turned its head towards her. Its face was human; she knew it would be, and even whose features she would see.

It was Timothy: her dead husband. His eyes stared at her from above grizzled, hairy cheeks, and he frowned as if in vague recognition.

Lana stood there and waited for him to come to her. She had been waiting like this for such a long time.

Standing on his back legs, Timothy lurched towards her, slashing at her with those long, lethal claws. He roared; the air shook. Birds took flight around them, rising from the underground to take to the sky. Lana felt slick warmth at her belly, and when she placed her hands there blood flowed across her fingers. She grabbed at the wound, trying to stop the flow, but it was no good. She was already dying.

She closed her eyes and felt her body being hauled into the air. She flew, slung up into the branches of the nearest tree, and then once again she felt those claws go to work on her stomach, slicing away her sense of self.

What felt like hours later she opened her eyes. The world was upside down. The bottoms of the trees were at the top of her field of vision; the rustling canopy was the ground. Her ankles ached. Her belly was empty. There was nothing there, just a cool breeze across the exposed inside of her gut. Steam drifted past her eyes, from the upside-down ground and towards the tumbledown, loosely-packed sky.

A small upside-down girl stood several yards away, fumbling with the hem of her dress. She was wearing the tattered remains of a school uniform, but her legs and feet were bare. Her small toes were filthy with soil. The trees and the foliage closed around her, keeping her beauty and her innocence close. The air held her like a gentle hand. She was part of this place now, and would never again be forced to endure the concrete agonies from which she had finally escaped.

"Goodbye, Mum." Her voice was like music; the sound played on and on, repeating even after the girl had turned around and begun to walk away, into the trees, heading into the world beyond the grove. Lana recognised the song; she just couldn't place the name of the singer, or join in with the words.

"*Not yet*," she breathed. Then the world – this one, and the one outside, where she never again wanted to set foot – went dark and the relentless sound of humming filled the emptiness that had always been inside her, taking away the fear at last. "*Yes*," she whispered. She was ready to go now. There was nothing left to keep her here.

EPILOGUE

HAILEY WALKED AWAY from her mother, remembering the dream she'd once had – the dream that had now become real. She entered the dense shadows between the oak trees, and was lost in darkness for a little while. But when she came out on the other side, free from the grove at last, she was bathed in bright sunlight.

It's like a dream. I don't hurt anymore.

Far off in the distance, down a vast hill and across an expanse of low-lying open woodland which lay at its base, there was a dense forest of younger oak trees. And beyond that – who knew? Perhaps there were vast cities to explore, deep oceans to navigate. Monsters she might need to fight. Or perhaps all that existed was the eternal forest, and the primeval oaks, and the baleful shadows they cast.

Beautiful, she thought. *It's beautiful.*

Finally Hailey realised that none of this really mattered. Whatever was out there was out there, and all she needed to do was be willing to discover it all. There was nothing left for her where she had come from; all she had, everything she would ever need, lay ahead of her, in the trees and the shadows of her new home.

She had somehow come upon the central truth of this place, this grove within the Grove. At last it all made sense, and she repeated what she had learned silently inside her head, like a mantra to keep her company on the long journey that lay ahead of her:

Everything is beautiful and nothing hurts.

Author's Note

The Concrete Grove does not exist, but it is in fact based on several council housing estates I've known, lived on, or lived near during my lifetime. The Needle, for instance, is based on the infamous Dunston Rocket in Gateshead, Tyne & Wear, and the idea for the circular layout of streets in the Grove was pinched from an old Scottish estate long since demolished.

I've tried to keep the geography of the North-East as true to life as possible, with only the occasional cheat invented to serve the mechanics of plot. Northumberland is, to my mind, the most beautiful part of England. Despite the fictional horrors I've placed there, I can't recommend the area enough for a visit.

The people in this novel are real, every single one of them. They had different names when I met them, and their circumstances might not have been 100% the same as the ones in the novel, but I've known and mixed with the real-life counterparts of Tom, Lana and Hailey, Francis Boater, Terry, and even Monty Bright. If anything, the real characters were more outlandish than the versions I've created for the story.

Gary McMahon
Leeds
2011

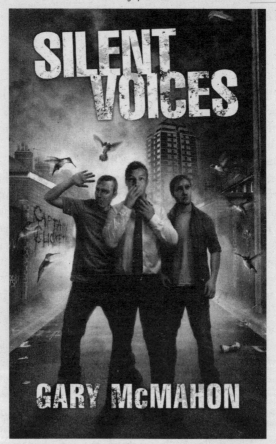